A. N. WILSON grew up in Staffordshire and was educated at Rugby and New College, Oxford. A Fellow of the Royal Society of Literature, he holds a prominent position in the world of literature and journalism. He is a prolific and award-winning biographer and celebrated novelist. He lives in North London.

A. N. Wilson

RESOLUTION

ATLANTIC BOOKS
LONDON

Published in hardback and e-book in Great Britain in 2016
by Atlantic Books, an imprint of Atlantic Books Ltd.

The author and publisher are grateful for permission to
reproduce a quote from Samuel Johnson, *The Letters of Samuel Johnson,
with Mrs. Thrale's genuine letters to him, Vol. 1: 1719–1774; Letters 1–369*, ed.
by R. W. Chapman, (Oxford University Press, 1952),
by permission of Oxford University Press.

Every effort has been made to trace or contact all copyright holders.
The publishers will be pleased to make good any omissions or rectify any
mistakes brought to their attention at the earliest opportunity.

1 3 5 7 9 10 8 6 4 2

A CIP catalogue record for this book is available from the British Library.

Hardback ISBN: 978 1 78239 827 1
Trade paperback ISBN: 978 1 78239 828 8
E-book ISBN: 978 1 78239 829 5

Printed and bound by CPI Group (UK) Ltd, Croydon, CR0 4YY

Atlantic Books
An Imprint of Atlantic Books Ltd
Ormond House
26–27 Boswell Street
London WC1N 3JZ

www.atlantic-books.co.uk

For Georgie

PART ONE

Setting Forth

The bride hath paced into the hall,
Red as a rose is she

I

1772

NALLY SAID,

—They're almost human. The hands. The eyes . . .

Nally had already named his monkey Plunkett. The choice of name had not been explained. George felt it would be a mistake to become too fond of 'his' monkey. Life was cheap at sea. Only a few days previous, one of the carpenters, Henry Smock, filling a scuttle, had fallen from the side and sunk in the briny without a trace. More upsetting, because more poignant, had been the fate of a swallow who had followed the ship from St Iago, which was where they had bought the monkeys. After a hundred and sixty miles at sea, the bird was still with them, sheltering, when able, in the rigging. On one occasion, rain and seawater in the foremast had collected in gallons, so, when the sails were oriented, a torrent had fallen, carrying the drenched bird with them. George had wrapped it in a piece of cloth, taken it back to the cabin, nursed it back to life. Reinhold, who was entirely capricious – and could easily, in another mood, have deplored sentimentality bestowed on a bird

– entered enthusiastically into its cult, even encouraging it to visit the Captain and to fly about indoors while they all dined together on *Sauer Kraut* and dressed albatross (shot the previous day by the master, Mr Gilbert). Even Captain Cook, who was as capricious in his mysterious way as Reinhold Forster – though with that silent Yorkshireman the whims and prejudices were held secret, whereas Reinhold wore more on the surface than was ever prudent – yes, even the Captain liked the swallow; called it a 'fine little man'. When, however, some days later, one of the cats got it, he was impatient with Reinhold's displays of emotion.

—It was a swallow – a bird. You let a bird loose – what do you expect a cat to do?

While Reinhold, the ship's naturalist, was saying, at the same time, talking *through* the Captain,

—You think it was no accident? That the bird was not *introduced* to the cat – to be blunt, *fed* to it? You think there are not some very cruel, ill-natured people on this ship?

—Ay – and some *difficult* 'uns 'n' all, was Cook's response.

So with the monkey, George was trying not to fall in love. The unnamed little fellow was holding a piece of raw potato, Nally's gift. Nally said,

—No, Plunkett, you got yer own spud!, and he lightly cuffed his monkey out of the way.

George's monkey seemed to appreciate the attention given to it. He sat still on the side of one of the rowing boats, while George, cross-legged on a coil of rope, intensely transmitted its likeness into a sketch-book.

—I mean, said Nally, the hands are like our hands, the eyes – well, you can see they're thinking something all right. There must be some *link* between them 'n' us?

Resolution

—I'm sure there is, Mr Nally.

—George, I keep telling you to call me Nally, or Pat, but not Mr Nally.

—And, George laughed, my father keeps telling you not to call me George.

—It seems daft.

They both laughed. George was seventeen, Nally a bit older, probably nineteen. Nally had been in the Navy since he was twelve.

—You couldn't look at that monkey now and say he didn't have a soul.

George had not sounded out his father on this difficult theme. George's job, apart from keeping Reinhold Forster company, was to draw the wildlife. Reinhold, lanky and clumsy in his gait, was coming on deck again now, brandishing a quarto volume of Edwards's *Natural History*, the wind catching its pages.—You must keep that cabin tidy, my son! Cabin! Bloody dog-kennel I'd prefer to call it.

George cast an embarrassed glance at Nally who, with the ninety-one other seamen, was squashed in the small and fearful discomfort of the hold, for whom a cabin of his own would have been an undreamed luxury. Nally, a hollow-cheeked young man with curly black hair and very green eyes, gave nothing away: indeed the clumsier Reinhold was, the more impassive was Nally's expression.

—Your books and mine, your sketches – all muddled and stuffed higgledy-hog. It is difficult enough to find things even if we were to keep them in some kind of order. But my point. This engraving in Mr Edwards's book. If you please! The *Simea sabaea* of Linnaeus which is sitting in front of you! Has not Edwards so much as set eyes on such a monkey? This is what we must ask ourselves.

—Well, I'm sure I never saw a man draw like young Mr George, said Nally pleasantly.

—He's learning, said Reinhold. His stiff manner implied that there was something almost offensive about being addressed by a sailor, albeit his personal servant. Nally had been assigned to this role on their first day. Reinhold was obliged to pay for the privilege. He had objected, saying that it was the least the Admiralty could do, to supply the ship's naturalist with a servant. Captain Cook had merely pointed out the simple regulations, and silenced further objections with a long sniff. Nally divided his time between his duties as an able seaman and his valeting and waiting upon the Forsters.

—Young Mr Forster is doing his job, Nally, said a pink-faced fifteen-year-old midshipman harshly, and yours is to be up the mainmast where you were asked to be.

—Ay, ay, sir.

The midshipmen were all gentlemen and spoke differently from the sailors. George, only half used to institutional life, marvelled at Nally's quiet acceptance of this young puppy's superior status. For a moment, George took his eye off the monkey and watched Plunkett and Nally, with more or less equal expedition, climb the rigging by the mainmast. Within minutes, they had become little stick-silhouettes against the sky.

Behind his monkey's grey head – for though called green monkeys, there was more grey than green – George watched the rhythmic swell and dip of the everlasting sea. It was a week since they had left the islands of Cape Verde and now were speeding through choppy waters south-east and south-east by east, with strong westerly winds behind them. And all they could see was the limitless ocean, an emblem already, to the seventeen-year-old boy, of his very existence. They had always been moving, he and his father . . . It was years later that he asked himself how his mother might have felt about the arrangement. George was the eldest of a large brood. There were five younger siblings in the parsonage-house in that bleak village in East Prussia. That his father wished to escape the place, had never wanted to be there in the first place, that went without saying. The burdens of his father's disappointments, these he could only begin to assess when he had endured disappointments of his own, just as the impenetrable relationship between his father and mother never came into any focus until his own unhappy marriage took shape. How could they have been happy, Reinhold and Justina? Johann Reinhold Forster, moody, selfish, book-mad and ambitious: he'd dreamed of being a great man of Law, or a Professor of Oriental languages in Berlin – just as – after the voyage with Captain Cook – he'd hope to become the Director of the British Museum. Only when George was a man who'd confronted his own professional setbacks could he begin to imagine the bitterness of his father, the linguist and botanist and would-be polymath, obliged to take holy orders as a means of earning a living, and reading the prayers to peasants in the hamlet of Hochzeit-Nassenhuben . . .

There was something of his near namesake Faust in Reinhold Forster's nature. Filling his study at Nassenhuben with many volumes, in many languages, on a variety of subjects he somehow wanted . . . mastery. No demonic contract was made – but there were moments of luck when the elder Forster would seize a chance. Once George was able to toddle, his father was never alone. The child learnt to read with his nose pressed close to a huge folio of Luther's Bible, and before he was six, he was reading the sentences back to his father and translating them into Latin as he went. It was the cleverness of his first little son, George, that was Johann Reinhold's ticket out of the village parsonage into the greater world. Father and son could become a Double Act. Johann, like Herr Mozart, could parade his little boy around Europe as an Infant Phenomenon. From his earliest years George began to acquire languages. His father conversed with him in Latin and pummelled him with a cudgel if he failed to understand. At family meals, the Latin conversations continued, deliberately shutting out George's mother from what they were saying.

—We have been at large, we Forsters, for a hundred years – we must stop drifting – and build a monument.

It was true. They had always been adrift, always journeying. George, for all his multifarious talents as linguist and scientist, would be famous as a *traveller*. The restlessness, the everlasting discontent of father Reinhold entered his own soul also, was part of the very atmosphere in which the family itself existed. George came into the world as a foreigner – from a long line of foreigners. Deprived of their modest lands and possessions in English Yorkshire by Oliver Cromwell – for the seventeenth-century Forsters, no less than their eighteenth-century European descendants, had the unerring instinct to support the wrong side in history. They had fled to Prussia. Germanized for more than a century before George's birth, by their century and mode of residence, his father was the Lutheran pastor of a village near Danzig. The Seven Years War was in progress when George was born – in '54 – Danzig and Pommerellen were occupied by Russian troops. Reinhold, with his gift for getting to know 'everyone' – and then quarrelling with them – befriended the Russian consul.

In the streets of Danzig where Reinhold went to hobnob with notables, you heard a multiplicity of languages – Russian, of which

Resolution

George had a smattering even as a young infant, English, Polish, as well as their mother tongue. Almost as soon as he could walk, George became his father's companion on those trips to 'the town', as he called it. (Later, when he became fluent in English, George would note how southerners and a few of the more sophisticated northerners would use the single word 'town' to describe *London*, whereas in Warrington, their next residence after Nassenhuben, 'Are ye' – or more often – 'Art goin' to tarn' – would mean *Liverpool*.)

In *'die Stadt'*, in the back room of the pawnbrokers, you would also hear that language which used so to puzzle George's childish ears, so like, and so unlike, German it was, as the ringleted old moneylenders, whose fur hats and shawls bespoke an exotic East, a universe away from the Forsters' Lutheran domestic simplicities, spoke in subdued tones, their bearded bright-eyed faces sugges-tive of an ancient pre-European world where the priest Ezekiel had seen the glory of their God beside the Euphrates, or the more minor prophets, Nahum or Obadiah, had held the corruptions of the rulers to account. Or, their intelligent expressions as they shrugged and weighed one point against another might have resem-bled that of their co-religionist Spinoza as he laboured over lenses in Amsterdam and meditated upon the very nature of moral reality. It was a while before the infant George figured out they were prob-ably, in reality, wondering how Pastor Forster could possibly repay his already ascending obligations. Far from regarding the money-lenders of Danzig as sinister beings, George grew up accurately considering them the indulgent godfathers of his father's insatiable bibliomania. The Forsters' few items of family silver, brought to Prussia from the English Civil War a hundred years since, had long ago been converted into an impressive collection of Coptic manu-scripts. Reinhold had made himself a master of the tongue, and of their theology, of Egyptian geography, and of travel literature from Pausanias to Marco Polo. He'd studied Michaelis's *Travels and Biblical Philology* – indeed believed Philology to be the clue to the Bible. Some of the pawnbroker minor prophets – the Obadiahs or Nahums of backstreet Danzig – shared Reinhold's book-passion and had even been invited to the parsonage at Nassenhuben to see the collection, had turned over the quartos and folios with astonished admiration.

—Please, please! His father would proudly indicate the top of his chest of prints, where a book-stand indicated a Gutenberg Bible and a folio of Josephus, illustrated with copper engravings which depicted the Roman army of Titus despoiling the treasures of Jerusalem. No one present was so indelicate as to suggest that the Coptic grammars, the folio of Pius I's *Travels*, the Hebrew lexicons and mathematical treatises on display had all been paid for by exchanges, some rash, some judicious, of Frau Forster's few remaining family jewels, or the silver including a goblet made in York and said by pious family legend to have been drunk out of by the Royal Martyr himself a short while before the Battle of Marston Moor. The author of the Book of Proverbs might well have been purely metaphorical in intention when he stated that the merchandise of wisdom is better than the merchandise of silver, or when he calculated that wisdom was more precious than rubies. His co-religionists in Danzig, when faced with the prosaic necessity of deciding the matter on a business footing, had felt constrained to calculate just how many books of wisdom on Pastor Reinhold's shelves could be paid for by just how many of Frau Forster's rubies.

George would always remember the day when the prophet Nahum, far from rolling his eyes at his client's extravagance (as was the wont of some of the other minor prophets of the jewellery quarter), actually suggested the purchase of all purchases – the book which determined the course of George Forster's life.

—Herr Pastor, you will never guess what came into Eyck's [the bookseller's] yesterday morning.

Reinhold, fondling George's six-year-old head with one hand and mopping his brow with the other, which clutched a handkerchief, had replied,

—Herr Rosenthau, I have not come to town to ask you for *more* money, merely to ask for an extension of the loan. I do not know how I *can* have spent so much.

It was a sentence he heard so often on his father's lips and which he would often himself repeat!

—Herr Pastor – there was genuine kindness in the prophet. He was a man of business but not a shark and he had been inspired by many of the pastor's interests, above all, his knowledge of Egypt – Herr Pastor, I want you to have this book, as a gift from us for you have been one of our best customers.

The prophet had not actually placed coins into Reinhold's hands. He knew that to give money, as such, to the pastor was like pouring water through his fingers. He had written a guarantee on a piece of paper and Reinhold, as fast as George's six-year-old legs could run – had hurried to Eyck's shop in Johann Nepomukgasse agog to see what the prophet had bought them – for Nahum had playfully withheld the title of the volume prized above rubies. And there it was! A magnificent quarto of Linnaeus's *Systema Naturae* (1735), the first great work of taxonomy. For the first time since Aristotle – but with so much more scientific accuracy and discipline – the attempt had been begun to categorize each genre of fish, bird and beast, each family of plant and tree, to classify and to define each species. It was a gift of stupendous generosity from the old prophet. For Reinhold and George Forster it became an invaluable tool, almost, for father and son, their *raison d'*être: for, from now onwards, they would scarcely walk outside the parsonage-house without the specific aim, not only of identifying every bird, fish, leaf and petal itemized in Herr Linné, in so far as such flora and fauna were to be found in East Prussia, but also – this was the challenge – they would set out to find species which had escaped the notice of the great Swedish botanist. In Reinhold, the lust for knowledge was a twofold thing, everlastingly co-existent with the pleasure of putting another in the wrong.

With what joy, if George's beady little eyes found a finch or a reed or a wild blossom un-noted in Linnaeus, would the pastor dispatch a letter to Sweden informing the great man of yet another *lacuna* in his survey. They always had a reply, even if Linné sometimes needed convincing that, for example, Baltic bog moss (*Sphagnum balticum*) really was slightly different from the commoner moss, *Sphagnum recurrum*. Most of the species George saw had already been noted in Linné's book – but it was by reading it that he learnt to be what we call a scientist, but what the eighteenth century called a natural philosopher. ('The tactless philosopher' was one of Reinhold's nicknames when they were living in London, on their return from voyaging with the Captain.) With his father George also helped the botanist Gottfried Reyger prepare his work on the flora of Danzig – *Tentamen Florae Gedanensis* (1764).

George was ten years old when escape from the parish of Hochzeit-Nassenhuben became a possibility. The Russian Empress Catherine the Great, herself a German, had determined upon a programme of colonization by German settlers along the Volga. (In the event twenty-seven thousand Germans, exhausted or displaced by the war, made the journey.) They were slow in coming, partly because rumour travels more readily than bedraggled refugee families, and the word was that the bare steppes were bleak and inhospitable, the local Russian commissioners harsh and despotic, the local criminals violent and efficient. What was needed was a German speaker who could survey the Volga region and counterblast the 'mischievous, injurious rumours' spread abroad concerning the plight of the colonies. The Russian resident in Danzig, Hans Wilhelm von Rehbinder, offered this delicate diplomatic role to 'the tactless philosopher'. Reinhold was so desperate to get out of Nassenhuben that he took his boy to St Petersburg almost at once – in the spring of '65. It was strange, looking back from an adult memory, George had no recollection that he had wept, on leaving his childhood village, the scene of all his life-experiences for a decade. He had felt no grief at parting from his mother and siblings. All he could recollect, of the setting forth with Reinhold, was that they were leaving behind, less a collection of souls, than an atmosphere, an atmosphere which emanated, like the smell from one simmering stockpot in the kitchen filling the whole parsonage with a stench of cabbage and chicken bones, from his mother's capacity for discontent. Her little headaches, necessitating tiptoes from her children, her 'blinding' headaches, which required an already shadowy house to be shuttered in darkness, her 'bilious' attacks, her rheumatick pains, and above all her simmering ill nature had poisoned all his early childhood, spoiling those innocent early times, when he still loved Reinhold without reserve, because he knew no other, no other object of love and saw no reason for his father not to be as he was. So it was that they set off for Russia as on a great jaunt, with joy and lightness in their hearts – *Heiterkeit*.

'The tactless philosopher' would have got nowhere in life had he only been tactless. He had genuine accomplishments. He knew seventeen languages, and was a considerable scholar. He was also a networker of the greatest skill. Those whom he would later offend by his clumsiness he had won by assiduous social talent. He made a great success with Grigorii Orlov, Catherine's favourite, whom she had put in charge of her colonization programme. With the sizeable Lutheran population of the capital he made friends – as with the Russian scientific academy. George for the first time in his life went to school – Pastor Büsching's school – where most of the lessons were conducted in German, some in Russian. By the time Reinhold had got his appointment – Imperial Commissioner to the Volga – George had learnt Russian. They toiled through the dark Petersburg winter – Reinhold persuading Orlov to buy him meteorological instruments and reference books, while networking in the international academic and diplomatic circles of the capital – especially among the English – until George had mastered the language. When the ice on the Volga had broken and the sudden spring returned to Russia, they were ready to set off on their journey – along the Volga's west bank to Dmitrevsk (Kamystuk), then across the great river to the Kalmuck Steppe, where the Forsters inspected the salt mines, north to the river Yeruslan and back to Saratov. As winter began again, in late autumn, the Forsters were prepared to return to Petersburg.

George remembered the hot summer as one of seemingly inter-minable journeys by straw-laden carts on sun-baked barges: of filthy inns, of relentless, scorching skies, of smelly 'popes', bearded priests in brimless hats and greasy cassocks, so dirty that you did not suppose they had ever washed in their lives, of foul-mouthed toothless women in scatterings of hovels which passed for villages, of the moonlit weirdness of the salt mines and their hard-faced German managers – so unlike the high cheek-boned mysterious

Resolution

Slavs of the villages – of the colonies, where they saw so much hardship and poverty, but where they refreshed themselves, almost wallowed, in hearing their own language spoken, of the gut-pains caused by brackish water, of the delicious refreshing *kvass* sold by old ladies carrying barrels on their backs down the main streets of dusty provincial towns, of bells clattering from gilded onion domes. And he remembered, too, the joy of improving, with every passing day, his skills as a draughtsman – chiefly drawing plants, but also birds and beasts, and as if to plumb the puzzle of Reinhold's strange character, the endless portraits of his father: the long face, which in some lights seemed sharp and clever, and in others, gormless; the moist lips which were sensual, the hooded eyes which were spiritual; the slightly crooked, long nose. At court, or when he wanted to impress, Reinhold wore a stiff Dutch wig, but often, on the road, he wore his long, wispy hair uncovered save by the large round-brimmed hats which had been his preferred head-covering since University days.

Throughout the Volga journey, and throughout the subsequent marks of the Petersburg autumn, both Forsters worked diligently. Reinhold had done extensive cartographical work – his map of the Volga region, much the most detailed to date, would be published in England in '68. Father and son between them had identified two hundred and seven plants, twenty-three mammals, sixty-four birds, fourteen reptiles and sixteen fish, many of them not in Linnaeus – all of which were chronicled in a learned paper, 'Specimen Historiae Naturalis Volgensis'.

All these were enough to establish the academic qualifications of the father-and-son pair. As a 'natural philosopher' Reinhold was triumphant, as an aspirant favourite of Catherine the Great, he did less well.

Orlov had sincerely wanted a report on the Volga colonies – the Russians needed to import more Germans to the sites to boost the economy of the region, especially in the mines. Some helpful criticism – relative to property law, inheritance law, and the settlers' need to feel politically represented – would have been in order. Reinhold, however, delivered a full-frontal attack on the Russian administration. He represented the German colonists as being in a condition similar to the colonists of America *vis-à-vis* the Government in London – unrepresented and economically exploited. The brutality of the Russian bureaucracy made life hard, sometimes intolerable, for the settlers. Having submitted his report to Orlov Reinhold found himself dismissed. There then followed a pattern which would repeat itself wherever he went – a wrangle about money. Reinhold claimed he had been promised the position of Councillor of State with a salary of two thousand roubles. The Government offered him a thousand roubles to shut him up. (In fact, Catherine, a wise though ruthless ruler, acted on many of Reinhold's suggestions to improve the Volga colonies, but by then he had cut his losses – or rather the losses of his creditors in Petersburg – and sailed for England.)

It was a stormy crossing. Twice they had to put in at Norwegian harbours and wait for the tempests to subside. The journey, which could have been accomplished in a few days, took the best part of a month. In the intervals of heaving, agonizing seasickness, George talked to those on board. He talked Russian to some of the passengers. From the sailors his sharp ears picked up a variety of English which, in the learned societies his father wished to penetrate in London, had to be tempered by a more measured version of the tongue. Reinhold's spoken English, after a lifetime of reading the language, was always accented, and his written mastery of grammar was never perfect. George spoke his several Englishes like a native. He would say – before they'd even docked at Harwich – 'If tweren't for this thur fuckin' storm we'd've been home two fuckin' week ago', or, 'T'First Lieutenant's a bugger and oi mean bugger.' (George was at that date unaware of the meaning of the term in any language.) He could also – the same First Lieutenant having taken a friendly interest in the lad – speak the officer's English and say that he thanked Lady—, or Sir Somebody—, for their condescension and had the greatest happiness in accepting their kind invitation. He had also, in the intervals of being sick, read a history of Russia and decided to write a translation of it into English.

His initial impressions never left him. Though he later believed Berlin to be the finest city in Europe, architecturally, and though Destiny would allow him to die in Paris – after a solitary year, separated from his wife and children – it was London which was most spectacularly teeming with intellectual and social interest. They had just about enough money to pay one month's rent for a small room in Denmark Street. Smoke from a neighbour's chimney flitted past the window in puffs. From the street below came the clatter of carriage wheels on cobblestone, the shout of traders, the seemingly unstoppable conversation of the inhabitants. In German, Vati had said —You see it is only a matter of time before Woide finds us something! Woide is our man!

A thin man, Reinhold's age, a friend of student days in Berlin, Woide seemed a frail figure on whom to hang high hopes. It was to Woide's house in Denmark Street they had repaired on landing – Woide occupied two rooms on the first floor.

—Woide understands more Coptic than anyone else in Europe, Reinhold excitedly told his son, and George, at twelve, did not question that this augured well for the future, though quite how

Woide, with his unstoppable excitement at finding someone with whom he could discuss Coptic scripts and paintings, might improve the Forster family fortunes, George did not ask.

When the first month ran out, they sold souvenirs from their Russian journey to buy themselves a second month – Tartarian coins, miniature icon-paintings, fossils. Woide, little by little, worked his magic, introduced them to the Swedish naturalist Daniel Carl Solander, and to Andreas Planta, one of the keepers at the British Museum, who was cataloguing the Natural History collection. Surely if Planta, a German-speaking Swiss pastor, could do such work, they could find paid employment for Reinhold Forster? Woide took the Forsters to scientific meetings at the Royal Society. He persuaded George to abridge Lomonossof's Russian history, translate it into English and sell it to a bookseller – which he did – to Mr Snelling, No. 163 next to the Horn Tavern in Fleet Street. Within no time they felt themselves part of a 'circle'. Solander, Linnaeus's representative on English soil, introduced them to Joseph Banks – then twenty-four years old – who had sailed with Captain Cook in the *Endeavour* to Tahiti, witnessed the passage of Venus over that island, and sailed on with the Captain to New Zealand. Plans were afoot to sail again – and if Banks required assistant naturalists in his entourage? Well, certainly, my dear fellow.

—Cook is . . . how shall I put this to you? Banks had guffawed – it was a noise which Englishmen of a certain class made, and it already slightly scared George. Ever met him?

—Kapitän Cook?

—Well, he calls himself Captain but he's not yet been gazetted beyond the rank of – *simple* soul – you get me?

Reinhold did not.

Resolution

—Is he not one of the finest navigators in the history of mankind – did not his skills as a cartographer show themselves when he mapped the coastline of North America? Is he not an astronomer as well as a sailor of valour?

—Yes, yes, no doubt – but – at heart a *peasant*. Father was a farm labourer in Yorkshire – did ye know?

Banks, it would appear, had been the real genius behind Cook's momentous voyage – they should not pay too much attention to Cook.

—But I say, sir! Your boy, what is this I heard? – Banks bowed obligingly to George – written a book? You must bring it to the next meeting of the Antiquaries, present 'em with a copy for the library.

And this was done.

The son of Mr Forster, honorary Fellow of this Society, a young Gentleman of not 13 Years of Age, but conversant in several Languages, presented a Copy of a Work, translated by him into English, entitled *A Chronological Abridgement of the Russian History*, translated from the original Russian, of Michael Lomonossof, Counsellor of State and Professor of Chymistry at the Academy of Sciences at Petersburg; & continued to the present Time by the Translator.

Thanks were returned to this young Gentleman for his kind Present.

Invitations followed – My Lord Lansdowne, Secretary of State for the Colonies, asked Reinhold to his table – offered him a post as pastor at Pensacola, West Florida. It was turned down. Solander introduced him to Joseph Priestley – of all the Englishmen he'd met to date, one of the most fascinating.

Priestley wore no wig. He was in his mid-thirties – four years younger than Reinhold – sharp blue eyes, a clear skin, a strong-boned jaw and a straight nose. He spoke of his passion for education.

—In England, a young gentleman can attend one of the older schools and learn nothing – nothing except Latin and rudimentary mathematics. He will go on to Oxford, if his path is to lead him to the Church or the Law, and just study more of the same. Of the modern tongues he will learn nothing – of Natural Philosophy, nothing . . .

He told Reinhold of his explorations into electricity and of his correspondence on the subject with Mr Franklin in America. He talked of his chemical researches. He was on his way to discovering what we call oxygen and he called, at this date, dephlogisticated air. He spoke of wanting to live in a world where boys and girls, equally, could pursue knowledge, discover the nature of Nature – of matter, of stuff, of what there *is*. He also spoke of religion, but in a manner which Reinhold did not wish to follow: indeed, Mr Priestley said,

—Do not most men and women if they are honest revere the teachings of Christ without any understanding that he was divine, or their Saviour, or the sacrificial Lamb of Passover? Do not most men and women who are *called* Christians merely want to live justly, to love mercy, to worship the Creator by the exercise of goodness?

Priestley told Reinhold that, partly with money from a like-thinking young businessman, the red-faced Mr Wedgwood, who was also at the table, he had helped to establish the Warrington Nonconformist Academy which had enjoyed a partial success.

—Ay, partial! laughed Wedgwood. We employ scholars to lecture our young scholars – men of science to breed up men of science. You canna expect men like that to be ushers, thrashing little brats into shape and mekkin 'em learn the tables . . .

—Ooshes? The word puzzled Reinhold.

—Ay, so we decided – did we not, Mr Priestley 'n' I – ter dispense wi' little 'uns – ter tell the truth they were so badly disciplined, so out of control they learnt nothing – yet they were being taught by some o't' foremost natural philosophers in t'world!

—But I have decided, for the time being, said Mr Priestley, to give up my teaching work. I supervise three of our meeting houses, and preach in all of them regularly. And my chemical research takes up more and more of my time.

—Which is why, said Mr Wedgwood, drawing his chest close and putting his face near to Reinhold's, we are looking for a new teacher at the Academy – one who can instruct the scholars in modern languages, and one who can gi'e lectures in Natural Philosophy as well.

—A man of science, fluent in the European tongues! said Mr Priestley.

It became a matter of some merriment, on Mr Wedgwood's part at least, that Reinhold's next question had been

—And tell me if you would be so kind – in what part of London does *Warrington* find itself?

Reinhold, when he first went to University in Berlin as an ambitious young student, had not imagined that at the age of thirty-eight he would become a schoolmaster in a small town near Liverpool. The pay was £60 per annum. It enabled him to bring Justina and the children over from Germany, and they lived as a family for five years. When he was in his late thirties – roughly the age that Reinhold had been when they went to Warrington – George would make a tour, with Alexander von Humboldt, written up and published as *Views of the Lower Rhine, of Brabant, Flanders, Holland, England and France in April, May and June, 1790*. Perhaps it was not until he made that journey, and made it in the company of an intelligent young German, that the mysterious phenomenon of England came into any kind of perspective. His father's sharp eye made him a taxonomist of brilliance. The same mind which could master the complexities of Coptic grammar picked out grasses, flowers, butterflies and moths which even an astute countryman would have missed. (His *A Catalogue of British Insects*, Warrington, 1770, was a product of these times.) So observant of British flora and fauna, Reinhold noticed almost nothing about the social complexities in which the human organisms were working out their place in the scheme of things. He professed admiration for John Locke, whom he had scarcely read, for the Parliamentary system, which he had not mastered, but he remained at heart a conservative German, a citizen of the *ancien régime*. The intricate morphology of British life, the fundamental chemical changes brought about in the organization of its very existence by the expansion of manufacturing trade, a phenomenon at this date unseen anywhere else in the world, appeared not to interest Reinhold. He saw the way to advancement as crudely simple – to acquire the patronage of the aristocracy, and ultimately of the King. Had he been less successful less early, had he been able to see by what an astonishing series of chances he came to be sailing with Captain Cook, in 1772, as his chief naturalist, with George as his illustrator and assistant, he might have trod less clumsily at his setting forth, and been less crushingly disappointed by his failure, after the voyage, to achieve advancement.

As events turned out, with only a few throws of the dice, the obscure pastor of Nassenhuben turned schoolmaster of Warrington was 'recognized' in learned circles. True, Reinhold was a man of abilities, but he was *naif* enough – conceited enough, his enemies would say – to suppose that ability is always recognized. He did not see the role of *luck* which enabled him to become a Fellow of the Royal Society, a Doctor of Civil Law at Oxford, a friend of Solander and Priestley, culminating in his becoming the naturalist on the most stupendous voyage in the history of world discovery. While he laboured as a teacher in Warrington translating Bougainville's *Voyage Autour du Monde* into German, Reinhold yearned to follow in the wake of the great Frenchman, to explore the South Seas and to bring back to Europe exotic plants and birds. Like a child whose greedy list of wishes was gratified each 6th December by the arrival of St Nicholas bearing sugar-plums and toys, Reinhold took all his good fortune for granted, scarcely conscious of the fact that he and George owed their place on the *Resolution* to the chance that Joseph Banks – who had accompanied Cook on the first voyage to Tahiti and New Zealand in the *Endeavour* – was an even more difficult person than Forster himself.

When the Admiralty had agreed the scheme for Cook to sail, with two ships, to explore the southern hemisphere, in quest of the putative Southern Continent, it was assumed that the naturalist on board Cook's sloop would be Banks, who was not yet thirty. Banks belonged to that robust species – deplored by Cook, never got into focus by Forster – an English gentleman. From a landed fortune in Lincolnshire he had been not merely to Harrow but also to Eton, followed by Christ Church, Oxford. There being no adequate lectures on botany in Oxford at that date, Banks had paid for the Cambridge botanist Israel Lyons to give a course at the more distinguished University in '64. A couple of years later with his Eton chum Constantine Phipps – aristocratic naval officer and a future Lord of the Admiralty – Banks had sailed to Labrador and Newfoundland, thus forming a collection, and catalogue, of specimens which established him as a scientist of international repute. He was the natural choice to serve as naturalist on the *Endeavour* when they sailed to Tahiti to observe the passage of Venus. Upon their return to England, Banks had received more accolades than Cook himself.

Cook, who was the son of a Yorkshire farm labourer and who had learnt the sailor's craft working on the 'colliers' – the ships which brought coal from Newcastle to Hull to London – could admire Banks's intelligence while refusing to be impressed by his 'side'. No one in the history of the Navy had a more practical grasp of equipping and packing a ship. He knew precisely what sort of ships were required for this voyage – small sloops, not great men of war, which could negotiate the inlets and coves of South Sea islands and, when more southerly latitudes were explored, withstand the snow and ice. Two neat merchant ships, built relatively recently at Whitby, were purchased – it being decided that the journey was so hazardous, a consort ship was needed as back-up in the event of one vessel meeting with calamity. Cook was to command the *Resolution* and Lieutenant Tobias Furneaux the *Adventure*.

The *Resolution* was taken to the dockyard at Sheerness – and Banks followed Cook down to Kent with his list of requirements. There must be room for his 'staff' – Dr Lind, the Edinburgh scientist; Zoffany, the painter; secretaries; his 'valet' (known to be his floozy, a woman in disguise); and two horn players – damn it, a man wanted a concert in the evening when his work was done.

—Mr Banks, this is a ship of discovery, not a floating music room.

Ignoring Cook's raised eyebrows, Banks had further insisted

that a huge cabin be built for his use on the upper deck, above which there was to be constructed a fully equipped laboratory with a roundhouse to accommodate the Captain. Perhaps Cook knew what he was doing when he actually acceded to these requests. By the time the carpenters had finished their work, the *Resolution* resembled a floating Tower of Pisa. There was laughter and mockery as she sailed out of Sheerness for a trial. Banks was on board. He had invited Sandwich – First Lord of the Admiralty – and the French Ambassador. It was as much as any of them could do to stand upright as soon as they got out to open sea for the imbalance caused by Banks's towering additions. Though the sea was not especially choppy the swell was prodigious – and the dinner provided for the French Ambassador was soon spewed on to the main deck. At the trial sailing, the pilot declared that the ship was so top heavy she could hardly carry a sail without capsizing. Clerke, Second Lieutenant, exclaimed,

—By God, I'll go to sea in a grog tub if desir'd, or in the *Resolution* as soon as you please, but I must say I think it by far the most unsafe ship I ever saw or heard of.

The vessel, through the pilot's skill, made it back to Sheerness. The next day, when Banks went down to the deck, he saw that Cook had already instructed the carpenters to demolish the laboratory, the luxurious cabins and all the other additions considered essential by the gentleman scientist.

—Cook? Cook!

The inscrutable Cook was himself capable of eruptions of volcanic rage, but on this occasion he controlled his temper.

—Mr Cook, I'd thank you, sir – *Mister* Cook . . .

—What in the name of fucking HELL do you think you are DOING?

—I am making the *Resolution* seaworthy, sir. I have removed four of her guns – if we are going to carry that weight it had better be barrels of *Sauer Kraut* to prevent the men getting scurvy – thirty deaths we had in *Endeavour* – I'm not having that again on any ship under my command.

—But my laboratory, my fucking CABIN – you – you—

—Ay, Mr Banks? As I told you when you demanded these things, the *Resolution* is a ship of discovery – not a floating laboratory, nor a floating concert hall where flute players can entertain the island lasses, nay, nor a lady's boudoir neither.

—We'll see about this! We'll see, Cook! What my Lord Sandwich . . .

But of course, neither Sandwich nor his colleagues at the Admiralty wished to send out a ship for the southern hemisphere which would capsize before it reached the Bay of Biscay. The *Resolution* was to be seaworthy. It was to be packed as no ship was ever before packed. Cook never allowed officers or crew to witness the packing – he alone, with the stevedores, would fill every available space with barrels of drinking water, barrels of *Sauer Kraut*, supplies of salt beef, salt pork, biscuits, ropes, sails, spare masts, Baron von Storisch's marmalade, spirits, stockfish, winter clothing. The crew and officers assembled. It was nearly ready to sail. All that was lacking was the team promised by Banks – for not only had he withdrawn his services as a naturalist, but Mr Zoffany had withdrawn as the artist. They engaged William Hodges as the painter. William Wales was to be the astronomer. Who could be found who would do the work of a naturalist? No one of Banks's wealth or fame, that was for sure. Banks, Solander, Lind, had all left Cook in the lurch. The Admiralty had to act swiftly. There was no time to be choosy. Banks and Solander both knew the Forsters through

Resolution

Daines Barrington, a lawyer and amateur scientist whom Reinhold had befriended. Their name was put up. Sandwich accepted it. A hastily drafted agreement, which would be the source of rancorous dispute when they returned home, was drawn up between the Admiralty and the Forsters, father and son. Parliament, at the behest of the Prime Minister Lord North, granted Reinhold the £4,000 which had been assigned to Dr Lind. Until the money was forthcoming, the King granted Reinhold £1,795 out of the Civil List.

For the schoolmaster on £60 per annum, it looked as if his fortune was made. With a part of his brain Reinhold was unable to grasp the simplest financial statistic – he knew and could not quite appreciate that the £1,795 was an *advance* on £4,000, not an addition to it. He knew that out of this money he must collect clothing and equipment, buy books, provide for his wife and family. To be a 'natural philosopher' was a rich man's game. Priestley could never have advanced as a chymist without the help of rich businessmen like Matthew Boulton or Josiah Wedgwood. In one crazy month, scrambling to prepare for their voyage round the world, Reinhold managed to spend more than £1,795, and to leave England as a debtor.

The scientific instruments, colours, sketch-books, portfolios, paper, herbals and three years' clothing cost him £1,200. On their travelling library he spent a prodigious £300. He had to leave £750 behind for his wife – for he and George would be at sea for three years at least. Almost the first thing that confronted him, on coming aboard the *Resolution* at Plymouth, was that he was expected to pay one of the sailors to be a personal servant to himself and George – in charge of their laundry, and cleaning the two little cabins which Cook had had hastily constructed for them, nearly abreast of the mainmast.

And thus it had come to pass, that in the month of August and the year of grace 1772, George Forster found himself on the deck of the *Resolution*, patiently capturing an exquisite likeness of a green monkey. Nally was right. It was impossible to look at the monkey-face and not to feel the presence of a personality. George felt the same about dogs, about quite a lot of animals, actually. He must have said something to that effect, for Reinhold was putting him right.

—The ratiocinative capacity, where is that in your monkey? The gift of tongues – why, even the language of a baby or of the most primitive savage is more complex than the squeaks and grunts put forth by your – oh I say, but oh I say! This is too much!

George's unnamed monkey was innocent. Indeed, only an hour or so before he'd dropped a tail-like turd over the side, neatly plopping into the salt ocean. Some other monkey, aloft, possibly Plunkett, possibly another, had scored this very palpable hit on the natural philosopher.

—But ever since they came aboard, I have said! But . . . lice, fleas. They are . . . but only yesterday a man, I saw a man tread in . . .

—I'll take your coat, Vati. I'll take it back to your cabin.

—He trod, he could have slipped. A man could have slipped, I find. But look – the shoulder. All down the sleeve of this coat – and is Nelly here? When you need him? Is Nelly?

George wondered at his father's capacity to think, after four weeks at sea, that their personal servant bore this name.

—I'll see if I can find Nally, Vati. But I can fetch your other coat.

—Hundreds of pounds each year. And the coat. You remember that tailor in London? Three identical coats and he charged the same for all of them!

Resolution

While George was in the cabin fetching a clean coat for his father, the bells sounded. Twice an hour, at each turning of the glass they rang, marking the division of the ship's day, always inducing, as they had during his brief periods of schooling – though George seldom had specially assigned tasks – the sense that he should be somewhere else, trying a little harder.

—You give it to me, George . . .

Nally had somehow been found in the lower deck and told that 'the professor' – one of the politer nicknames bestowed by the men on Reinhold – was in a 'paddy'.

—It's just down that sleeve, I can . . .

—Not at all, George, no trouble at all.

George had felt an instant rapport with Nally. He had never had a personal servant before, not one specially set aside to attend to his needs, and the needs of only one other. Though an ordinary seaman who, in the intervals of attending to the Forsters, did his bit, cleaning the decks or mending the rigging, and, though popular with his mates, not the least standoffish, Nally appeared a little apart from them. Though he maintained his smiling appearance while those around him swore or raged, it was unimaginable that he would himself ever use 'sailor's language'. Nothing appeared to ruffle him. His smile suggested some quiet secret which he was in no hurry to share with the rest of the world. George wondered whether this secret was not simply Nally's superior intelligence.

He took Reinhold's coat. Only hours later it was hanging in its closet again, odourless, as clean as the day it was made.

—My father will want to wear this for dinner.

—Naturally, Mr George. What about his shirt?

—Untouched, thanks, Nally.

—So, limited damage.

They both allowed themselves a little laugh.

—Well, Jem's been enjoying himself down in the kitchens after yesterday's sport.

Jem was Pattinson, the ship's cook, with whom Nally enjoyed discussing receipts. Two of the Lieutenants had shot seabirds – an albatross and a booby – and, to the general rejoicing, the master had supervised the netting of a shark.

—It's going to be a fine albatross pie and shark steaks with gull egg sauce.

Very occasionally the Forsters ate in the gun-room with the officers but normally the 'gentlemen' – the surgeon, the astrono-mer, the naturalists – ate at the Captain's table in the 'cabin'.

Mr Wales, the dry-skinned, cold-eyed astronomer, to whom both Forsters had taken, from their first coming aboard, an instant dislike, quizzed George, while they gnawed their way through the pie, about his mathematical exercises. The man was not his schoolmaster. How could he imagine this was dinner conversation – quadratic equations! The two officers brought in to leaven the talk of the gents talked to the Captain of ship's business – but the Captain was a taciturn fellow and had a Boswell or a Plato been commissioned to write down the table talk of the hero, they would not have covered half a page. As was often the case, Reinhold's was the voice which dominated the table.

—I do not say that, like the rat, the monkey actually carries disease – but it was a mistake – I should say most definitely. A mistake. Allowing the sailors in such numbers to buy these crea-tures. I mean one or two as, so to say, specimens. One who could perhaps be killed and stuffed. But you see only yesterday, a man stepped in . . .

Resolution

Captain Cook's silences were impenetrable. Did he not hear? Did he consider the defecatory habits of monkeys an unsuitable topic for the dinner table? George could not decide, though it seemed to the boy, as his father talked and talked, that the Captain was always on the verge of a reply, as though his firm lips were closed, lest words escape them which he might later regret. The filthy habits of the monkeys had not gone unremarked. Later that afternoon, the second mate, during a breezy swell, made a precipitous stride across the main deck. Concentrating upon holding his balance, and not seeing that he had planted his shoe in monkey-dung, he fell backwards, cracking his head against a sharp corner near the masthead. He did not lose consciousness but the incident was witnessed by the Captain who had been standing, as he so often did, staring out towards the limitless sea and the unknown horizons.

—Mr Clerke.

—Ay, ay, sir.

—Call for Mr Patten to dress Mr Marra's head.

—Ay, ay, sir.

—And, Mr Clerke.

—Sir?

—Order the men to throw every monkey overboard.

—I beg your pardon, sir.

—I think you heard me, Mr Clerke. Throw the little shitters overboard. Bekoss enoofs enoof.

It took not much more than quarter of an hour for the order to be passed around the ship. George's unnamed monkey was one of the first to be grabbed by an able seaman who was kind enough to say 'I'm sorry, boy' as he took the elongated black hand of the monkey and hurled it into the air as if it had been a ball. It happened so fast, George did not see his face, though he heard the creature shriek as it flew into the sky and then hurled downward into the foaming green of the seawater. More terrible was the fate of Plunkett. A tearful angry Nally tried to hold on to him.

—You're not taking Plunkett, you're not, you can't—

—It's orders, you fucking fool. Give o'er – Nally, let go the fucking monkey.

—No. No.

Plunkett was gibbering and squeaking as the sailor grabbed him. George saw his large eyes. Years later, a memory of that terror-stricken expression would return to George when, among the stinking baying crowds of Paris, he watched the chemist Lavoisier being trundled in a tumbril to the guillotine.

And on they sailed to the Cape, which they reached at the end of October, and where they spent a little over three weeks.

1784

GEORGE'S MARRIAGE BEGAN, AS IT WOULD END, WITH another man squeezed between them. Therese had begged George to allow her to bring Assad on the first part of the wedding journey. She had seemed, as the wedding day approached, so unwilling, so regretful about the whole idea of marrying, so taciturn, that George had actually felt glad of Assad's company; a third party was someone to whom they could both talk. In bleak East Prussian inns they had talked of Rousseau, of *Werther*, of Göttingen friends . . . The coachman was plainly unable to 'make out' the trio. Were George and Therese brother and sister, and was Assad her sweetheart? There was no obvious family resemblance. George at thirty was a small man, thin, with springy hair which appeared to sprout haphazard from his head rather than to 'grow'. His skin had never recovered from the scurvy he had contracted on board the *Resolution*. It was greyish, pitted. Many of his teeth had fallen out during the scurvy attack and those which remained were orange verging on mahogany in tone. Therese, with lustrous thick black hair and a high colour, had a squint. In all their years of marriage George never knew beyond question whether she was looking at him with one eye or avoiding his gaze with the other.

There exists a condition of self-consciousness in which memory plays a part, but which is not in itself memory. Time, if not suspended, has ceased to move in chronological order. In the smelly old leather coach bound for Vilnius, his right shoulder bruising the left shoulder of his bride, he remembered, but more accurately re-entered, all but re-enacted, the many journeys with his father, above all that uncomfortable journey down the banks of the Volga in '66. To use the simple word 'memory' of a bundle of associations summed up in the coach of his wedding journey would suggest a temporal sequentiality, and would also suggest conscious or total recall. It was not that he said to himself —This foul coaching inn twenty miles east of Warsaw reminds me of one near Danzig where I threw up and where Vati picked that quarrel with the local constable . . . Or, this moment when my wife – how strange that phrase is – my wife! has repeated her (German) words slowly as to an idiot or to a recalcitrant child asking for an omelette rather than the 'baked eggs' swimming in rancid fat which had been proffered by a filthy Polish hand. It recalled the inn at Harwich when slowly and three times Reinhold had enunciated in heavily accented English —I said that for stale fish vill ve not pay – words which mine Host of the harbour-front's King's Arms at first did not understand and then would not accept. Now, in Poland, his adult stomach involuntarily knotted itself into the same embarrassment. In Harwich in his late teens, he'd blurted out to the waiter —The fish was stale, we couldn't eat it! Now, his Polish less certain than his English, he suggested an omelette, or failing that, bread and cheese. It was almost as if the same waiter stared in puzzlement as if to ask —If you know my language why didn't you speak up earlier?

The English waiter had said – *Farndja tungven?* It was only about an hour after hearing the syllables that George had realized what they had meant. For a moment, in '84 in Poland, revisiting this moment of '70, consciousness had floated. The sensation involved recall but it was not a simple act of memory. Just as the slave boy in the *Meno* appeared, by his grasp of mathematical principles which he had never been taught to carry within himself the recollection of some prenatal – indeed preconceptual – spiritual existence, a soul's memory of eternity before the putting-on of human flesh, so George sometimes felt that real life, his soul's essential, timeless being, were like a collection of loose drawings in a portfolio; could be rearranged in any order. Here he was sketching the penguin in a limitless expanse of Antarctic whiteness, possessed by a feeling of ecstasy – whether induced by the extreme cold or by the Holy Ghost, or both – who was to say? Here was one rude waiter bringing filthy food, and here is another. He knew, of course he did, that events occurred in order but their significance was not necessarily temporally sequential; nor was the mood induced by the experiences, and if he asked himself, in that coach journeying eastwards with his bride, why he felt quite so wretched, the answer might have been a semi-articulated belief that the same experiences come round and round like the grotesquely painted animals on a carousel. Though he'd never been married before, he felt, as he sat beside his wife of ten days – *here we go again*.

Perhaps we learn how to be married, as we learn speech and manners, by copying our mother and father? Perhaps the children of those unsuccessfully married cannot hope themselves to be happy in wedlock? If marriage, like language, is a learnt knack, then Reinhold Forster resembled one of those who had passed a lifetime in a foreign land without bothering to converse with the natives, nor learning much more than a few phrases in which to command waiters or servants to bring food or wash clothes. That there had been physical intimacy between his parents George recognized – it was attested by the existence of himself and his siblings. Of friendship between Reinhold and Justina there was none. As the coach rattled eastward, however, George the married man could not attribute all his misery to his father's example. Quite enough had happened in the previous two weeks to make anyone unhappy: Therese's declaration in the days before the wedding that she passionately loved Assad – one of the librarians who worked for her father at the University.

She named him 'Assad' after Saladin's deceased brother in *Nathan the Wise*. Lessing's play was 'all the rage' among Therese's circle of friends, and the young bluestockings – all daughters of academics at Göttingen and nicknamed *die Universitätsmamsellen* – eagerly passed it from hand to hand, aware that its central idea – the equivalence of Judaism, Islam and Christianity – was offensive to the fuddy-duddies. Assad, whose real name was Friedrich Meyer, could not have looked less like an Arab prince. The twenty-six-year-old blonde man had rosy cheeks and those easy, German good looks – good skin, good bone structure. Of course, his passion for Therese fed a passion for Lessing, and they quoted chunks of the poet to one another. Only a few weeks before, as her hateful father ponderously reminded her, she had been madly in love, 'sick, body and soul' – her old dad cruelly quoted to her from her diary which his wife (her, even more hateful than Dad, stepmother) had read while tidying her bedroom – for another young man. Oh, how she hated them! Oh, how she hated the step-mother's philistinism —What good is *reading* to a girl? You'll never get a husband with your nose always stuck in a book! Her father, the old philologist, weakly acquiesced in this view, partly because he never dared stand up to the bitch, and partly because he genu-inely despised novels, and disdained her taste for Richardson, or Rousseau's *Emile*, or *The Sorrows of Young Werther*.

At fourteen, the girl had appeared enraptured with George Forster. Even his ugliness had recommended him, for the teeth had fallen out during his world-encompassing voyage and the skin had become pock-marked while he had painted boobies and petrels, while he had escaped icebergs, endured tropic heat, seen naked savages dancing before their carved fetishes, run from the Anthropophagi in New Holland.

She lov'd me for the dangers I had pass'd, and I lov'd her that she did pity them.

But there was the world of difference between the fourteen-year-old girl, listening to the travellers' tales of the celebrated scientist from Kassel University, and a twenty-year-old woman, married to the man, with his appalling breath!

—She's lucky to get *any* man, with that squint of hers.

That had been one remark by the stepmother. Overheard. And

it was not George's fault that the woman had said it – but it had made Therese hate not her father's wife – she hated her already, always had done – but the man *they had chosen for her*. Therese knew this wasn't true – not wholly true. She knew 'they' had been initially dubious about her growing intimacy with George. She knew that one of the bonds she had with him was that both she and George wished to escape their fathers. Once Professor Heyne, however, had accepted young Professor Forster as a potential son-in-law, it had come to feel like an arranged marriage, something stitched together by the men behind her back.

Unable to bear her hatred, hurt by it more than he knew what to do with, he had acquiesced in all her whims. It was actually he, George, who proposed that Assad should accompany them for the first leg of their journey east. Rather than protesting at her supposed 'love' of the man, rather than asserting his authority, telling her that she was not *his* – all of which might have persuaded her that he needed her, *loved* her – he had proposed that Assad came in the coach. Much of the time – for there really had not been room for the three of them to travel comfortably – George left the pair together inside while he shivered beside the coachman on the box above, pulling his collar about his ears and holding his tricorn hat by the brim lest it be carried by the wind that blew, cruel and uninterrupted, from the faraway Urals across the relentlessly boring wastes of East Prussia. Though it was only September, it felt, with every mile they lurched east, as if they were entering a winter of eternal dark and cold. Why had he been so acquiescent in her childish crush on Assad? No 'real man' would have done that. Frozen not only in body but in thought, and doggedly not listening to the Polish coachman's flow of anti-Russian, anti-Protestant, anti-Jewish, anti-human rant, he attributed his weakness

of willpower to ancient habits of mind in which he had always suppressed his emotions, said the opposite of what he felt: this was
the habit engendered by being Reinhold's travelling companion
since early boyhood. He knew there was an absurd melodrama in
self-pity. Yet, loving his father had been the tragedy of his life, not
least because – a fact which dawned on him only when he had left
Reinhold in England and, as a young academic, came to take up
his post at Kassel University in '78 – he did not very much *like* his
father, perhaps never had. The fact was too shocking to admit, until
he had been free of Reinhold, and to the end of his life George
did not like to articulate the fact. If he did not like him, however,
this was a minor detail, for from a time which pre-dated conscious
memory, he had learnt to love Reinhold. It had skewed love for
him. His idea of intimacy was with one he did not like, with one for
whom, internally, allowances had perpetually to be made. Therese's
refusal of his bedroom advances in that succession of awful inns –
Posen, Warsaw, Bialystock – his *acceptance* of this refusal – what
had this been except, in part, a continuation of life with Reinhold,
in which over and over again, George had learnt never to complain
at being given the uncomfortable side of the bed, or eating the less
palatable of two cutlets brought to a table? Later, when different
tactics were tried, when at an inn near Bialystock, he had become
angry, and he had forced himself on her, torn at her nightdress
and pulled it upwards to reveal her pubic tendrils which made
him wild with lust, she had wept. He tried to rape her but it would
not work – it simply wouldn't penetrate her – and her tears made
him revisit emotions which were terrifying. His uncontrolled rage
had not been with her alone as she both frustrated him and, at one
and the same time, filled him with pity, but also with Vati, who
seemed to be in the room beside them, oppressing him, dismissing

his amorous propensity not only as an outrage against bourgeois Lutheran virtue but as an interruption to *work*. Thus, in Tahiti, 'We need more drawings of those plantains – you can swim any time of your life – you might never see those plants again!'

While nearly every man aboard the *Resolution* had bathed in the blue water, and many of them gambolled with the island beauties, nakedly and uninhibited, George had sat, with his thick woollen stockings, buckled shoes, cotton shirt, worsted vest and coat, drawing the Tahitian flora.

Sometimes, quite explicitly, Reinhold would exclaim,

—Aargh! It disgusts a man. The way these human *beasts* behave! Twenty times in my head have I written a letter to my Lord Sandwich. A letter. That a Captain in the Royal Navy could allow such passions to rampage through a ship. Why, a petty thief is flogged on the main deck before all his shipmates, these people. But they go unpunished when they . . . when they . . . Has the Captain no control over these *beastly* impulses?

It had never been explained how Captain Cook could have restrained the amorous instinct itself as it surfaced in nearly a hundred sailors who had not seen a woman in months. George could never imagine, either at the time, or in his memory, whether Reinhold knew what it was like for his son to set eyes on so many naked women in Tahiti. Clearly he wanted to protect the boy, to preserve his virtue . . . And his own, perhaps? But his manner implied that only wild beasts, depraved creatures, could be charmed by the hair-tossing smiles, the open, white-toothed invitations, the firm round breasts of these young women. To the end of his life George would be haunted by them. The habit of *Onanie* to which even before the voyage he had become addicted was now fuelled by thoughts of those laughing girls. Their black hair reaching to the small of their backs, their laughter and evident enjoyment of life. Respect for and love of his father, fear of the desired object – for the island girls terrified him, and the effect they had upon him shook his being. These experiences conspired to twist and mould his unexpressive temperament.

So it was, as he sat, squeezed and cold against Therese as they rumbled together eastward to the wretched future, sat opposite her in unpleasant inns, sometimes trying to catch, sometimes to avoid, the glance which came from one or other of her squinting eyes, or lay sleepless beside her in flea-infested mattresses, that their soul-journey was not merely one which trundled painfully towards the future but also one which dragged with it the inescapable past, all its frustrations, angers and disappointments. Hence it was, sitting beside a grumpy, tear-stained twenty-year-old Therese with her tired head on his shoulder, and his conscious mind telling him he was sitting with a young bride, that his soul was trundling along the same rutted track it had always followed, the companion of the inescapable father. Others might have learnt to love as the Tahitians apparently loved, naked and smiling in the southern sun. George had learnt to love all right, but his love-object had been his father, so that love for him could not exist without the accompanying emotions of irritation, guilt, frustration.

They'd married, George and Therese, both agreed upon this on those occasions, over the eight years they were together, when they were able to talk about it, to escape their fathers. The paradox of the situation was that, although they hardly ever saw Reinhold – who was by now established as a Professor at Halle, for the whole eight years – he remained omnipresent in the one place in which he was as firmly entrenched as in the best cabin on the boat – inside George's head. Professor Heyne, on the other hand, whom they saw quite often, and with whom, when they did not see, they maintained a copious correspondence, was a man whom eventually Therese could put behind her – though perhaps this process of release was not complete until she had also escaped her husband and her unhappy marriage.

When she was thirteen, still smarting from her mother's death (which happened when Therese was eleven), and her father had married the twenty-five-year-old stepmother she hated, one of the Professor's friends said – in her presence – staring at her as if she were nothing better than a joke,

—Herr Hofrat, she's an ugly little thing, eh? She'll either have to make her way through comedy or by her wits.

—Don't speak to me of her wits. They'll scare off the men. That's what Georgine [the hated stepmother] says. Says we must send her to a boarding school where she can forget some of the things she's read. Tells me I should lock up my book-case and keep the key hidden!

That large grey book-case! Behind its criss-cross grilled doors and its dusty grey silk was concealed what – once discovered – could never be undiscovered. Its secrets could defy the best endeavours of cruel silly mistresses trying to make her read vapid French fables. She had already read Rousseau, Voltaire, Diderot, and – to her the most intoxicating of all the *encyclopédistes* – the Baron d'Holbach. Even before she had read ten pages of *Le Système de la Nature* she had known what it was going to disclose – it was actually a secret she had known for some time. Its truth had come to her in church, attending the interminable Sunday morning services with her father and her siblings. When her mother became ill, and the pastor came to assure Professor Heyne that God loved his poor flushed, wheezing consumptive wife, Therese had known that the words were meaningless. Reading the Baron d'Holbach merely confirmed, in the most heady, most joyous way, that her hunch was right. Some of the other *encyclopédistes*, such as Voltaire, persisted in saying that the machinery of the universe demanded the existence of . . . a clockmaker. Therese asked herself – what if it was a mistake to look for a Cause? What if Nature simply *was*? What if Spinoza was right and *Deus* was simply a word for *Nature*? If HE were to 'exist' it was impossible to use such a word of HIM without inverted commas; we would have to reconcile ourselves to living in a universe presided over by a monster of Cruelty, who *wanted* her charming, funny mother to be dying of this terrible disease – wanted her to have lost her babies – one a stillbirth, one killed by a smallpox inoculation – wanted all this and, not content to make her mother suffer so, sent the pastor to the door to say that the First Cause had sent all these horrors upon them out of love.

Therese never said a word about her secret to her father – though she whispered about it to the other *Universitätsmamsellen*, some of whom thought she was merely parading it as an exhibitionist trick, an affectation, and some of whom thought it was wicked. Only when she read Baron d'Holbach did she know she was not alone in the world.

Her parents' marriage had been a love match. Therese had watched the love die, in the mother, and in the father continue its reproachful burn. She believed that Christian Gottlob Heyne went on loving his first wife – she was also Therese – until he died in 1812. No doubt he could not help loving her, but everyone else in his family – especially his daughter – felt as if they were being punished for the mother's inability to love their father with the slavish passion he bestowed upon her. The stepmother made pretences – she openly regarded hers as a marriage of convenience.

She kept house for the 'old Professor' – as he had become in her eyes (he was after all twice her age) – and shared his bed. He gave her the house and money. One of the reasons Therese hated her stepmother was that she made her father happy.

Therese Weiss had been the daughter of a court musician and a woman who had been something between a nursemaid and a governess to one of the royal children of one of the Princes in Dresden. When her mother suffered an early apoplectic stroke, Therese Weiss took over her mother's duties. When the Princes grew too old for her, a position was found, as 'lady's companion' to an ageing noblewoman. Her thirst for knowledge was satisfied in the library of the old lady's late husband – her cultivation and good reading immediately impressed Christian Gottlob Heyne when they met. The other thing which impressed him was the fact that, during a bout of illness, she had been visited by her elderly lady's Lutheran chaplain, and been converted to Protestantism. It was an act of great courage, since it cut her off from all her surviving Catholic relations, who were horrified by her choice. Not only did Heyne share her faith, he admired her courage, and moral admiration, fuelled by amorous attraction, made her everlastingly his *femme idéale*.

She for her part had admired Christian Heyne's intellectual integrity and tenacity. Born in Chemnitz he was a year older than she was. His father was a linen weaver who found it difficult to make enough to feed his family, but who was generous enough to recognize his boy's remarkable intellectual gifts. Money was somehow borrowed to pay for books, and paid back by ingenious means. Christian made money as a schoolboy composing funeral speeches, Latin epitaphs, dinner-speeches to celebrate the achievements of local big-wigs. He found a free place, with board, at a local school. His excellent Latin became more than excellent, prodigious. He studied Law at Leipzig but the attorney's office or the Bar were never to be his *métier*. It was Latin that was his passion. One of the Saxon Gort ministers at Dresden, Count Brücht, took him on as household librarian and Latin tutor to his children. He was in this position when he met the love of his life. Within a year or two of his marriage to Therese Weiss he was offered the Chair of Languages and Antiquities at Göttingen University, and his career as a great philologist began – he laid the foundations not only of Latin but also of Germanic Philology, identifying the cognate forms of Old High German, Gothic, Norse and Old English.

There was time enough as he laboured over his grammars and dictionaries, and prepared his dry as dust lectures, for his wife's love for him slowly to die. Therese, their third child, watched the process with her too-observant squinting gaze. True, whenever he emerged from his study his first act would be to seek out his wife. Even in company he could not resist holding her hand possessively, stroking her arms, expressing endearments: but anyone could see her sinking into depression.

Frau Heyne was not a housekeeper. The maids were idle. The Professor's house was live with bugs, mice, even rats. Klauss, the half-mad butler, sat all day in his little boxroom next to the kitchen. Beside him on the small round table were his spectacles, a yellowing old copy of the *Frankfurter Allgemeine Zeitung*, a flask of schnapps, and a small dish containing bread pellets, lumps of stale cheese and the like. If a rat stuck his nose out of the wainscotting or poked his head through a hole in the floorboards, he would be rewarded with a little snack.

Upstairs, Therese remembered, her mother's little boudoir was never tidied. Piles of clothes gathered dust: and to the dust was added powder, some of it sweet-smelling talc, some of it the rice powder she used for dressing her wigs. When these wigs were removed, the daughter, whose own hair, young and springy, fell into ringlets on her shoulder, would note the oily coils which clung to the elder Therese's never-washed skull. Behind the pungent French scents with which her mother soaked her clothes and her bedding, there were other earthier smells, sometimes the acrid scent of armpits strong as cat pee, or that other rodenty smell which came from Frau Heyne's head when she took off her wig. Careless as she was about housekeeping and – as such – personal hygiene, the Professor's lady would take immense care in the application of beauty-spots and lead-based cosmetics to her face when she was expecting a visit from an admirer. Once the Professor was known to be safely fixated on his folio of Saxo Grammaticus or Einhard, his lady would tie a once-white yellowing handkerchief in her window as a signal for the admirers to pay court. These included the toothy, vivacious writer Friedrich Wilhelm Gotter, and a Law student named Johann Nikolaus Forkel – later well known as a musicologist and especially as expounder of the genius of Bach. Sometimes little Therese, literate from the age of four, adept at cut-out figures, precocious and conceited, would be allowed to sit as the little *salon* formed itself in Frau Heyne's dusty quarters. Later memory made the daughter suppose that a *salon* was what, principally, it was, where Geller, Haller, Klopstock, Young ('Night Thoughts') and Richardson would be eagerly discussed. Sometimes, however, if Frau Heyne had a solitary gentleman visitor, the intrusive Therese, bursting in to show him a folded paper which she had cut out, and which unfolded would reveal a row of dancing figures hand in hand, would be aware that her presence was unwanted, and the gentleman, on his knees and holding

Mama's hand as she sat in her little nursing chair, would tell her to 'run along'.

Göttingen – the small society of intellectuals, of the Prince's Court, of University and professional folk – the couple of hundred who were entertained in one another's houses, and who attended Baron Munchausen's 'evenings' – took an indulgent view of Frau Heyne's dalliances, even went so far as to say there was nothing improper about them. She does no more than accept devotion – she is like Petrarch's Laura, or like the female aristocrats of Medieval Provence, accepting the chaste worship of the troubadours. Even if 'more' took place – Heyne had only himself to blame. This was 'Göttingen's' view – he had risen, the linen weaver's boy, in part by his own endeavour, but largely through patronage – Therese had bestowed a favour on the young Professor by marrying him. The Baron had granted Heyne the privilege and title of *Hofrat* soon after he had arrived at the University. Yet he persisted in absenting himself from society – thinking his 'work' came first. What had he, the foremost philologist in the history of Europe, to do with powdered wigs, embroidered coats, touching lace-mittened aristo-cratic paws with his new-shaven lips as the fools pretended to play cards, and in the background, unheeded, a string quartet played Mozart? Their 'discussion' of the latest books or ideas seldom rose above the level of dinner-table tittle-tattle. They met so often to gossip about one another. Well, let them! So he had dismissively instructed his wife when she had implored him to go with her to the court.

Baron Munchausen – a cousin of the purveyor of tall stories – died, to be replaced by one Brand, a smooth-faced fellow with a pretty daughter. Frau Heyne sickened. They'd known, she and her husband, long before 'Göttingen' knew, and certainly before the truth dawned on Therese, what the coughing of blood, the flushed cheeks, the fevers and the sweats foreboded. She died when her daughter Therese was eleven. There was not much attempt by the sluttish maids to tidy the little boudoir in which they laid out the body: so when they gathered round the open coffin, and looked at their mother's still marbly waxen face, it was as if there was a ghostly presence. The closet, carelessly stuffed too full of unwashed clothes, burst open, and a cascade of linen fell on to the dusty carpet as they stood there beside their mother's corpse. Marianne, who was crying, immediately became their father's enemy – fights between them became frequent – Christian striking her face with the back of his palms. Carl who also quarrelled openly with his father soon left to join the army. (He perished in the Russian campaign in '94.) Little Therese, inside her head acting the role of Rousseau's Sophie, became the submissive model. Women – Jean Jacques taught this – *make men into what they want*. With the *Universitätsmamsellen* she whispered about the Rights of Women and the non-existence of God. ('Since I have been able to think I have been unable to pray.') All the father saw was an obedient little squint-eyed *Mädchen* trilling Gellert's pious song as she sat at the fortepiano – O *Lord My God!*

Secretary Brand's daughter Georgine married the widower Heyne. He was a grieving, bungling, bad-tempered man in his late forties: she was a briskly efficient twenty-five. There was never even the suggestion, the polite fiction, that it was a love match. She had the status of a Professor's wife, and a position in Göttingen. He had a much younger woman who kept house far more efficiently than the woman he had loved, and who appeared to enjoy the bedroom intimacies. Mimi was born in '79, Nette in '80, Philipp Eduard in '82, Frize-Friedente in '83. By then Therese, dispatched to her insufferable boarding school, had planned her escape. It could only be through marriage.

So these were their pasts, George's and Therese's, as they rumbled eastward to Vilnius, their childhood and adolescent experiences, like the luggage strapped to the bulk of the diligence, weighing them and swaying them, as the wheels slithered over sandy roads, as the landscape became ever flatter, ever more boring. At length, they approached the little city, fringed with dunes and flat-topped pines, past hovels on the outskirts of town which they both at first took for pigsties until they saw the round hostile Polish faces peering out of their doorways, past several churches with white towers and onion-domed cupolas, and into the cobbled main square. The apartment which had been assigned to the Professor and his bride was the central floor of a brown-stuccoed, flat-faced house in the middle of the square. Dabrowski, the University administrator, was there to welcome them – to arrange for the stowage of their luggage, to introduce them to two servants, a married pair called Kuminski, who bowed and smiled and spoke bad German to them. Dabrowski supervised dinner for them at the inn, told them how excited the Faculties were by their arrival, how eager for George's inaugural lecture. George thought he'd start by talking about the botany of the Pacific Islands.

It was only a matter of minutes, when the meal had been ordered, and, famished, they had begun to devour a delicious dish of cabbage stuffed with ground meat and a vegetable sauce, before Dabrowski – an earnest young man with straw-coloured hair and sore-seeming pink eyes – had asked George the inevitable,

—Please share with me, if you could bear it, sir – what was it like to sail with Captain Cook? Naturally, we have all – *all* – read your *Voyage Round the World*!

Resolution

Therese, too hungry to mind, filled her mouth with mashed potato and the melting meaty cabbage, wondering if all meals for the rest of her life would be like this – people eagerly asking about the Captain.

That evening, left alone together in a bed whose sunken straw mattress made their two bodies slither together in its declivity, neither Therese nor George had ever felt so alone in their lives. Neither of their mouths dared say it, or ask it, but their bodies asked it, whether this was the most fundamental mistake of which two human beings are capable, marrying the 'wrong' person. Both were so miserable and, suddenly, under inadequate blankets, so cold, that when they both wept, they held one another out of pity.

George's way of dealing with the mistake which was their marriage was to be out much of the day, teaching at the University, chairing meetings of his colleagues, putting his miscellaneous writings in order. Therese's way of dealing with the mistake was to behave, by a supreme act of will, as if it were no mistake. She learnt rudimentary Polish. She had an 'evening' to which the Forsters invited University husbands and wives. They played music. She made George twelve shirts. She re-read much of Rousseau. The worst thing about the 'mistake' was the extent of their anger with one another. She said,

—Since everyone wants to know, why not write another book about the Captain? Your work on botany could wait? *Cook the Discoverer* – there's a good title!

To which he, furious, replied,

—What do *you* know?

Behind her apparently harmless suggestion – and it was a good suggestion and one he acted upon – was *her* rage. She actually dated the moment when doubts about George had turned to hatred. It was after they had become engaged. On his last visit to Göttingen, her doubts had been suspended: they had talked of Lessing, of Herder, of English novels – she had imagined that this was how their future relationship would be. And then, a few days after he'd left to see his younger brother, working for a bookseller in Berlin, one of her father's colleagues, Herr Böttiger, had told her how much he was enjoying reading 'Über den Brodbaum', an article which George had given him just before he left.

—It is an essay on the most fascinating question of all – causation. Origins. Where do the different species in Nature *come from* – are they affected by environment? Is Goethe right, does all life stem from one single cause?

And Therese had felt a stab in her stomach which was as painful as if she'd heard George had screwed her best friend Caroline Michaelis. He'd been prepared to talk to the little woman about novels of sentiment: but there was another world which was only suitable for the chaps – the real voyage of discovery into an ocean of new knowledge. This was to be conducted on a shipload of males. The sting of hatred she felt for George, seeing 'Über den Brodbaum' in Herr Böttiger's hand, was something which never entirely left her. She tried all manner of methods – pretending it did not matter was quite inefficacious. Trying to *make* him talk about his paper on the Breadplant as a *way in* to discussing the origin of species themselves. This merely made him clam up: for, he sensed her anger, felt her 'making too much of it', so the subject became *verboten* between them. So she fell back on the Rousseau method. She became Sophie, made shirts, kept the apartment neat, resolved to pretend to enjoy herself in bed, in the hope that, in sexual matters, pretence could turn into something real, or almost real.

Resolution

In that mid-terrace, upper storey apartment in that brown flat-faced building in the square not far from the University, their first child, another Therese always known as Rose, was conceived. In that apartment, while Therese sewed those dozen shirts, and as they inhaled the pungent cooking smells from Maria's kitchen, George wrote what Therese considered his best book – *Cook the Discoverer*. During short winter days, so reminiscent for George of childhood days not so far away in Danzig, when iron-hard ice and snow lay under foot for five months, when it was so cold it hurt to breathe, when Vilnius, its little streets, its wooden houses, and its Romish churches always full of people at prayer, lay under a grey damp blanket of winter mist, he revisited in his mind the warmth, the bright colours, of Dusky Bay. Gliding to the University – you couldn't walk, skates were worn at all times outside – to give his lectures, and feeling the flecks of icy hail sting his cheeks, he would recollect the strange primitive sculptures of Easter Island and the bright cerulean sky behind them; and as day ended at three in the afternoon, and Herr and Frau Professor Forster ate their dinner together, usually in silence with a book propped open at their plates – trying to avoid one another's gaze – he would involuntarily recall the spontaneous welcome given to the sailors of the *Resolution* by the smiling, round-bosomed girls of Tahiti.

The pathos of their lives together, their loneliness, their shame at having got themselves into this thing, when it now seemed so blindingly clear that they were ill-matched, their almost constant catarrh, and stomach pains, the smelliness of their apartment, the discomfort of the furnishings – not one settle or chair where the body felt truly comfortable – above all the awkward discomfort of the bed – these horrors would often make them weep. Sometimes if they were drunk the sheer awfulness of it all made them laugh sorrowfully. In such moods they would hug one another. In these sad clinches sometimes they both wept, sometimes one wept while the other groaned with cynical laughter; in one such clinch, after several months of marriage, coition, for the first time, actually worked. He had become reconciled to the fact that he would never enter her – that however hard he tried to force or persuade her, Nature would not allow it to happen. And then, beneath the blanket, in the candlelight, while she still read Jean Jacques, it happened. She put down her book on the little round table beside the bed. It would be putting matters too strongly to say that she gave the impression of enjoyment, but her petulant, spoken interruptions —Hey, hey, not so fast – I'm not a horse – you don't need to canter . . . Hey, stupid – not there – *here* – implied at least the possibility of improvement. Then, after a few days, it was back to normal. He would be rejected with a jab of her elbow —Not *now*. No, no – George.

She only ever used his first name when she was correcting him or upbraiding or denying him.

After the entry, however, the penetration of the ice floes, it seemed possible to his male optimism that 'things' would improve between them. They began to talk to one another, as they had done in the days of courtship at Göttingen, about books. Lowering her guard, and in desperate need of talk – how she missed Assad, how she missed Caroline – she would ask him to read aloud to her. He read from *Cook the Discoverer*, my God it was good. And she read to him from *Emile*. And she would carefully avoid the subject of science and Philosophy and she would feel unexpressed fury for him as he avoided it too.

If they spoke of Goethe it was not of his colour theories or his idea of the origin of species, but of *The Sorrows of Young Werther*.

Resolution

—I remember coming to London after the voyage – and every-one you met was talking about it. Has there ever been a book quite like that?

—It starts with such joy – and neither Werther nor the reader can guess what an emotional precipice he is standing upon!

She wanted to go through the story letter by letter, to talk of the terrible despair which love brings with it – but he said,

—I can remember finishing the book in my little bedroom in Percy Street. It is such a pretty street – it looks out over rolling fields, and in the distance you see the hills and woods of Hampstead. And for about half an hour, although I had never been in love in my life, I felt I knew what it was to love, to feel this . . . this really rather absurd emotion.

Her silence told him he had said quite the wrong thing.

—I mean, it was absurd to kill himself. That, surely, anyone acknowledges.

His nervous laugh, which, he supposed, came as an attempt to placate her, to subdue her anger, always had the opposite effect.

—That is how you see it? Absurd?

—Yes.

—Love is absurd?

—No. No . . .

Allowing his voice to trail away, refusing to say anything which could rescue the situation, he allowed her to think – or as he furiously said in his silent hate – to 'think' – he'd said love, rather than Werther's extravagant self-regarding suicide, was absurd. But damn it – it *was* absurd, this talk of love when all it was, was Nature, forcing human beings to continue the species. And in that cold week, Rose was conceived. Their first born child. Neither of them knew how to leave a dispute, or an unpleasantness, behind. It was several days after their *Werther* squabble that she said to him, as he came into the room hoping for peace, even daring to hope for an evening of pleasure, perhaps a game of cards,

—It wasn't your saying love was absurd that made me so angry. It was your refusal to *discuss* it – you thought I'd been stupid, you thought I'd failed to distinguish between Werther's selfishness and—

—but you had—

—What did you say?

—You had failed to distinguish—

—So the little woman can't think. She can read novels but she does not even understand *them*. That is why we do not even bother to tell her about our *real* interests – our scientific papers we do not even show to her.

—I'm sorry – what is this about?

—Surely *you* are not so stupid that you need me to spell it out. And thus was their sad setting forth.

PART TWO

New and Awful Scenes

With sloping masts and dipping prow,
As who pursued with yell and blow
Still treads the shadow of his foe,
And forward bends his head,
The ship drove fast, land roared the blast,
And southward aye we fled.

I

1772

THEY WEIGHED ON 23RD NOVEMBER AND FOUR DAYS LATER,
in a high sea and brisk wind, George celebrated his eighteenth
birthday: a fine dinner of roast albatross and *Saur Kraut* at the
Captain's table, after which they all toasted him in the excellent
brandy which had been brought aboard at the Cape. Returning to
their cabins they reeled – unsure how much this was owing to the
swell, and how much to the Captain's good Cognac.

A kind of dew settled on everything and it was impossible to be
dry. At five in the morning, waves lashed the side of the ship and
through the seams of George's cabin a flood of sea water squished
over his bedclothes. He was in time to rescue the portfolio of
sketches which he kept, wrapped in oilskin, on a shelf above his
door. He was especially pleased with his bird paintings – a watercolour of a petrel and a pintada had both been accomplished since
he left the Cape.

—It's as if you could touch their feathers, Nally had said. Jesus,
what I'd give to have that gift – to be able to draw.

—You have other gifts.

—I'd be pleased if it was true, George, and that's a fact.

Nally was there next morning when he came out of the cabin, drenched, in the dark, holding the portfolio. Nally, even in pitched darkness, was an immediately recognizable figure. George could sense his presence even when he couldn't see it.

—Sure have you been sick?

—Nally, where are you?

—With a swell like this it can do you good to vomit.

The words were yelled at the wind.

As light returned they were aware of Dr Sparrman, the young Swede whom Reinhold had met in Cape Town, and persuaded to come aboard.

—The wages they offered your man – Nally was scandalized – £500! It would take me a lifetime to save a sum like that and they give him £500 – not that I grudge him. He's a nice quiet lad. There'll be some persuading the Admiralty to pay up, I'd say.

—The Captain says my father will have to bear the cost himself.

For the last week Reinhold and the Swede had been inseparable: whenever time allowed arranging plant samples collected in South Africa. George had had the runs ever since his birthday dinner, and took no part in the scientific work – dividing time between the privy and the sketch-book – and the everlasting conversation of Nally.

—Talking the old Latin the pair of them like a couple of priests.

As the glimmer of dawn brought Nally, soaked rigging, mainmast, the sea itself into clearer light, they heard Reinhold's voice,

—*Incubuere mari, totumque a sedibus imis –*

and the Swede's response,

Resolution

—Sehr gut! *Ponto nox incubat atra. praesentemque vivis intentant omnia mortem . . .*

How little, when they had studied the *Aeneid* at Pastor Büsching's school in Petersburg, had George imagined he would ever, like the ancestor of Rome and his companions, be cast forth onto the brine, and feel the journey as an emblem of some greater destiny.

—My dad would say, the priests could get away with gabbling Double Dutch for all we'd notice it – *et in saecula saeculorum* – that's one of the phrases—

—Indeed it is.

—George—

—Good morning, Vati.

—I heard you in the night. I heard you get up twice, thrice, to squitter. You should not let this looseness, those gripes, so to say, continue. Dr Sparrman will help you.

—Sure and I've told him he ought to try and vomit, said Nally.

Later that morning all hands were summoned on deck. The sea was lashing them and the roar of the wind made it difficult to hear the Captain's words. Cook, upright and unbudgeable as a mast, in his tricorn hat and his thick cloak from which the rain splashed in thick drops, bellowed,

—and I want every man of you at once – to put them on – We are going – very likely – [lahkla] – where no man has ever been – we are going to a land of ice and snow – and every man of us will come back alive. That is my duty to you – to the Royal Navy – and to God. And by God you must obey me. You must wear—

The words were lost in a tempest's howl.

Meanwhile, the quartermaster distributed the thick Magellanic jackets, the woollen Fearnought trousers and the thick red woollen hats. You could remove the Fearnoughts to shit and for no other purpose. This order created splutters of merriment among the midshipmen.

—Hear that, Forster?

At first George thought Midshipman Burney was making a jest about his weak bowels: but there are no secrets on board ship.

When the Lieutenant tried to check their impish cruelty, Burney unconvincingly said,

—It was the tossing of the waves, Mr Clerke, we referred to the tossing of the waves – not Mr Forster's—

—That's enough, Burney!

How did they know? When had he been seen?

Certainly, once everyone on board was swathed in the thick woollen garments there would be small temptation to remove them. Not only would the process be unwieldy, but the thermometers were falling rapidly. Even at dinner, though the woollen hats were laid aside, the cabin was so cold they were glad to be wearing their protective layers of warmth. The Captain was in expansive mood.

—I've studied Bouvet's journey till I could tell it by rote, chart his passage with my eyes blindfolded. Course, he was travelling from the coast of Brazil, but we're soon going to meet up wi' his course. The ice were unusually far north in '38 when he did the journey – he reached his icy cape on 1st January—

—which, being the Feast of the Circumcision he called it Cape Circumcision, said Reinhold. But before you tell us any more, Kapitän, I am sorry. Sorry. But I must. I must revert to the condition of my cabin . . .

Wales, the astronomer, cut across Reinhold, with

—and I imagine our difficulty will be to see how far south we may reach before we are wedged in—

Resolution

—Ay sir, by field ice. That will be our challenge. The floating iceberg we may by God's grace avoid, but – the field ice. I heard tell of a Greenland ship frozen solid in the water a whole nine week. We'd scarce survive that. We must – *must* – go as far south as God permits. That is the object of our voyage – to find the Southern Continent. But I shall risk not one man's life for it.

—We all have colds already, sir. My son has a disturbed gut – for some days diarrhoea – and the state of our cabins is a desolation – I could say without hyperbole, a disgrace.

—We'll go down as far as we can, Mr Wales. And if we fail to make it this time we'll retreat for New Holland or New Zealand for a while, and then return.

—Are you saying to me that the state of our cabins—

—The Captain was not saying anything, said Mr Wales. I take it upon myself to speak for the rest of us that if you have complaints about the accommodation they could be made to the master – and if your son is ill he could be referred to the surgeon. What he does in the privy and how comfortable you are in bed – these are not subjects for the table.

There was an awkward silence.

—Kapitän, does Mr Wales speak for the company? I have never before considered my conversation needed correction.

—We'll see tomorrow. They've been devilish days but we've made good progress – sixty sea miles yesterday, I reckon – so we'll see tomorrow. It's the fog that's worst. The *Adventure* were out of sight altogether today.

For two weeks they plunged south, the two ships sometimes losing sight of one another. Every man aboard the *Resolution* had a cold. The oakum had worked out of the seams of the ship, which was leaking. It was near impossible in their lumpy winter clothes to keep clean but each man, despite the cascading temperatures, was obliged to display his bare hands for inspection at six bells each day. Any with dirty hands had their allowance of grog stopped. So too those with frayed cuffs or torn.

—This is a Royal Navy vessel, said Cook. I'll have a healthy ship, a clean ship, a safe ship.

Two men were flogged for pilfering – two lashes only, but as Nally said,

—You could almost see the blood freeze on their backs by Jesus as the cat hit them, poor bastards.

Cook distributed needle and cotton to the men to make them 'shipshape'.

On some days the rigging hung so thick with icicles that it was impossible to manipulate the sails. They did no more than tack this way and that, trying to keep moving without collision with an iceberg.

—Mr Wales, Dr Forster, would you be prepared to reconnoitre our position – make an expedition in the jolly boat?

This on a day when the fog was so thick you could not see from one end of the deck to the other. George went with his father, the astronomer and the master. Nally volunteered to be one of the able seamen who rowed the craft. There was an eerie quietness as they rowed into whiteness. They tested the temperature of the water – 32° – and tried to gauge the currents. If the whole experience of being at sea transformed George's concept of time, this expedition in the jolly boat intensified the sense of temporality suspended. He would think of it in later years on the many occasions when he lay on a bed of sickness. As he lay dying in that cold truckle bed in the rue des Moulins in '94 this universal whiteness, this blanket of cold oblivion, this sense of being, yet not being, of bobbing and gliding into the unknown, with Nally's knees pressing his own, returned.

The jolly boat was out two hours. For those who had gone on the expedition it could have been two years.

—We nearly thought we'd lost you, Mr Gilbert, Mr Wales.

Vati found it in himself to mock himself.

—I was so frightened it silenced me, Kapitän Cook. Even I was lost for words.

The master said,

—We couldn't see a bloody thing. We could have been any-where.

—I know how you feel, Mr Gilbert.

The expedition happened in the week before Christmas. There was no possibility in these circumstances of finding the Southern Continent. Conscious of the hell through which he had put his men, Cook was determined to let them enjoy Christmas Day. He began the day with church – the Lord's Prayer and the Collect. In his *Journal* he wrote:

At Noon seeing that the People were inclinable to celebrate Christmas Day in their own way, I brought the Sloops under a very snug sail least I should be surprised with a gale of wind with a drunken crew.

There was plenty of rum for all of them. One of the hogs which he had been taking to breed in New Zealand was roasted. His own cabin was crammed with the gentlemen, and as many officers and petty officers as could be squeezed in, the others eating as usual in the gun-room. They drank Madeira, claret, brandy and rum. From below decks where the men were enjoying rum came the roar of

A. N. Wilson

song. Although there was the slightest of swells, everyone to be seen on deck swayed from side to side as if in a typhoon. In the afternoon there was a boxing contest, which the Captain and his officers appeared to enjoy as much as the men – only Dr Sparrman and Reinhold protesting at its barbarity as inebriates lashed out uncertainly at their opponents' faces, as teeth were knocked out and blood spurted, to the baying satisfaction of the audience. So much had been drunk that the pugilists felt brave enough to strip off and fight bare-chested.

—That's a grand lad, that one – Nally had somehow found George – just look at the sinews on the boy. The sinews.

—This is worse than the barbarities of Rome in its decline.

—But the men are enjoying it, Vati.

—That is what makes it so . . . so . . . *nauseating*.

Nothing distinguished the men of the *Resolution* so impressively perhaps as their ability to live with a hangover. Those who on Christmas Day had been scarcely able to stand upright could be seen early on the Feast of St Stephen clambering up the rigging with the confident handgrip of gibbons, heaving ropes, swabbing, scrubbing, patching the leaking seams with fresh oakum, regardless of throbbing heads and queasy stomachs. In spite of the cold and in spite of their frail bodily condition, there was constant reefing of sails and striking of top gallant yards as the proud sloops ran to the east at a rate of about twenty miles per day. Two weeks into the New Year – '73 – the Captain, with his impeccable navigational instinct and skill, steered sharply southward and on 17th January, just before noon, those aboard the *Resolution* became the first human beings in history to cross the Antarctic Circle – latitude 66°36½'S – four and a half miles south of the Circle – and longitude 39°35'E.

Resolution

The air had cleared, and they could see – the limitless miles of field ice, and the bergs, green in that midday light. Did any of them but know it, they were within seventy-five miles of the Southern Continent they sought.

For a week or two they cruised, gingerly fearful of being trapped in field ice, searching in vain for land. By the beginning of February, the appearance of penguins and petrels made them suppose land must be near.

—Where birds are, land is – this is Law.

—I would have agreed with you, Dr Forster, said the Captain, peering at the strange birds that swooped and swam, half waddling nuns, half graceful divers – but where *is* the land? We must discard the dogma. I wish I knew where the buggers found fish to eat. Mr Gilbert's been trawling wi' 'is net day after day and not a dab, not a tiddler has he caught. We could all do wi' a fish dinner.

The number of penguins following the ship was immense. Some of them outstripped the *Resolution* and swam ahead in the water. Others strained out of the sea and stood in formation on floating ice-sheets: small penguins, black above, white beneath, identified by George as *Aptenodytes papua*. Nally netted one for him and he painted its portrait before lowering it again into the water. From the beadiness of its eye and the semblance of a grin in its half-opened red bill, it seemed to take a satirical view of humanity.

Such cynicism as the bird appeared to express would surely, George thought, have evaporated, could it have looked with emotionally intelligent eyes on the fixed, fine-boned face of the Captain. Having tacked east and south for a week, Cook now resolved upon one last attempt to sail due south. Like a fencer who with coulé and glissade revolves his epée waiting for a chink to appear in his opponent's guard before cutting to the triumphant patinando,

Cook was determined upon one further lunge upon the mysterious south. George would never forget the concentration upon that honest face, the set of the very straight lips, the frost on his brows and on the rim of his tricorn hat as he stared resolutely at his aim. While other naval heroes had sought ships to fight, wars to win, Frenchies or Spaniards to cannonade into dark water, Cook was in pursuit of knowledge, his conquest would be a conquest of the future. Already, for the rest of the human race, the world was larger because of James Cook.

Further, further, further south to what George in his book of the voyage called new and awful scenes. Seals played on the larboard bow. Common and sooty albatrosses wheeled over the masts, with common and black-banded petrels and black shearwaters. Whales surfaced and spewed, huge islands of flesh, and a gigantic iceberg, a vast island of ice, loomed to leeward. As night-time approached on 18th February, the word got out that the sky was full of portents. Even those mariners who would have needed sleep, in readiness for an early watch, left their hammocks and came on board to witness the wonder of the Southern Lights, immense curtains of colour shimmering across the frozen skies.

—Die Himmel erzählen die Ehre Gottes, said George's father spontaneously and no man aboard would have contradicted him. While Mr Wales with his telescope and instruments made scientific notes – it was the first anyone ever knew about this Australian counterpart to the Arctic phenomenon of the Northern Lights – most of the men stared upward, awestruck by the colours – streaks of green, purple, orange – the wide extent, the sheer majesty of what they beheld – and beyond the skeins of coloured light they saw the bright stars and were speechless with what they felt.

Resolution

Next day, everyone on board heard that land had been sighted, but it was an illusion. Huge icebergs loomed. Two jolly boats were sent out to collect ice, for the bergs were fresh water, which could be brought back and stowed on the quarter-deck and in the sheep-pens. Everywhere they looked there were whales surfacing and ice-islands towering. A gale blew for a couple of days. Snow and sleet pelted upon them. Cook tacked south and north of the Antarctic Circle, but his conscience would not much longer allow him to take risks with the lives of the men. By 24th February they had sailed past over a hundred icebergs, and found themselves, after some squally weather and heavy sleet, surrounded by vast floating islands, green and white, which towered over them, many times taller than the mainmast. The waves dashed and foamed against their icy walls creating glories of light, colour and movement no less stupendous than the Southern Lights in the heavens. Hodges and George were busy with their pencils and brushes.

—We shall return! Captain Cook told the men at prayers the next morning. We shall find our Southern Continent. No one knows more than I do what valour you have all shown, what hardships you have endured. You need your rest and our good ship needs an overhaul – so does the *Adventure*, I dare say. So we're turning round now and we're New Zealand bound! If you think I haven't noticed how cold it is – our breeding sow farrowed nine pigs. This afternoon every one of which, poor little blighters, perished o' cold. I've seen your chilblains and your blue noses!

As he announced an additional measure of grog in appreciation of their hardships the men all cheered.

He did not veer north, he edged north, sailing east for ten days, covering a hundred and fifty-five miles, moving slowly. They saw the Southern Lights again, and then began their progress, north by north-east towards New Zealand. They sailed through torrential rain and gales. The ram, stowed with two ewes, had not been idle and when the time came for the lambs to be delivered extra care was taken to keep the animals warm. A makeshift byre was wedged between the master's cabin and Reinhold's.

—You will, of course, not expect me, Mr Gilbert, to stay—

—I don't know where else you want to sleep unless you can sling yer hammock below with the crew – and even there there's little room enough.

—You joke . . .

—Of course I joke, you silly bugger.

—And you think the Kapitän will not have something to say when he knows that on one side of my bedroom there are sheep bleating and pissing and on the other there are goats butting and shitting and my cabin is soaking wet and—

—You'd win a contest at belly-aching, Forster, wouldn't you?

—On the contrary, my stomach is in order. I keep nearly all my woes to myself. *Quocirca vivite fortes fortiaque adversis opponite pectora rebus.*

—Very likely.

—That is my motto and that of my son. Live, therefore, as brave men and turn a brave front to adversity.

—So that's your motto.

—So that's my motto. But to sleep in a shit hole with sheep and goats. Did the King of England expect this of a philosopher when he asked him on board? I could by now be the Director of your British Museum – instead I chose – and my son chose – to come on board the *Resolution* – but to sleep as a man sleeps, not in a midden, not in goat shit. Mr Gilbert? Mr Master? I asked you a question and could, I hope, be accorded the courtesy of a reply.

Resolution

One morning, George counted the days and realized a week had passed since he had seen a penguin. The gales, too, subsided. There were seals, skuas. The sea winked with bright sunlight. On Lady Day a voice came from the crow's nest —Land ahoy! It was New Zealand. There was a great swell, and rain pelted down, as the Captain, allowing himself a smile, applied a telescope to his eye and recognized the prodigious cliffs, the sheer slopes, the wooded hills, broken by the white gush of cataracts, the abundant, fertile welcome of Dusky Bay. Two leagues up the bay, he let go his anchor for the first time in four months. The pinnace was lowered. Mr Gilbert and four hands rowed out with their nets to ensure a fresh fish supper for all hands.

II

1785

NEITHER OF THEM WANTED THE QUARRELS. SINCE THEY WERE both intelligent people, they learnt various tricks of avoiding these, though sometimes involuntary irritation led them to slip. Desperate to keep together some semblance of conversation – if only to avoid embarrassing Marie, who stared, puzzled, at them as she served their silent meals – he began, cautiously, to show her his *Cook the Discoverer* book – even, after dinner, to read passages aloud to her as she breast-fed Rosechen. (Marie had tried to persuade Therese to find a wet nurse, had even impertinently suggested in broken German that the sight of her feeding the child would lessen George's ardour – poor goose – did she really suppose that since the child's conception there had been much of *that*?)

—What sailor would have eaten walrus, sea lion, polar bear, penguin, petrel or albatross without the good example of their Captain . . .

This made her jolt with laughter . . . and Rosechen momentarily lost the pink rubberiness of the nipple. George stared at his wife's swollen veiny breast as it happened, feeling interest but no lust.

But some of the time her comments irritated him.

—*Truth – that was the mission of all the great men with something to teach the human race. Truth, the relation of things to one another and to us . . .*

—Don't make it preachy. The best bits are the narratives – that passage about the New Zealanders, and Captain Cook visiting their huts, his courtesy. That was good. Let his passion for truth be clear in the story . . .

—Well, perhaps we have read enough for a day.

Instantly, though a quarrel was (just) avoided, a cloud of wretchedness returned, like the acrid coal smoke which billowed down the chimney and into the parlour when the wind changed direction.

—My God, I hate feeding this baby!

—Why do it?

And the veins on the wet breast and the little hand which clawed it, having seemed fascinating, became instantaneously disgusting to him. He knew that pretending not to hear what she called after him, as he left the parlour, would make her angry. Equally he felt himself too angry to stay in the room. So their days went on.

And then, one day, when he was out at the University – lecturing to the ladies of Vilnius on botany, a course he conducted in French – and Marie was cleaning his study and the baby was asleep, Therese looked out of their window and saw a Russian naval officer dismounting from his horse. Within twenty minutes of his having rung the doorbell, been admitted and given tea while a boy was sent to the University to bring George home, Therese knew that the officer was their saviour. He was a sea-captain named Grigorii Ivanovich Mulovskii. The news he brought was that the

Empress Catherine wished to finance another great voyage of discovery. Five ships were to set sail to the South Seas and to take up where Cook, on his third, fatal voyage, had been cut short.

—He won't speak of the Captain's death – even though he has almost finished his book on the *Discoverer*, he has not written . . . how he died.

Mulovskii, who was about her age, smiled politely at Therese's need to involve him in a marital tension.

—Captain Cook's last voyage, as you know, took him down the west coast of America. He sailed the Bering Straits. He visited the westernmost tip of Alaska, which he named Cape Prince of Wales. He came to Siberia, and then down the west coast of America and into the Pacific. Then of course—

The Russian was a handsome man. George could see Therese's squinty eyes taking in his muscular thighs in his nankeen, the blue coat, the braiding. The firm wrists emerging from his gilded cuffs. He saw the Slav's brow and the smile which played over thick, sensual lips. Already, only a few years into marriage he noted his wife's devouring coquettishness, but in this case, the fact of his noticing it had no more emotional effect on George than if he'd observed the colour of her dress. For his mind was racing ahead. Mulovskii was spelling out the details of the Imperial Russian voyage. They would go to London together, George and he, to purchase no fewer than five vessels – perhaps going to the north to buy merchant ships from Cook's old haunts in Yorkshire. George would be engaged as chief scientist and chronicler of the voyages. The terms were to be absurdly generous and he could have as large a team of researchers, draughtsmen, botanists, astronomers, bag-carriers and servants as he required.

—And, he stammered, Hawaii. We would – we would visit Hawaii.

Resolution

It was in Hawaii that the disaster had occurred. Therese knew that George found it quite literally too painful to contemplate. The dear old *Resolution*, accompanied by a ship called the *Discovery*, had sailed into the Hawaiian archipelago – Cook called them the Sandwich Islands – after they had explored the west coast of America. (The *Resolution* had a new young master, one William Bligh, much admired by Cook for his seamanship but hated by the men for his abrasiveness.) The islands' first European visitors had been sent by the Spanish conquistador Juan Gaetano, in 1555, but they had remained a Spanish secret, so well kept that the world knew nothing of them until Cook's arrival. The English ships first took in the island of Murci in November '78, though they did not land. A chief had come alongside in a canoe, his skin encrusted with scabs, his eyes inflamed with drinking kava, and presented the Captain with a fine yellow feathered headdress which he had worn proudly. Cook had not, at first, wanted to stay, however, and the *Resolution* and the *Discovery* had sailed southwards until it became clear to him he had made a mistake. Both ships were leaky and needed repairs; both crews were ill: he himself was exhausted and the outbursts of bad temper which were legendary even in the days when George had sailed with him were now a frequent feature of life. They were all drinking too much, when, after stormy weather – and it took nineteen days of blowy seas before they could put in at the easternmost part of Hawaii – Cook bought sugar from the natives and eagerly began the manufacture of a rather deadly beer – 'which was', he told his *Journal*, 'esteemed by every man on board.' It was not true – the men complained the beer was making them ill. He ordered the men aft and roared at them that no sugar cane could make them ill. Next day the cooper, William Griffiths, started drinking from one of the barrels and pronounced it 'sour' – which produced such rumbles of dismay among the crew that Cook believed them to be on the edge of mutiny. Griffiths was given twelve lashes.

The bad atmosphere aboard the British ships was matched by a sense that the islanders were not their friends. Cook lowered the anchors on 6th January and was welcomed with some ceremony. Accompanied by priests to their *heiau* or village temple, he had taken part in a ritual meal, and allowed himself to be wrapped in a red robe. He had found it difficult to swallow the lump of putrid hog which he was given to eat on this occasion. The scabby old man who had come aboard the *Resolution* in the previous visit turned out to be a king, and he returned to the ship with Cook for dinner.

There was trouble, however. The natives who followed the British sailors were pilferers. One of them, caught in the act of stealing clothes, was brought on board the *Discovery* and flogged. The sailors in their turn were stealing sacred images from the islanders on Maui – acts considered blasphemous. They even torched the temple. Cook's officers believed, in spite of these actions, that the people of Maui regarded him with reverence, even with worship.

At the beginning of February there were gales and the short voyages round the islands had shown the necessity of mending both ships before they put out once more to sea. There was a month's work here for the carpenters. The foremast of the *Resolution* needed replacement. The main topmast of the *Discovery* with that of the *Resolution* were requisitioned to be used as sheers. So, a little humiliatingly, they staggered into Kealakekua Bay, establishing the carpenters and sail-makers in huts to replace the masts and make the ships seaworthy. The Hawaiians, however, showed little respect. One 'rascal' got aboard the *Discovery* and stole the armourer's tongs. He escaped in a canoe, pursued, unsuccessfully, by two midshipmen in a cutter, firing muskets. Next day, the sailors found the owner of the escape-vessel, the canoe, and beat him with their oars. The next disaster was that the *Discovery*'s cutter was itself stolen, leaving much of the crew marooned in the ship. Cook, loading his double-barrelled firing piece, decided to act. He had always in all his voyages insisted on his peaceful intentions. He had never wished to 'conquer' the indigenous populations of the lands he discovered. On the other hand, nor could he brook the humiliation of their stealing with impunity, nor of their treating Englishmen with disrespect, nor of their mockery. He had always believed that the use of firearms was a last resort, but that if they were used, they would subdue the savage instantly. In Hawaii this proved not to be the case.

Some of the officers who had been ashore were attacked by the Hawaiians. The crews of two boats were pelted with stones.

—Mr Cooper, Cook said to his First Lieutenant on the *Resolution*, the behaviour of the Indians obliges us to use force. They must not imagine they have gained an advantage over us.

—And if they resist us, sir? asked the young master.

—There will be no resistance, Mr Bligh. I am very positive of that. The Indians will not stand the fire of a single musket.

With a party of armed mariners, commanded by Lieutenant Molesworth Phillips, Cook made the decision to go aboard, to make their way to the king's house. They found Kalaniopu'u asleep, and at gunpoint he agreed to accompany them back to their boat. Cook had meant to tell the villagers that if they restored his stolen boats and the other items, he would release the royal hostage. By the time they reached the shoreline, however, a huge crowd – thousands of angry people – were waiting. Some of them threatened

Cook with stones and sticks. The mariners fired into the crowd, killing one or two people. Then Cook fired his loaded musket at a man. He was instantly set upon, stabbed from behind.

—Get back to the boats! he was able to call out before he was hit again.

His officers and men obeyed him, crowding into the pinnace and rowing at speed back to the *Resolution*. The cutter from the *Resolution* rowed back to give the men cover, continuing to fire into the crowd.

Cook was dead; so were four mariners. The islanders took his body. It was impossible, in after time, to be quite sure what the islanders had done next, nor was it apparent why they had acted as they did. Some of the sailors believed that the islanders, aware that they had slain a great man, had identified him with one of their gods – Lono. There seems some evidence that in his visits to the *heiau*, Cook, when arrayed in a priestly cloak by Kalaniopu'u, had been addressed as Lono. In Hawaiian mythology, Ku is the God of War who enacts a ritual battle each year with Lono, a fertility god. Evidence for the identification of Cook and the Gods seemed scant enough. Clearly, however, they had recognized his high status. When the next day Commander Clerke – who succeeded Cook and took charge of the expedition – went back to the islands to beg for his remains, he was treated with respect. There were to be no more killings.

Some days later, the carpenters finished work on the new mast, and as it was carried to the boat to be transported to the *Resolution*, the men were met by a long procession of natives, carrying green boughs, hogs, fruit, roots and beating drums. The chief, who led a gang of wailing natives, presented Commander Clerke with a bundle, which he gently carried back to the ship. The body had been burnt – roasted rather than utterly cremated. The bundle contained the scalp and all the long bones, the thighs, legs, arms and the skull, missing the jaw. The hands were wrapped separately. No flesh remained on any of the bones, except upon the hands – the right hand was instantly recognizable, bearing the scar between thumb and forefinger which he had borne since, as a young sailor, he had suffered an exploded powder-horn off the coast of Newfoundland.

The next day, the chief was rowed out to the *Resolution* in a canoe, bringing another bundle: the Captain's jaw-bone, his feet, and the twisted broken musket. The remains were put in a coffin and late in the afternoon of 21st February, they were lowered into the waters of the bay. The mast was fixed. The *Resolution* sailed for home.

George could not write these things, though he knew them, and had determined with great concentration to find out all that could be known. He discerned very soon, not the obvious things he had already surmised – that the scene of the Hawaiian tragedy was a muddle, a riot, whose exact details would be impossible to recapture – but other, more troubling truths. What had his own *Voyage* book been, written with the deliberate intention of attracting a public sale in advance of the publication of the Captain's own *Journals*, but a form of disembodiment, a scalping, a severing of limbs? Yet he too, like the islanders who had taken Cook to pieces, worshipped the man he had dissected, worshipped in a way he could never revere another person. The journeys of discovery which Reinhold had initiated when he first opened Linnaeus or took the boy down the Volga was a voyage of fits and starts: an unsatisfactory chaos of explorations. True, Cook had not found the Southern Continent. True, he was murdered before he had completed his explorations of the American western seaboard or established the existence or otherwise of the Northwest Passage, but nonetheless there was a purity of purpose, a simplicity of aim, an integrity of intellect, a majesty, a stature about this man which made him, indeed, possess qualities which in certain human usages could be termed divine. George finished his book by ignoring the fact that Cook had been buried at sea.

In my passionate Enthusiasm I now think of him at this moment, as one of the beneficent heroes of antiquity borne aloft on eagles' wings to the assembly of the blessed gods. Were he, from the heights of Olympus, to cast a glance earthwards, he would see the academies of science who crowned his endeavours with honour in his life time bestowing upon him an immortal garland; he would see the tears of abject sorrow flowing, throughout Europe, for a noble man too early cut short; he would see the History of his Voyages, a more lasting monument than bronze or marble. He would also see the blossoms of Friendship strewn upon his grave.

And now the Russian officer had brought George the chance not only to immortalize the Captain in prose – to 'cash in' as Therese mercilessly called it – but also to follow in the hero's footsteps, to sail again to the Pacific – without Vati, without Therese.

The prospect offered by Captain Mulovskii filled both the Forsters with a joy which was almost unseemly. They had never been like this with one another before. What had weighed, so horribly, was the knowledge that there was no way of escape. Therese's letters home from Poland, her graphic complaints to her father that George had been violent with her, forced himself upon her, provoked merely paternal denunciations, and a short, infuriating note from the stepmother – did Therese not know what was expected of a wife, and with a little care and *practice* – oh how odious that word was – it was the duty of a wife to please her husband and to give him children. Did she know how very *angry* her letters made her father? Georgine must ask her to desist from sending them.

Separation, then, could only be achieved by death, or by a miracle. (They both, silently, severally, hoped for the same death – George's, for Therese's *grasp* of life was too total for it to be entirely possible to imagine the planet without herself upon it.) And George could never shake off the instincts – *thoughts* would be too definite a term – of *Sturm und Drang*, *Liebestod* and the Romantic sense that life should be short and intense. Only when the Russian offer had been made did either of them realize quite how unhappy they had been, quite how desperately they both yearned for the mistake – their marriage – to be . . . not set aside, for they knew that it could not be quite undone; but . . . They wanted to be able to live. Ever since their going away to Poland this burden, their mistake, their inability to be happy, had hovered over them. It had wasted so much time! They had escaped, they were resourceful people, into the narcotics of literature, work, even a little society when they found German-speakers. The minute, however, that the narcotic had worn off, when the volume of Rousseau had been placed on Therese's table, or when George laid down his pen and stopped writing sentences about the Captain, the waves of misery would return.

Now, however, with furniture, books and clothes packed, with a tearful Marie taken leave of, with a post-chaise heaving lumberously to Warsaw, they could almost have been mistaken, by

A. N. Wilson

other passengers, for a little Trinity of love, the parents and the gurgling Rosechen. The plan was for Therese to reside at Göttingen with their daughter during George's year at sea. Either she would find an apartment of her own or she would reside with Caroline Michaelis – now married to the district medical officer, Böhmer. In Göttingen, she would be free, with Caroline, to lead an intellectual life. She would have the run of the University library. She would be surrounded by like minds. Nor did she object, with the prospect of separation so imminent, to basking a little in her husband's fame: for Mulovskii's offer, the Empress Catherine's offer – to enable the young man who had sailed with Cook to take again to the high seas – made George's fame universal. At Warsaw, he dined not once but twice with the King. Stanislas was an intelligent man who asked in detail about the state of the faculties in Vilnius, about the chemical discoveries of Mr Priestley and M. Lavoisier, about electricity and Mr Franklin.

The journey out in '84 had been unendurably slow. The journey home, with its changes of horses and coaches and the same inns no less uncomfortable, was all positively enjoyable.

—We'll be going through Halle?

Her question was natural enough. Six years had passed since he had seen Reinhold. He could not quite articulate to himself, still less to her, why he would not. He dreaded his father's envy of this new voyage? He could not endure the advice which would stream from Reinhold's mouth? Of these things he was sharply aware. Beneath their crystalline surface, however, was a feeling, having penned the final paragraph of Cook the Discoverer, and crowned the Captain on Mount Olympus, he had also enthroned him in his heart, finding a father for whom no apology need be made, a father for whom *pietas* was unmingled.

Resolution

—Let's go through Weimar. We can make the pilgrimage!

There was no need for him to *name* Goethe. Perhaps, in suggesting that they actually visit the author, he hoped to lay to rest the demons who flew out during their first strained conversation about *Werther*. Both of them had met the great man before – indeed, Therese's father is actually mentioned in the novel when, in its early, sun-filled pages, before the Sorrows begin, Werther meets a young student who was reading, among other things, notes taken during a lecture by Professor Heyne, on the Primitive Ordering of Society in the Homeric Poems.

But, delightful as it was to see Weimar – Goethe was not there. He had started on his Italian Journeys. They dined instead with Knebel – who was the tutor to the young Prince – and with Herder the Moderator (*Generalsuperintendant*) – and talked of Homer, of folk-songs, of Philosophy (of which Herder was writing an enormous history). Herder expanded on his theme, that human civilizations like human individuals have births, maturities and deaths.

—And what of us, smiled Therese, are we in our maturity or on our death bed?

—We? When I talk with you – you are what? Twenty something? And I am forty-two. I think you are the future, waiting to be born! But if you mean is the Holy Roman Empire on its death bed? Is our broken, fragmented Germany with its Grand Duchies and Prince Bishoprics and Electorates, with its Cardinals and Princesses – if you mean is *that* on its death bed – dear woman! It has already died. It died the moment America sent the English packing.

—You think there will be a Revolution in Europe? she asked.
And George, just as eagerly,

—That we will overthrow thrones and altars?

So it was not to the old Göttingen that they returned the day after next. It was to a new world of infinitely exciting prospects.

She renewed her giggling flirtations with Meyer almost as soon as she stepped into her father's house – there he was, Assad, the mysteriously annoying collusion between him and Therese instantaneously resurrected. George had had no choice – had he? – but to accept her old assurances that her 'love' for Assad was innocent – the sort of 'love' her mother had encouraged in her visitors.

—Look at the way my father behaves! Even to greet us, when we've been gone two years, he scarcely comes out of his study. Poor Mummy never *saw* him, she loved him—

Yes, but you *don't* love me, was the sentence George left unspoken.

—It's only like you and Sömmerring – you and Captain Cook.

—It's not like Sömmerring – none of my friends said . . .

He could not finish the sentence, 'say they are in love with me.' No one had ever *said* they were in love with him and as far as he knew only one person ever had been in love with him – that with disastrous results. But there was no time any more to mind. Mulovskii wanted to accompany him to Copenhagen to look at ships. There was a whole team to assemble. Bayly – astronomer on the *Adventure* when Wales was the astronomer on the *Resolution* – had been enlisted. In Denmark they met a number of artists, botanists, cartographers and philosophers who wished to be involved. Mulovskii went on to London alone. George came slowly home to his wife, preparing to take leave not only of her but also of Germany. He came through Lübeck with its many-masted harbours and wooden-gabled houses. He stopped in Hannover and saw one of his sisters and he spent New Year in Charlotte Kestner's house – she'd had several long marvellous letters from

Goethe in Italy. Yes, Herder was right, the old world was on its death bed, a new one was waiting to be born. It was a palpable feeling – you could almost see it in people's faces, as the bells rang and 1788 began.

Nothing prepared him for what would be awaiting him in Göttingen: a letter from Mulovskii in London. The previous August, Russia had declared war on Turkey. —This won't affect things – our expedition? George had asked, and the Russian's reply had been —I do not see why it should.

Now, the state of things had changed. The letter was in French. *Tout à fait désolé . . . l'Impératrice s'interesse beaucoup en les recherches de M. Forster . . .* But war was war. All expenditure must be devoted to the defeat of the enemy. Until hostilities ceased, the expedition must be regarded as cancelled.

George stood in the panelled hallway of his father-in-law's house as he read this letter. His hat was on the marble-topped table. He had not even removed his travelling coat as he stood there with the paper in his hand. Therese and Rosechen had come out to greet 'Daddy' but while he looked at his mail and removed his outer garments and read the letter, they had gone back into the little green parlour with its silhouettes – made by Therese – of her mother and father, brother and sister, on either side of the little chimney piece. Caroline, with her thick shock of hair falling loosely over her shoulders, was there – and the ridiculous Meyer. When he came into the room, Caroline said,

—Your face! You've seen a ghost!

—The Captain's? asked Meyer, and the three of them all laughed.

He tried to suppress his hurt and his fury by falling to his knees to kiss Rosechen – but shy, not having seen her father for two weeks, she hid her face in her mother's skirts.

Then he told them what was in the Russian's letter.

The implications of it did not sink in all at once. All that had been making them happy for the last months had now been removed from them. Irrational anger with one another surfaced: it was somehow not bearable that they would have to take up the struggle of married life with the prospect of the limitless future.

One weekend, when he heard her taking leave of Meyer and calling him 'Darling', George's temper snapped.

—This *cannot* go on.

—I don't know what you are talking about.

—You know perfectly well.

—You have your friends.

—You know this is different. Why do you always like to argue with the use of false analogy?

—There's nothing false. I have not hidden my feelings for Assad. It was you who invited him to come on our wedding journey. Assad—

—God damn it. I won't continue with this Assad nonsense. He's bloody Meyer and I won't have it – do you hear?

This had never quite happened between them. They had had rows. In the bedroom he had on a number of occasions tried to force himself on her, and though penetration against her will had proved impossible they had physically wrestled. That had been behind closed doors, however, only overheard by Marie. But now they were wrestling in one of the public rooms of her father's house. He had grabbed her shoulder and was shaking her. She pummelled his chest. She was weeping with frustration and rage.

—O you are a tyrant – I have no freedom—

—You mean you take liberties – liberties no man could allow his wife.

Resolution

—Oh God, oh God, God, God!

—What in the name of Heaven are you fighting about?

The Professor had appeared at the door.

—I will *not*—

George was still so beside himself with rage that he could not release her and continued to shake her shoulders.

—O Daddy. Daddy, you see – now you see . . .

And her sobs were uncontrolled.

—Yes I do, said the Professor quietly.

George released her. He could not look Heyne in the face.

—I think you should leave now, sir.

—I shall go to my room, mumbled George.

—I mean, I think you should leave this house.

While he packed his belongings, the house seemed numb as if the doors and walls had been blockaded with bolsters. Then, now and again he could hear muffled voices. His stepmother saying,

—but you wrote such happy letters from Vilnius . . .

and Therese muttering something in reply, and Heyne saying,

—My poor child.

George had no real idea where to go. When, after an hour or so, he had packed, he went in search of the nurserymaid, Beata.

—Where is Rosechen?

—I think she's curled up with her mother.

The maid spoke in the thickest of Westphalian voices. She looked at him reproachfully as though he had been beating both his wife and his child.

—I am going away.

—So oi ears – *surr*.

—I want to say goodbye to my child . . . to my—

He did not need to justify himself to a nurse, but her stares made him stammer with shyness.

—The worst thing, Therese said a month later, was your not even bothering to say goodbye. Just walking out. I can understand your being angry with me – but not even wanting to see your child before you went to Berlin.

Berlin had seemed the obvious place to go. His brother was still there, working as a publisher. There might even be work to be found. Besides, natural curiosity made George want to see the Prussian capital with its new King – Friedrich Wilhelm was a very different fellow from his militaristic genius-uncle Frederick the Great.

He and Therese had sensed something different about Prussia on their journey home. There had been road works everywhere, and now, as he showed his Westphalian passport at the border, he could see not only the construction of a new highway, but what seemed to be a trench.

—Canal, isn't it? the customs officer replied, to his question. England has 'em – we're moving with the times.

As he approached the outskirts of Berlin he could see that the old wall, with the little gate on the Brandenburg road, had been demolished: three-quarters constructed, the new Brandenburg Gate's great neo-classical pillars soared confidently to the skies.

His old Kassel friend, Samuel Sömmerring, was paying a visit to the University to give a series of lectures on human origins. The pair had not had a chance of a proper conversation since they had been colleagues together. George had not known Sömmerring was going to be there – they met by luck in the scientific faculty building where George had gone to leave his card, in the hope of meeting some of the professors – perhaps – who knew – finding work?

Resolution

Goldhagen, the Professor of Natural Sciences, had lately died, and even if George stood no chance of succeeding him, he might pick up a more junior post in the general all-change brought about by Goldhagen's departure. Seeing on a noticeboard that Sömmerring was to lecture that afternoon, George simply joined the crowds on the assembled benches. George loved Sömmerring, who was a year younger than himself, but at the same time the reunion awoke feelings which he had put to one side – suppressed from sheer embarrassment. Recognizing his friend's long intelligent face, sharp nose, fleshy lips was to be reminded of the episode in his life of which George was most ashamed. The reason he had left Kassel and gone into Polish exile. It was in Sömmerring's company that he had given free rein to the side of his nature which was the least becoming, the most absurd, so that to set eyes upon his friend, in his formal dark cutaway coat from which a medal was suspended on a ribbon, and its crisp frill of shirt front and white cravat, was not to see what the rows of students saw – an embodiment of scientific reason. George, by contrast, felt as if he were seeing a man with whom he had been on an especially shaming debauch. He and Sömmerring were upright men: they did not drink to excess or visit bawdy houses, but George, looking back upon his last year at Kassel, was to create embarrassment of the same potency as might possess the soul of a respectable citizen when he looked back with incredulity at an evening of excess. What? Did *I* do *that?*

George and Reinhold, when in London, had been admitted to a Lodge of Freemasons, and although it never crossed Reinhold's mind that such professional success as he enjoyed was owing to anything but his own talents, the son felt that much of their British success derived from their Masonic connections. Freemasonry for George was not primarily connections by a collective of networking and self-promotion. Nor was it a branch of arcane knowledge. He saw each Lodge as a beacon of hope for the earth, a place where men of different backgrounds and faiths could meet as equals, where privilege based on rank counted for nothing, where humanity in future might use reason to create a fair and just political system as they had done in America. *Dann ist die Erd' ein Himmelreich und Sterbliche den Göttern gleich* – then is the Earth a Heavenly Kingdom and mortals like the gods. In Kassel, as he had taken up his job as a Professor, the Head of the Faculty had greeted him with the secret handshake. Just as for some men the erotic impulse or a taste for alcohol cannot be held in check and, once indulged, leads on to orgiastic intemperance, George had a weakness for mumbo-jumbo. In the embarrassed years since Kassel, in the moments of recollection when he had been able to confront what he had done, he had asked himself whether the observation – the bent towards fanaticism – was not precisely a side-effect of his intense devotion to the life of the mind; whether, precisely because he had devoted ninety-five per cent of his life to rational discipline, his mind did not crave, as a sort of intellectual equivalent of *Mardi Gras*, five per cent of sheer silliness.

He and Sömmerring, whose friendship at Kassel had begun as a shared passion for botany, astronomy, anatomy, the new chemistry, joined the Rosicrucian Order which had been assembled by some of their Masonic cronies. Now you could not imagine a truly sensible person, such as that embodiment of sense, Captain Cook, being taken in for five seconds by the 'secret knowledge' supposedly handed down from the medieval figure of Christian Rosenkreuz – with its muddling of magic and mathematics, with its childish and obviously modern 'traditional' rituals, and its strange mingling of the wisdom of old Egypt and crackpot scientific theory. Perhaps the battiest Rosicrucian of them all, in George's lifetime, was an English doctor called James Price who revived the age-old fantasy of the Philosopher's Stone which could turn base metal into gold.

Perhaps George's dire financial difficulties (he'd inherited Reinhold's inability to manage money) predisposed him to believe Price's absurd theories. Not content, however, to read Price's literature, George had introduced his name into his University lectures at Kassel – and had even made public attempts, by a combination of bogus chemistry and mumbo-jumbo formulae, to turn quicksilver to gold in the University demonstration room. The laughter of his students saved him. He had seen at once that he had been duped, that the whole Rosicrucian episode had been a species of brain-fever. It had also left him with a hangover of shame, which was why he'd accepted the King of Poland's offer of the Chair at Vilnius. Time to move on.

Now he was in the audience to hear Samuel Sömmerring addressing not only a hundred young students, but as many again grown-ups – distinguished academics and members of society. Sömmerring's career did not appear to have been damaged by his dalliance with the Rosy Cross. He had left Kassel for the Chair of Medicine at Mainz and was now regarded as the leading German anatomist.

Sömmerring's lecture was a masterpiece, not only of scientific exactitude but of humanism. He described to his audience the theories of human origin, and of the differences between human races, which had been current when he began to study medicine. Many people supposed that savages, in Africa, or in the South Seas, were of a different species from Europeans, perhaps that they had smaller brains, or different hearts, lungs, livers – which made them more 'backward' than, say, Frenchmen or Russians. At Kassel,

Sömmerring had been privileged to work in a University town sponsored by a Landgrave who not only had an extensive menagerie, containing baboons and chimpanzees, but also employed as servants many former African slaves who had worked in the plantations of the American Republic. As these slaves and apes died, it was possible to dissect their cadavers in scientific conditions and to compare them with the corpses of Germans.

—Gentlemen, I can tell you this after several years of research. There is a kinship – you cannot deny this kinship – between human beings and the apes. The hands, the facial expressions, in many areas, the cousinship, so to say, is visible. The differences, however, are greater than the similarities. Can an ape talk? Can an ape form grammatical sentences? Does an ape possess what we could recognize as a moral sense? Now let us turn to our African brethren – for that, gentlemen is what they are. Beneath the brown skin, and beneath the frizzier hair there is a human being who cannot be distinguished from a German. No difference in brain, or heart or in any other anatomical particular. Consider, gentlemen, the implications for this in our day when, for all our claims to be enlightened human beings, we take poor men and women, and their children, and, merely because we are rich and they are poor, we allow them to be purchased as if they were chattels. Gentlemen, when I showed this paper on anatomy to my friend the English chemist Mr Priestley, he showed it in turn to his friend Mr Wedgwood. And he made these . . .

Sömmerring held up a medallion showing a kneeling African in chains. Around the rim of the medallion were the words, AM I NOT A MAN AND A BROTHER?

—Gentlemen, those words are not the words of sentiment. The world will change when it realizes the scientific truth that we are all indeed brothers, identical in physical composition, equal, surely, in the eyes of Our Creator.

The words brought the entire audience to their feet in an ecstasy of applause. Naturally, afterwards, audience members clustered around the speaker. As George pressed forward, he found himself looking at a familiar shoulder, the unmistakeable slope; the hair on the back of the neck a little greyer now, but not white. He was a few months short of sixty. The coat was not the very one in which its wearer had sailed to New Zealand and back but it was of exactly the same homespun light brown cloth which he had worn since early manhood and which George, more sensitive in these matters, had always felt a little too countrified for meetings of the Royal Society in London, or for academic assemblies in the Prussian capital. Tapping the shoulder, George said,

—Vati.

The elder Forster covered his surprise with bonhomie.

—A change, eh? Ja ja! To hear the German language spoken here? The new King brought in the reform at once, of course.

There was something in his bustling, pompous manner which almost suggested – not quite – that the new Prussian sovereign, who had in fact never met Reinhold, had overturned Frederick the Great's ban on the German language upon his personal recommendation. Until Frederick's death all lectures in the University and indeed all public discourse, in the Reichstag, and among departments of the civil service and the military, had been conducted in French.

—It was moving, the ending.

—How do you mean?

—I found Sömmerring's conclusion very affecting.

His father gave him a sharp look, as if to check a display of emotion.

—I was pleased he mentioned Mr Priestley and Mr Wedgwood.

—Well, I mean – if ever there was a stunt! The brotherhood of mankind.

George felt it all, all over again. His father's refusal to be impressed by another's achievement. His (surely deliberate, for he was an intelligent man) inability to remember the slogan correctly, and his apparent inability to see how nearly, and with what inspiring optimism, it expressed both moral aspiration and scientific fact.

—There's Sternfeld!

And for a moment the father left his son in the crowd, elbowing his way towards the elderly academic in a powdered wig who was standing near the lectern.

When he eventually got to speak to Sömmerring, all embarrassing recollections of their Rosicrucian adventures fell away.

—My dear George, what brings you to Berlin?

—Your brilliant lecture?

—No, but seriously.

—This and that.

Sömmerring was being 'dined' by the University, but they agreed to meet after dinner. George ate at his inn with his father. Reinhold, who must have felt hurt by his son's failure to keep in touch over the previous few years, determinedly showed no such emotion. His talk was of generalities. He alluded to his publisher son. George wondered whether to tell his father that he had written *Cook the Discoverer*. Reinhold, either truthfully, or with a very good air of bluff said,

—I'd heard. It could be successful.

He sniffed.

—All the same, some original scientific research might have

been more to the point. Whatever became of that paper you were going to write on Meiner's *Anthropology?*

Gnawing on a rib-bone of pork, later in the meal, George asked his father, who was attacking a third dumpling,

—How's Mother?

Reinhold continued to eat, giving a sly look, as though the inquiry were some kind of trick question. The thought crossed George's mind that his mother might actually be dead and that his father, in order to avoid seeming an object of pity, had paused before answering. Later, George came to a different conclusion, believing that his father's hesitation had been caused by reluctance, perhaps by actual inability, to shift the subject of talk away from himself or his own opinions.

—Only, he said at last, she has always known Berlin is my great love. Here I studied. Here I hoped to devote myself to scientific research for the rest of my life had not poverty forced me into the ministry and that hellish little parish at Nassenhuben. A man of my interests and abilities at Nassenhuben! Of course when we heard that Goldhagen was dead and the Chair of Natural Sciences at Berlin was vacant . . . well, she has established herself in Halle now with her little circle of knitters and chocolate-drinkers, but she understands. It would be more fitting for us to be here. The Chair . . .

—They've offered it! Vati, this is wonderful news.

—Not in so many words. But Sternfeld this afternoon . . . Put it this way, I came away *optimistic* from the fellow's lecture. But I *ask* you – lecturing on niggers! The brotherhood of man!

He laughed and drank his beer.

—If your friend had met the savages of New Zealand, as we have, he'd have told a different tale.

Sometimes with his father, sometimes alone, sometimes with Sömmerring, George paced the streets. It was not a city he could love; more barracks than city, with uniformed soldiers everywhere.

—They seem to have a soft spot for the new King.

—Well, he's rebuilding – it'll be a fine thing, the new Brandenburg Gate – and they love him for lifting the State monopoly on tobacco. But – well, we've been down that road, eh, George?

Friedrich Wilhelm was a mystic, a devotee of Rosicrucianism – appointed Johann Christoph von Wöllner, his fellow Rosicrucian, Minister of Finance.

—And I don't like this edict he's just promulgated against the 'Enlightenment', forbidding preachers from enlightened interpretations of the Bible. Kant has been silenced – isn't allowed to lecture at Königsberg.

—Only forbidden to lecture on religion.

—It's a bad principle, said Sömmerring, we can't have kings telling us what to think. Only the truth is worthy of homage.

After ten days, Reinhold went back to Halle. George kissed his father. He had heard from Sömmerring that 'the tactless philosopher' had been as good as his name, telling Sternfeld, who chaired the selection committee for choosing the new Professor, that he would be a 'fool' not to choose him, and accosting a Professor of Natural History in order to inform him that the mistakes in his last paper could be blamed on his ignorance of *A Catalogue of British Insects* (Warrington, 1770) by J. R. Forster.

—This came, were almost the last words his father spoke to him. Reinhold produced a letter for him from his pocket – it was forwarded from Halle.

It was a letter from George's friend Zimmerman, informing him that the Empress Catherine deeply regretted the cancellation of the expedition. She could not reconcile the expenditure on such an enterprise in time of war, but she would like Herr George Forster to come to St Petersburg and be part of her intellectual entourage. He would be a Professor at the University, have his own secretary, be free to pursue his research.

It was an agonizing letter to receive. On the one hand, it solved his two most urgent problems: absence of income, and the need to get away from his marriage. On the other hand, St Petersburg was not Germany. It was far away – from his child, his friends, his roots. His childhood memories of the place were not of the beauty he knew it possessed, but of intolerable cold, of long dark winters, of drunks in the street, of smelly, bearded priests. Therese wrote to him every other day, hysterical letters, letters which were trying to turn themselves into a novel. Her heart was broken by their quarrel. Why did they quarrel? Why could they not start again? Her father, who had taken her side, was now angry with her again. By the same post came a letter from Professor Heyne saying that he regretted asking his son-in-law to leave Göttingen. Therese, it stated, had not been honest with her father. She had concealed from him the reason for her husband's anger. Heyne had convinced himself that the flirtation between Therese and Meyer was in essence childish, innocent, but no husband could be expected to endure it. Now, Meyer was the one who was banished. He had gone to England: hoped for a librarianship somewhere.

Both Heyne and Therese urged George to 'come home', but he was ill. He lay up for two weeks in his inn with jaundice. Sömmerring, a qualified doctor as well as a professor, made assiduous visits. George's brother, the bookseller, tried to cheer him up by saying that *Cook the Discoverer* was selling briskly. Reinhold wrote, failing to take in the fact of his illness, asking him to go to the University and inform them that their letter, offering him the Chair, had seemingly gone astray since no word had come and he needed to make plans, to resign his Chair at Halle, to find a house in Berlin commensurate with his new status (or maybe a house came with the post?). It truly was unaccountable that no word had come.

Prostrate with jaundice, George could not go to the University. He already knew, from Sömmerring, that Reinhold had not even been considered for the post. It was a difficult letter to write to his father, informing him of this. When Reinhold replied he made no allusion to the dashing of his hopes. Rather, he reminded his son that, among the distinguished guests at their house in Percy Street, when he was waiting to take up his duties as the Director of the British Museum, had been the Prince Duke of Anhalt-Dessau. His house and estate at Wörlitz were more or less on George's way home to Göttingen. Wörlitz was an ideal place for convalescence.

Strangely enough, George did remember Prince Franz very fondly, and he wrote proposing himself for a few days. He did not regret this. His strength began to return as, on legs still wobbly after a month in bed, he walked with the Prince in his well-planted park, took in the lake, constructed to resemble the Bay of Naples, with a miniature Vesuvius which, by means of fireworks, could be made to 'erupt'. The new, classical palace of this whimsical potentate contained, together with the somehow surprising presence of a wife, an enormous collection of Wedgwood. There was a Wedgwood chimney piece depicting the hunting of Calydon the boar, there were Wedgwood medallions, Wedgwood busts, and in almost every room a naked Ganymede wiggling his buttocks.

The Prince was a sympathetic man, fourteen years George's senior. George found himself able to talk to 'Father Franz', as the tenants on the estate at Wörlitz called him, in a way he could never talk to his own father. Reinhold gave out every indication that he did not want to carry even the smallest part of George's burden of unhappiness. Not being told about his son's marriage problems he conspicuously failed to ask a single question either about his daughter-in-law, or about his grand-daughter Rose. Whereas Franz –

—She's very clever, your wife. Met her when she was growing up – met her when I've been to Göttingen. My word! The *Universitätsmamsellen* they called them – she and Fräulein Michaelis and their friends. Nothing they couldn't talk about. She must be pleased she married an intellectual!

George reflected sheepishly that they seldom talked.

—She must be lonely, said the Prince.

When George came home he resolved to try to woo his wife all over again, to make things right with her, to respect her, to try to talk to her of his intellectual interests. He now regretted the thought that poverty would force him to Petersburg. He need not have done so. In his absence in Berlin, Professor Heyne had secured a post for him, as the University librarian at Mainz. Therese was momentarily able to enter into his feelings, his relief at not going to Russia, his determination to save the marriage. She became pregnant again. Clara, their second daughter, was born a few months after they had been installed in their new life in Mainz.

PART THREE

Affinities

*O Wedding-Guest! This soul hath been
Alone on a wide wide sea:
So lonely 'twas, that God himself
Scarce seemed there to be.*

I

1773

THE CAPTAIN WAS THE FIRST TO BE EXAMINED, BY MR
Patten. Every man on board submitted, even Reinhold, who, having
engaged Dr Sparrman at his own expense in Cape Town, elected
to be seen by the South African doctor. To kill his embarrassment,
as Sparrman peered between his legs, Reinhold talked.

—Can we say the Europeans brought any benefit to the Americas
which could possibly compensate them for this Columbus-borne
scourge? And again here. The Kapitän was right to insist on our
all – *all* – undergoing . . . when he was first here – with the
Endeavour – he believes one of his own officers took the plague,
the filthy disease.

—Ay, sir, to the North Island.

They had all heard the Captain's speech that morning.

—We've been six months at sea. No point in being mealy
mouthed about it.

As if to emphasize his bluntness of approach, here the Captain's
Yorkshire accent had been especially strong. *Maily mouth dbah teet.*

—One of the worst things on my conscience is that when we first came to New Zealand five years since in t' *Endeavour* one of my own officers – so it would seem – infected a woman on the North Island. There's no cure for this disease – you all know that. You know, 'n' all, what it'll do t' ye – the nose on your face collapsing and turning to jelly, the pain of it – terrible – your wits and your eyesight gone. But I'm not judging any man. You've been away from shore a long time . . .

The Captain had been reluctant to judge, Reinhold rather less so.

—It is hard, impossible, not to detest the memory of that man who first disseminated this venom among these brave, spirited people.

The doctor was fond of Reinhold but he could not resist asking,

—There's a certain redness about your balls. You have not had unwise dealings with a woman since leaving England?

—You know that could not be the case.

—As the Captain said, we are all human. It is the strongest impulse in a man.

—It would have been better to stab the object of his lust than to . . . poison her in this way. The man, the man who – and you think I could do a thing like this?

When it was George's turn to be examined, he chose to be seen by Mr Patten. It was an ordeal, lowering his breeches.

—Is that a bit of a spot you have there? A blemish?

No words would come in reply to this inquiry.

—Would you mind lifting it up a bit so I can see the other side of it?

Terrified that this action would lead to the onset of an erection, George obeyed.

—Probably just been a bit rough with yourself when you last saw that Master all lads are so fond of.

Momentarily George felt himself accused of unnatural vice with Mr Gilbert, the ship's master.

—I would . . . *never*—

—All boys are friends with Master Bates, just don't overdo it, eh? Saps your strength. Pull your breeches up.

How did Patten *know*? George wished he had joined the queue for Dr Sparrman who had a comforting lack of comedy in his nature and would surely not have descended into banter. And what was overdoing it? There were some days when desire was so over-powering that *doing* it, far from dispelling lust, stimulated desire more painfully, as if increase of appetite had grown by what it fed on. Then – inseparable as father and son were during the days at sea – his father would say —That is your fourth visit to the privy since breakfast? You have the squits?

Perhaps this was Reinhold's way of telling him not to do it? Perhaps his secret was no secret at all, and everyone, Nally, the midshipmen, even the Captain knew it. Most painful of all were those passages in the Holy Scripture which seemed to say that God knew. *Herr, du erforschest mich und kennest mich. Ich sitze oder stehe auf, so weisst Du es; du verstehest meine Gedanken von ferne* . . . He understood our hearts, but could He forgive us? Was it not wasting the precious seed of life? Was it not trivializing the impulse which He had implanted in us to multiply the species, to make other human souls, not merely to give ourselves filthy pleas-ure? Surely if He forgave this sin He would condone it, He would be like Mr Patten with his manly laughter, his implication that boys will be boys. Oh, why could human beings not be like those species who had a mating season? For long ice-bound months, the father penguins stood with one egg, kept warm on their feet and sheltered by their feathery legs, while their mates waddled for miles to find fish. The penguins did not go in for self-abuse, they could concentrate upon being penguins, whereas, for George, this habit which was so compulsive drove out all useful, creative or intelligent mental acts and therefore in some sense prevented him from being George. Nothing, nothing, not prayer nor resolution – nor even his attempt to trick himself into embarrassment – *Vati knows why you slipped back to your cabin – he knows you do not need your pencil box or your pocket-volume of Horace* – could stop this all-consuming, humiliating, exhausting, depressing need. Oh, so depressing, the lowering of spirits which followed each squirt, but even the knowledge that it would be the result, the shame and the sadness could not stop him.

—And you, lad, with Mr Hodges, you're the two artists, you come along o' me – it was the Captain who was addressing him – and we'll pop yer dad and Mr Wales in the launch. They can do some Natural History and we'll take Mr Gibson our gallant corporal since he says 'e knows t' lingo.

George and his father liked Gibson who was a marine; even more they liked the Captain's easygoing attitude towards him. Gibson had sailed on the *Endeavour* voyage in '69 and deserted on Tahiti, where he had taken a wife, and acquired the belief during the year or so of his association that he understood what she was saying. (More than many of us'd say of our womenfolk, was the Captain's judgement.) He forgave Gibson when he came back to England and specifically asked him to travel on the *Resolution* to act as an interpreter. The language in Tahiti bore kinship to that of the New Zealanders, or so Gibson had his shipmates believe.

Resolution

—You should do it in oils, Mr Hodges – were Cook's awestruck words as they crossed the long cove, light rain pattering blue-black water, verdant, sheer slopes soaring above them, and beyond the rain, glowing over the mountain, a rainbow. Little songbirds, linnets, sang so close to their heads, they almost expected them to land on their hats, while on the water were blue duck, brown tern, and the black and white oyster-catchers. As the pinnace-men rowed them towards the rocky shore, they could see a low-lying hut thatched with flags of the flax plant and covered with bark. Out of this edifice came a blue-lipped woman with a child on her back, followed by a little boy and a girl who waved to their visitors. The woman called something into the hut, and there emerged an old man wearing a coloured mat with dried albatross-skin in his ears. He was followed by some younger men.

Captain Cook stood in the bow of the pinnace and, as it nudged the rocks, he threw his handkerchief out as a present; then a couple of the medals cast by Matthew Boulton in Birmingham, with the head of George III. The New Zealanders watched. The young woman with the baby seemed to think his actions comical. No one picked up the objects. Somewhat with the air of a conjuror attempting a new trick, Cook now produced a blank sheet of white paper from his pocket. Then, hatless, he sprung from the boat on to the rocks and walked towards the natives. He held out the paper to the old man.

—Peace! he hollered.

The elder was visibly afraid of the Captain who was by a good foot the taller man. His hand shook as he took the paper, but Cook then grasped this tremulous hand, enfolded the man in an embrace, and rubbed noses – remembering from his previous visit that this was the polite form of salutation there.

The next day it became apparent why the young woman had laughed when the Captain cast down his gifts, and why she had not picked them up. The respectable women stayed indoors. It was assumed that any gift, however small, was taken in exchange for favours. Sailors, both from the *Resolution* and the *Adventure*, streamed towards the shore, some swimming rather than waiting for the jolly boats.

—You canna stop it, it's *nature*, Dr Forster.

—That they should do it so flagrantly, not even trying to hide themselves . . .

—I know, I know . . .

—After all your warnings.

—At least there was no case of *that* among them.

—On the *Resolution*, yes – but did all the Adventures submit themselves to their surgeon for examination?

—We don't like it, Dr Forster, but believe me, I've worked with sailors all my life – in the merchant service, in the Royal Navy – you can't change nature. You sometimes have to turn a blind eye.

—They don't *all* behave like this. Why can't they be like Nally?

The Captain gave Reinhold a quizzical look.

—There hasn't been trouble with that one?

—With Nally? Sometimes a little slapdash maybe. The coffee he makes is too weak.

—That's not quite what I mean.

—What sort of trouble might Nally have given?

—Your boy would've said if there'd been trouble? I know he's a shy lad, but he'd have said?

Not caring to admit when he did not understand, Reinhold changed the theme. Next time he ran across George, however, he asked him,

—You haven't had trouble with Nally?

—What kind of trouble, Vati? It isn't true what the men say about him.

—What do they say?

George paused.

—You're not to get Nally into trouble.

—What is it they say?

—They say he supports the new ideas. Thinks all men should have votes and send members to Parliament – that kind of thing.

—Is that all they say?

—It's all a lot of nonsense.

It was conspicuous that Nally was among those who didn't go ashore in pursuit of the women, preferring to sit on deck darning, which he did with great deftness and concentration.

George knew the words, in at least five languages, for what the men and women were doing, so openly, so shamelessly. During his obsessive solitary lustful reveries he had assumed that these activities were what he wanted, more than anything in life, to pursue. Watching the sailors and the New Zealanders rutting changed his perspective. His own visits ashore, with Mr Hodges or his father, were sketching trips or expeditions to collect botanical specimens. Sport, too, occupied them – they shot a number of seals, and after a few curled lips almost every man aboard pronounced the meat as good as beefsteak. There was hardly a part of the district, however, when engaged in these occupations, when one did not come across some naked bottom bouncing up and down on a woman, sprawled on a rock; some other woman fellating a midshipman against a tree; or one of her friends on all fours while a group of ratings took it in turns to approach her from behind, their masts swaying shamelessly in front of them, their nankeen trousers round their ankles.

The energy of it all, and the openness, frightened him. Presumably the ones who did *not* indulge – Nally, say, the surgeons, the Captain, Reinhold, and quite a lot of the ratings – only abstained for fear of disease; they were all men, this was what they *wanted* – a thought which troubled him so much he was for a few days abstinent from his secret vice. He had never considered, until the scenes so shamelessly displayed in Dusky Bay, how much *loss* the activity involved: not merely loss of dignity, but loss of something else for which he could find no word. It was perhaps loss of self.

The *Resolution* was overhauled and ready to sail as the New Zealand winter began. The *Adventure* had in the meantime explored Van Diemen's Land. Cook devoted the next five months to sailing in the South Pacific. There was a delightful month when the two ships sailed in convoy with gentle breezes and blue-green bobbing water. Then bad fortune hit the *Adventure* whose Captain, Furneaux, never took enough care of the health and diet of his men. Their cook died, and many of the Adventures had by then gone down with scurvy. They had also several outbreaks of venereal disease after their sojourn in New Zealand, throwing open once again the question of whether this ultimately derived from the European visits in '69 or whether in fact the disease was indigenous. Some of the scurvy cases improved when, after a period in August of being quite becalmed, they reached Tahiti and were able to eat fresh fruit and vegetables once more.

George had become a seaman. At their first setting forth, the movements and noises of the ship had been alien, the frequent nausea, the numbing sameness of each nautical day, with the ringing of bells, with each half-hourly turning of the sand in the glass. Now he was used to all of it, the morning summons by Nally, the often inconsequential, gentle conversations they had together, their shared fondness for the ship's cat, the everlastingness of the limit-less sea, the timelessness of days adrift, the unutterable strangeness of being out of sight of land for weeks on end brought a calmness which made him dread the moment when land was descried. Ship life somehow suited the hidden innerness of his adolescent moods, the countless hours of mental drift, when he was conscious, but unfocused, aware of human voices but in no necessity to con-verse or understand what was being said, whether it was Reinhold prosing about the life of migrant birds or midshipmen pursuing their relentlessly arch humour. Moreover, cocooned by the ship's empty routines and surrounded by the automatic busy-ness of sailors swabbing, climbing, mending, stitching, rigging, the specific erotic torments and onanistic preoccupations were on many days containable. Loneliness was sad but there was a comfort in loneli-ness. Instinct told him there were worse things than the low-level gloom of his adolescent life, which was at the same time paradoxi-cally quickened by sharpness of outlook, an intensity of awareness, so that the taste of salt on his lips and face, the dampness of the breeze on his skin, the rise and fall of the turquoise swell, the voices and faces of the sailors, the exact colour and texture of the plumage of an albatross, were all vividly present. His capacity for observation was so sharp that it almost hurt, the sheer excite-ment simply of existence itself. And then it was land ahoy and the monastic repetitiveness of ship life was once again threatened by exposure to the human how d'ye do, the complexities of the social.

A month or so of exploring the island life of Queen Charlotte Sound. Then the purity and pleasure, after the beginning of June, of open sea: pleasure for George at least, though the Adventures all grumbled to the point of mutiny about sailing through squalls and rain, and Reinhold, half tempted to outdo them in self-pity, half anxious to show himself the better seaman than Captain Furneaux, said,

—You see the justice of their point of view. Anyone in charge of a vessel pulls into harbour for winter, sits so to say, sits the storms out. But Furneaux is not a man of science and our Kapitän *is*. We *must* press on – Furneaux with his more limited perspective does not quite see this.

When the *Adventure*'s cook died, the Captain of the *Resolution* sent over one of his own reliable shipmates, a man called Chaplain. Scurvy and VD were by then rife on the *Adventure*. It was essential to roar onwards over the waves in the hope of reaching the Society Islands before the crew of the *Adventure* started to die. The Resolutions, doggedly fed by their Captain on the barrelled remains of the *Sauer Kraut* and whatever fish could be hauled out of the ocean, were tired, but fit and proud.

Yet while for Captain Cook this beginning of his Island Sweep, his visit to Tahiti and the other Society Islands, was a feat of endurance and a voyage of scientific discovery, for George these weeks had been part of the inward journey made by all of us at some stage of youth, in which erotic preoccupations were to the fore. His terrier, Blanche, caught the mood and mated with Reinhold's spaniel, Octavian. Blanche gave birth to ten puppies at the beginning of August, and one of them was stillborn. Another of the dogs on board, a New Zealand puppy whom Nally had rather adopted, fell on the dead puppy and ate it.

—There are too many dogs on board! Of this one cannot doubt. Yet we have a rooted objection, based on prejudice, to eating them!

—You're right there, Dr Forster. I've eaten dog – tastes like mutton. But an Englishman thinks twice afore he'll eat his dog.

Resolution

At dinner Reinhold pursued his theme – that if only the English poor could be persuaded to eat their dogs and cats their cities would be cleaner and their diets more nutritious.

For George, the coition of the animals, the talk of devouring, were all alarming reminders of the predatory *centre* of Nature's cycles of eating, slaying, breeding, eating. When in his guilty note-books and journals he put a small 'o', more often several 'o's for *Onanie*, he became ever more aware of how much this solitary vice was a retreat from the powers of Nature, which with attractions as strong as gravitational force were trying to absorb him into the procreative, destructive and alimentary processes without which life itself would cease. His overwhelming consciousness of these things, his sense of being held back by his solitary eroticism, from involvement in the entire system of Great Creating Nature, his longing for, revulsion from, involvement in that system, dominated the days before they reached the Society Islands, making of these exhilarating days a journey of the imagination as much as of the sea miles. Temperatures rose to the seventies. At the beginning of August they sailed past a group of small islands, the Tuamotu, whose sandy palm-clustered shores had never been seen before by European eyes. They changed course northward. At night coming out to pursue his vice beneath the stars, George luxuriated in the slapping of the ink-black water against the *Resolution* as they breezed along through warm night air, and he gazed at the silent, cruel brightness of the moon shedding its cold white radiance on the choppy sea surface. And at dawn, five o'clock, on 15th August they saw the volcanic outline and high peaks of Osnabruck Island.

It was an indication to George of how much this voyage had entered, in its present phase, into a metaphor of erotic journeying, that when he published his *Voyage* in '77 it was appreciated as not only a travel book but as a variety of erotica. James Boswell, who sought out George, made it clear that the arrival of the *Resolution* in the blue waters off Tahiti formed part not merely of his geographical dreams but of his inner sexual *Mythos*. Enthusing to his friend and hero the great lexicographer about George's evocation of island life, Boswell provoked the put-down *Don't cant in defence of savages*. It was obvious why. Johnson, who fought his demons with iron self-control, had given up going backstage in the London theatres because the actresses excited his 'amorous propensities'. George's Tahiti – a little like the exactly contemporaneous and more coarsely phallocentric and priapic *Roman Elegies* of Goethe – evoked a new, liberated world. His Tahitian islanders were Adam and Eve before the Apple, or at any rate semi-naked examples of a humanity unimaginable in the confines of bourgeois Lutheranism, the closed *Pfarrhaus* of the mind in which Reinhold, while managing to produce six children, dismissed these impulses as a filthiness, a distraction from the life of reason.

—And it really was the case, sir, pressed the Scottish nobleman, his glowing pink face moist with lubricity. They came, the island lovelies – swimming out to you – their brown boobies like buoys afloat in the . . .

He had neither completely nor fully written such a sentence clearly, for Boswell, as for so many of those who purchased his *Voyage*, this was one of the great set-pieces, as the tired, dogged little sloop the *Resolution*, a metaphor of English pluck and common sense, tacked about to the south end of the island, avoiding the reefs, until the population of Tahiti, or so it seemed, paddled, drifted, swam towards them, some in canoes, some simply swimming in the water. Common sense, John Locke and empiricism met with physical passion, papayas and coconuts.

Resolution

Symptomatic of George's change from preferring life at sea to life on land was the feeling of boredom which overcame him whenever the *Resolution* put in, or tried to put in to land. Here in fact he showed himself the landlubber, for never was Cook more the seaman than when gauging a suitable landing-space and, having made the choice, coming in to shore. The better part of two days were spent in landing in Matarai Bay. At break of the first day Cook realized the *Resolution* was not more than half a league from the reef and that she and the *Adventure* were in danger of running aground. For the whole day the *Resolution* was full of bustle, the Captain and the officers shouting. The swell of the sea was thumping the poor little *Resolution* against the reef. With three or four hundred fathoms of rope, a warping machine was carried out into the water, but still the sloop stuck fast. The aim, George was told, was then for a kedge anchor and a hawser and the casting anchor with an eight-inch hawser bent to it, to be used to cut away the bower anchor. The pinnaces were then lowered and oarsmen by means of ropes managed to heave the *Resolution* away from her stuck position. It was then necessary for them to go to the rescue of the *Adventure*, which was well and truly stuck and which, in order to get properly afloat, had to lose two of her anchors.

George both admired the practical skill with which these complicated operations were effected and felt numbed by the old sense of boredom which all the practical operations of seamanship always awoke in him. During the arrival at Tahiti, however, the detachment, sense of inadequacy – he scarcely knew what the famed warping machine actually was – mingled with quite other feelings, as the islanders bobbed about them.

Even while Captain Cook halloo'd, and his officers supervised, for hours and hours, the saving of the two sloops, and their eventual safe harbouring, the Tahitians were holding up baskets of apples, plantains, bananas, coconuts. They brought promise of an alternative Pelagian universe in which the fondling of flesh was no more guilt-ridden than munching upon a yam. Cook, in his *Journals*, Reinhold in his, conveyed the social and commercial exchanges which he and Captain Furneaux had with the natives. The exchange of nails and medals for fresh meat (hogs) and fruit. There were the expected courtesies, the solemn pouring of glasses of Madeira, in the grand saloon of the Captain's cabin, for tattoo'd King and Prince. There were the predictable mishaps, as well. Dr Sparrman was set upon by natives and robbed of everything but his trousers. On Reinhold's part there was the tireless botanizing, and on George's part some of the finest of his watercolours – of the white-winged sandpiper and the red-rumped parrot. Reinhold formed a particular attachment to a Tahitian chieftain named Potatow with whom he believed it was possible to hold conversations about such esoteric questions as theology and life after death. For George, however, the whole of the Tahitian experience was merely a backdrop to what happened one afternoon as he sat with his colour-box and sketch-book near a well-planted piece of shrubland. As he carefully put down on paper a likeness of the *Barringtonia speciosa*, capturing the veins in every leaf, the delicacy of the firm jutting stigma, the velvet of the petals, the pistil and the stamen, he was aware of being watched, and looking up, he saw her. She was naked to the waist. Jet black hair hung over her shoulders. She sat for about an hour, watching him, hugging her knees through the grasses of the skirt which covered her upper thighs. Unlike the men, the girls were not heavily tattoo'd but there were decorations on her upper arms. He wanted to give her the painting because she watched with such evident admiration and because he knew himself to be getting better and better. At the same time he did not want to think he was treating her like a prostitute, so he waited for the sunny air to dry his work while he said his name, and she said hers, which was something like Rye or Rai or Ray. She was about his age – or seemed so. Sometimes in later years he wondered whether she had in fact been much younger. He wanted her more than anything but his shyness, his simple inability to act, his total absence of experience, would undoubtedly have led him to pack his colour-box and go back to the jolly boat, had she not taken his right hand and stroked his index finger, and then guided this finger to touch her breast.

An hour later, when he returned to the ship he scarcely noticed his father's reproaches.

—We were going to send a search party – for some minutes to go off into the woods, yes, but – two, three, maybe, hours. This was a cause for concern.

They met twice more, he and Rai – he formed all kinds of fancies in his head – that she was a ray of light, *Viva el Ré* – but part of the poignancy of their association was that there was no chance of conveying such fancies. When the two sloops left for another of the Society Islands – Raiatea – she came alongside the *Resolution*, standing on the shoulders of a young man and waving a flowering *Barringtonia*. She tried to throw it towards him, but it had no chance of reaching the deck and he watched it floating on the bright blue surface of the ocean as if it was the embodiment of dashed hopes and lost dreams.

He had not fallen in love: he had fallen into something almost as intoxicating. He had fallen into an enchantment, and waking hours had the quality of dream. Those fantasies of poets, such as the comic scenes in Shakespeare's *Midsummer Night's Dream* in which the characters open their eyes and see a new glory in their love-objects, this was what he saw, and new glory, too, in the world.

Raiatea was just as paradisal as Tahiti, the same light sand, wind-blown palms, blue waves. Cook, Furneaux and their entourage were entertained to a *heeva* – in which the islanders of both sexes, naked to the waist, hieratic young men and thigh-thrusting maenads, made a frenzied dance before them.

—*Heeva* – that's what they call it.

—It's a sort of ritual dance, Nally.

—That would be right. Quite reminiscent of the Captain when he loses his rag.

It was an analogy which gradually came to be adopted by all the Resolutions. The Captain, a man of such a sensible and well-balanced disposition, had occasional outbursts not just of petulance but of a rage so wild that, without speaking, he would sometimes jump up and down on the deck as if seized by some of the psychic fury which had animated the Polynesian dancers, their wobbling breasts, jutting pelvises, jabbing arms.

Strangely enough, he danced a *heeva* before they left Raiatea. Did *she*, George wondered – she who was his chief preoccupation, derive her name from this island? Might she come, like Venus born from the seashell on the waves, floating over the seas towards him if he yearned for her with sufficient fervour?

It was probably because he allowed his head to be filled with such daydreams that the unfortunate incident occurred. George and Reinhold, with Nally, Dr Sparrman and a few others, had made a small excursion to the north part of the island. George suddenly said he would like to hire a canoe, perhaps try painting the island from the water. Reinhold indicated a likely-looking native, who was standing beside a jetty, and the boy set off towards him. George had a gun over his shoulder. As he tried to indicate his wish to hire a canoe – pointing, and making pantomimic movements suggestive of an oarsman – the man grabbed the gun and a tussle ensued. The man was bigger and more muscular than George, and what followed, which happened in a matter of seconds, was that Reinhold reached for his own gun. Seeing that the man had George's rifle and was intending to make off with it, paternal instinct and a sense of natural justice guided hand and eye. Reinhold was a good shot, responsible for many of the booby, tern and wild duck which had appeared, fricasseed, at the Captain's table. He peppered the thief's arse with loose shot, not enough to kill a man, but enough to make him drop the gun and scarper.

At first, when the Captain heard of the incident he was inclined to laugh it off, but for Reinhold it had not been a laughing matter. It had summoned up from his vitals a consciousness of how much he loved his son. It was not the prospect of losing his son's rifle, it was the prospect of George's death, which had made Reinhold reach for his gun.

—My son, Kapitän Cook, might have died. This is another example – no – I must say this. I am sorry but I must speak. Another. I must. Example. On Tahiti Dr Sparrman was half murdered, robbed, left for dead in the woods. We look to you to protect us, sir – not to leave unavenged an attack upon one philosophical gentleman – and to treat as a matter of merriment the near murder of another.

Those who witnessed this tactless lecture did not include George but they did include Nally.

—You could see the veins coming out in the Captain's forehead. You know how it is when the wrath is in him. Boiling in him. And the quietness descends. The ominous quiet. Like the moment after you've lit the touch paper, and there's that silence before the cannon blasts off. And I'm not so sure your Da noticed the silence, the way the rest of us noticed it. Then by Jesus off goes the old twenty-four pounder and, oh George, the look on your Da's face. Doctor Forster, says the Captain, I'll not have my authority undermined. Have I not said, time and time again . . .

. . . Nally's reported speech attempted no 'imitation' either of the Captain or of Reinhold, but he was a good narrator, conveying the different speakers by pauses and by slight alterations of facial expression . . .

—My first speech from the foredeck before we left Plymouth . . .

. . . it was the Captain who spoke . . .

—insisted this was not a warship. We are not conquistadors, sir. We are men of science. We will defend ourselves if other men attack us but we will not open fire on them. By God, sir, that's . . .

Nally's voice trailed away. Then a pause and a tautening of his thin, sucked-in cheeks as he 'became' Reinhold.

—You give orders to *me*, sir? You speak as if I were one of your *ratings*? You give orders that I may not fire – quite safely – a few pellets in the po of some savage – to defend my son's life – you upbraid me in front of Mr Wales, Mr Pickersgill – in front of these little boys. Jesus, George, the midshipmen didn't like that part, I can tell you. Oh Jesus. And then your Da said he demanded satisfaction. And the Captain says he had not heard the remark, that officers in the Royal Navy, oh dear me, do not accept challenges from German village dominies and he could take it – he was banned from entering the Captain's quarters for the rest of the voyage.

—Banned? But, Nally, where will we eat?

—Gun-room, I suppose.

—With the little boys.

Painful as the quarrel was to contemplate, it was hard not to finish the conversation with a laugh on both sides. Three days later, First Lieutenant Cooper approached Reinhold and told him the Captain would be obliged were Dr Forster to attend him in his cabin. A stiff conversation had ensued. The Forsters were reinstated at the Captain's table. This was a relief to George, who had found the conversation of the midshipmen, who messed in the gun-room, uncomfortably reminiscent of his two experiences of school, in Petersburg and Warrington. He disliked boys, their coarseness, their banter, their determined facetiousness. All the midshipmen seemed to be carrying on an everlasting joke at his expense, exemplified, though not explained, by the fifteen-year-old Elliott asking Harvey, slightly younger, whether he had done any good drawings lately. It was plainly an allusion to George's activities: and made the boys laugh so much they all but spat out the seal-steak through which they were ravenously chewing.

—I did a lovely drawing of a booby.

Whoops had turned to howls, made worse by George's scarlet, furious silence.

At the end of June, they put in at Tonga. July saw some of the pleasantest weather of the entire voyage as gentle winds bore them into the New Hebrides basin. In September they sailed due south, and by October when New Zealand came in sight, they were finding it difficult to sail in tandem with the *Adventure*. The wind was too strong, on 22nd October, turning to gale force, to allow them to get into Cook Strait. Eight or nine leagues south-south-east of Cape Palliser, the Resolutions lost sight of their sister ship. By the very end of October, violent winds, some of the most furious they had encountered, blew them in sight of the Kaikoura mountains in South Island. So great was the gale, they were forced to lie under the mizzen staysail.

At the very beginning of November the storms passed.

—*Cras ingens iterabimus aequor.*

Even Nally could recite the line – it was a shared joke between him and George. Reinhold said it so often when they took their course once more over the mighty main. The brave little sloop got under sail on the Feast of All Hallows and, once under sail, was directed under Cook's sure guidance, past Cape Campbell and into Queen Charlotte Sound by the next flood tide. Off Cloudy Bay, he took a course across the strait to the coast of the North Island, and found an inlet, east of Cape Terawhiti, where he could anchor safely in the bay. It had been a terrifying three weeks and it ended with a desolating sense of loss. For, the *Adventure* was nowhere to be seen.

I I

1789

—IT'S LIKE A PARADE.

—It is a parade, darling.

—Parade!

—Better than the circus, said Wilhelm von Humboldt, one of the many young men who came to their apartment.

—George, Humboldt doesn't want to talk to the baby!

George was standing at the window of their apartment in Mainz. Beneath, in the street, a procession of thirty-five, or so, *calèches*, elaborate rococo carriages, painted, some with flowers, others with the coats of arms of their occupants, passed through the main street to the great Romanesque cathedral of St Martin of Tours. Most of the coaches were barouches – known in the Mainz dialect as *Pirutsche* – open two-wheelers – whose occupants, powdered and bewigged like the liveried footmen who attended them, waved to the crowds who lined the pavements and cheered. After these local noblemen and women came a long ecclesiastical procession, boys and girls in white garments, scattering rose petals, gold-vestmented acolytes holding a gilded umbrella over the Host as it proceeded on its wobbly journey to St Martin's, and behind this spectacle, and the boys swinging incense-bearers, came a procession of robed clergy, the last of whom, borne on the shoulders of boys on a golden throne, was the Prince Elector himself, Archbishop Karl Josef Reichsfreiherr von Erthal, a golden mitre on his powdered periwig, rings on the fingers of the purple gauntlets which he held out, half in salutation, half in benediction as he passed.

—He's looking up at us, said Humboldt.

Some of the other men in the room – Jacobi, Herder, Huber (a young protégé of Schiller's to whom George had taken a shine) – clustered at the window to see the phenomenon of the long-faced seventy-year-old cleric.

—The paradox is the Catholics are more liberal than we are, said Humboldt.

—It's true, said Jacobi. The new King of Prussia bans Kant from lecturing on religion. Dear old Erthal there made our George his librarian.

—He's a great admirer of yours, said George. It wasn't just flannel. When he spoke of you to me, asked me about you, he had been reading your work on Spinoza.

—I bet he denounced me as a heretic.

—He does not go in for denouncing. Little by little the old man seems to be holding out his gloved finger to the modern world, the new ideas.

—Spinoza's were hardly new ideas, said Therese sharply. It's simply that he exposed the sheer absurdity of believing in a personal God over a hundred years ago and still they're at it – look at them.

—It's like a parade.

Resolution

—Yes, darling.

While Therese spoke to Jacobi of Spinoza, George kissed his daughter's cheek and walked round the room holding her; the exaggerated bounce of his steps made the child laugh.

Before Rosechen, George had resigned himself to a life without love, or life without conscious love – for he was clever enough to know what had lain beneath the frustrations and irritations of life with, and without, Reinhold. This, though, was love riotous, love obvious and shared. So happy was he in his love for his daughter that he scarcely noticed how much it irritated his wife. He could only think that it – the love – it – the child – it – their having at last a shared love-object – could give her pleasure.

How, in any event, could Therese not be happy, here, after the monstrosity of life in Vilnius? Their new-built apartment was far grander than anything either of them had lived in before – its pillared entrance hall below, its delicately bannistered stone staircase, its large, symmetrical panelled rooms, with acanthus-carved dados and ceiling-roses. Rosechen's world was not to be the pinched narrowness of the parsonage-house, nor the closed world of old tyrannies. Light would pour through her large unshuttered windows. Reason would open and shut her inquisitive eyelids. That room with its big apple-green panels, its round marble-topped table in the centre, its scrolled chairs with lion's paw feet, would come often into his mind as he travelled. The room contained at that moment his hopes for his child, his life together with that child; it also contained the cleverness of his bright, young friends with their eager faces, and the strong personality of the women – above all of Caroline, just widowed, with her dark brown locks falling on her black-silk shoulders, and of Therese, whose animation intoxicated them all. George would remember how he had falsely supposed that Wilhelm von Humboldt, almost whooping with merriment at Therese's every observation, was going to become the 'new Assad'; but he would also remember how, as he clutched and bounced Rosechen close to his chest, and as the child gurgled and giggled, he had felt a happy toleration of Therese's nature. Perhaps she could not really function unless those around her were in love with her. Perhaps she needed Wilhelm, gasping out thoughts from Spinoza's *Ethics*, needed Huber and his thoughts about the latest play by Schiller, needed those intellectual young men to adore her as they shared the life of the mind. And perhaps the paradox of her friendship with Caroline Michaelis – now the widow – was this: whereas a beautiful woman is said to need a plain friend, and Caroline, with her full sensual red lips, glossy seductress eyes and cascades of chestnut tresses, was almost embarrassingly beautiful and Therese, dumpy and squinting, very much not so, their roles were much more symbiotic. Therese needed the beautiful friend to demonstrate that she was no bespectacled frump. That she was the companion of Caroline in seductive frivolity, just as Caroline and the other *Universitätsmamsellen* needed the well-read daughter of the Göttingen Professor to give them ballast, to advertise to the young men that they could flirt as much as they chose, and perhaps, who knew, enjoy something more than flirting, but not unless the men took the women seriously as intellects.

—George is given an easy time by the old Archbishop. There is a quintet of dusty underlings who do his work for him in the library – which is only open half the year. The other half of the year the court moves to Aschaffenburg, so George can get on with his writing.

—He tells me he is translating Hakluyt's *English Voyages*.

Resolution

This was said by Wilhelm's younger brother, Alexander, a sweet-faced boy who looked much younger than his twenty years.

—I wonder about him sometimes, said George's wife. We hear of English sailors at breakfast and dinner every day.

—We want more of his own work, said Alexander, giving her a winsome smile. The translations are of course interesting, but his travel-writing, his descriptions of the harbour at Tahiti as the *Resolution* dropped anchor, this must be one of the greatest pieces of German prose since the Luther Bible.

—I can see why he likes you, said Therese archly. But he has to do translations because we are always in bloody debt. Not surprisingly since he made me have another of these encumbrances.

Alexander von Humboldt, possibly the cleverest human being who has ever lived on this planet, stared at Therese with complete incomprehension.

—He hasn't noticed, darling, said Caroline.

—I know. And I can't tell whether that is very VERY flattering or very VERY insulting.

In a low voice which Alexander could not catch, Caroline cooed in Therese's red little ear,

—Women only half exist, darling, for such as he.

—But Wilhelm isn't like that . . . ?

—Very much not.

And with a moist index finger Caroline stopped Therese's lips.

The Humboldt brothers were not the Forsters' discovery, far from it, but they had burst upon them from the moment of their arrival in Mainz, and immediately, Wilhelm, at twenty-two, Alexander at twenty, had been clear annunciations of a new dawn.

When their father died, the mother had asked Goethe how she should educate the two boys. The monster-ego poet of Weimar, perhaps already dreaming of the demonic intellectual journeys of Faust, proposed an experiment – that the brothers should be crammed with knowledge, told all there was to know, allowing them the chance to explore every possibility of action and aesthetic appreciation. Even old Professor Heyne, Therese's father, was persuaded to Berlin to teach the brothers Greek. Wilhelm learnt languages and literature from University professors. Alexander was taught all that was then known of chemistry, physics and mathematics. Both studied Philosophy with Kant. Later, the mother would force Wilhelm into the diplomatic service (his last posting, after the Napoleonic wars, was as Prussian Ambassador in London). Alexander became, like Novalis, an inspector of mines, but from his first readings of George Forster's *Voyage*, he had pined to become a traveller, and, long after this story is done, he would travel through Central and South America, and publish, in the French language, a thirty-five-volume account of the geography and Natural History of those lands. He became what Goethe had wanted him to become, a universal genius, living deep into the nineteenth century, and dying in 1859.

1790

THE RHINE WAS IN LOW WATER. IT HAD BEEN A DRY SPRING. The skiff made slow progress. The hills, dotted with vineyards and medieval castles, swooped and soared. The thought came to George that, had Mr Hodges depicted the scene, it would have been all hills, trees, vines and ruins, their little skiff two brown triangles against flat water, and the three men who sailed it – Humboldt, himself, and a playwright called Iffland who had come for the journey as far as Koblenz – would have been no more than the pin-sized savages who adorn that painter's romanticized depictions of the South Seas. This was the journey which transformed George into a Romantic, and, when they read his accounts of the Rhine, its walled towns, its colossal rock formations, its mirror-water-surface, the journey made the sensible Germans sensitive – the cloth traders and clockmakers, the wine merchants and salt miners – became Nature mystics. Though it delighted the fancy to think, as the waters flowed past St Goarshausen, that the Rhine maidens would lure river passengers to their deaths on the rocks which jut out of the waters, George saw the waters themselves, and the great sky, and the rocks, as the truly 'romantic' discovery. Nature not legend lifted the soul into its mysterious silences.

Resuming a journey by sail inevitably prompted memory, memory which young Humboldt and Iffland implored him to open and to share, of the blue seas and sun-gilt islands. So, as their little boat glided almost noiselessly downstream, the silences were dotted with discourse of King Potatow, of canoes filled with smiling men and women offering plantain and coconuts, of exotic flora, of feathered cloaks and ceremonial meals at which no one present entirely understood what the other was saying. Of Rai and the gap in her white teeth and her long curtains of black hair cloaking her chubby shoulders, he said nothing; nor of Reinhold, his energetic capacity to collect botanical specimens only rivalled by his ability to rub up shipmates the wrong way. These memories were not for sharing, for they were, as he now saw more clearly than ever before, memories of love.

A. N. Wilson

Perhaps it was the passage of time, perhaps it was the curiosity of his listeners, perhaps it was the unlocking of love in his heart by little Rosechen from whom he'd parted in Mainz with such tears – but, whatever the reasons, he knew that this journey of his and Humboldts, was going to be transformative. Already he saw the world with new eyes. Whereas, ten years before when he had first travelled alone, and passed through Paris on his way to Germany, and looked upon the Gothic intricacies of La Sainte Chapelle with blank indifference, now, in the cathedral at Cologne, which he had seen many times, he was transfigured by the Gothic. The swooping, fluted columns of the nave and their capitals of leaf-fringed stone were revelations. On the cathedral's shadowy paving, he stood looking up, up, upwards, transfigured into the architects' purposes. Hitherto, taught by classical severities, George had supposed the arrangement of stone upon stone, the creation of arches, doors, columns, windows, roofs, was a classical, ordered thing, an imposition of mathematics. These architects, however, having learnt a mathematics superior to the Roman – from the medieval Arabs, which enabled them to construct pointed arches, had soared into a different aesthetic, in which stone could become spreading branches, in which a building, rather than defying the organic green, the crushed leaf, could enter the natural sphere, rather as, in Ovidian myth, an escaping damsel could be transformed into a laurel bush. Nor were these experiences of aesthetic ecstasy, in the presence of Nature – the Rhine and its waters – and of the Art–Nature marriage achieved by Gothic, even for a moment at variance with the ardour for scientific knowledge evinced by his young companion.

For several months before the voyage, Humboldt had been at work on his first major scientific work, on the basalt to be found in the Lower Rhine regions, so that while they exclaimed at the beauties of the Rhine, they were also analysing its very constitution. Humboldt was beginning to realize that basalt was volcanic, formed underground through an uprush of molten material, and hardening instantly as it burst from the surface of the earth and met the cold air. The pillars of basalt thrown up by Nature posed deep thoughts – when had the volcanic eruptions occurred? Surely far longer ago than Science, let alone Theology, had for centuries supposed? So, Geology and Poetry both had their pillars. From Cologne they journey to Düsseldorf, from Düsseldorf to Aachen, where the tomb of Charlemagne, father of modern Europe, prompted thoughts about the condition of contemporary Europe, since the French convulsions of the pervious summers, the white marble throne on which, since Charles the Great, so many German emperors had been crowned seemed so plain, so unostentatious that, George felt, it could be taken as a satire on all the thrones of the world. To journey on, through Brabant and to see those parts of Flanders still under the rule of the Austrian Empire was to feel the obsolescence of modern political institutions.

From the Low Countries, they took a packet boat to Dover. To be at sea once more, to hear the huge sails flapping their dragon wings above their heads, to feel the heave and bobbing of the vessel and to hear waves slapping the wooden sides was to re-enter, however briefly, the *Resolution*.

Whenever the sloop put in at a new haven, there had always coexisted, beside the tedium of finding suitable harbourage, the technical challenges of casting an anchor, the fear of the human. When the shoals and shallows of the treacherous reef had been successfully evaded, and the first human face, peering from behind a rock or a banana-bunch, had been spotted, would the inhabitants recognize the Captain's peaceful intentions? One of Cook's greatest gifts, beside his courage and his uncanny genius as a navigator and cartographer, was his ability to move with friendly confidence among the natives, to demonstrate his essential friendliness, to enfold their hands in his hands, to rub noses. Perhaps any traveller's success in his journeys depends upon the measure to which he has cultivated these gifts. As the cross-Channel ferry approached England, that summer of '90, George remembered the first time he and his father had arrived there in '66, and thought: Reinhold could not rub noses. When he and George had come ashore, had they presented enough old nails, beads or rusty medals? Had they entered with sufficient show of deference into the hierarchic ceremonies? Had they displayed enough gratitude as the Royal Society or the University of Oxford had wrapped them in the English equivalent of a feathered cloak? Though learned and noble Englishmen might have offered them the learned or noble version of a fruit drink served in a coconut shell, Reinhold had never quite known how to respond with the required combination of sycophancy and swagger. Though he had outwardly learnt the syntax and vocabulary of the English language, he had not really understood its organic grammar. He had not realized that when a favour was offered, there was not necessarily any truth in the offer. When favour was indeed given with diffidence, as if the gift were of no account, Reinhold had not seen that this diffidence was not to be taken at face value, nor that when an Englishman shrugs modestly and asks you not to mention it, he actually wants you not merely to mention it, but to gush, to set it to music. The Admiralty, and Parliament, had conveyed great honours on the Forsters by making them the official naturalists on the *Resolution*. The £4,000 given, if spent more judiciously, might have defrayed Reinhold's costs, and if the airy mention of future appointments or emoluments, the Directorship of the British Museum, for example, might not have been exactly meant, there probably would have been rewards, honours, positions for the asking had he asked with due deference, had he known when to ascend the dais in his grass skirt, when to place the feathered headdress on a grateful head, when to swallow, however unappetizing, the proffered putrid delicacy.

The Captain was dead, there was no chance of introducing Alexander to him, but George had it in mind to visit the Widow Cook in the famed farm at Mile End. Here, for all too short a time, had lived the goat which had accompanied Cook on the first voyage, to Tahiti, upon whose collar were inscribed words composed specially by Dr Johnson:

> *Perpetui, ambita bis terra, praemia lactis*
> *Haec habet altrici Capra secunda Iovis*

('After a double circumnavigation of the globe, the goat, second (only) to the goat that nursed Jove, has this reward of her milk that never failed.')

The goat, alas, who had survived the journey to the South Seas and back, had expired in '72 not long after being installed in Mile End.

The Captain had not often alluded to his home life, but when he had done so, it had been with warmth. Once, finding Reinhold and George together on the deck, discussing Latin literature or plants, or swapping quotations, the Captain had remarked,

—You're a lucky man – you're both lucky – to have each other.

—You have sons to be proud of, sir.

There was that slight pause, often noticeable in Cook's discourse with Reinhold as if the naturalist had stepped a little too far, as if perhaps the father, and not another, might decide the suitable emotion when his own sons were in question. After the pause, though, a smile.

—Ay, I have 'n' all, whether they follow me into the Service, we'll have to see. James and Nathaniel have it in mind – we're hoping to send 'em to the Naval Academy at Portsmouth.

—Start them young!

—James isn't ten yet, Nathaniel seven – Hugh's the babby.

—Happy the man who has his quiverful.

—Ay – we're lucky to have them. We thank God, sir, though we've lost three, Mrs Cook and I.

It crossed George's mind, during this conversation, on a gently breezy blue day sailing from Tonga to New Zealand, that when the Captain was staring silently at the ocean, as he so often did, his mind was very likely with his lost children, or with his wife on the farm at Mile End; whereas he suspected that when Reinhold's family were out of sight, they were out of mind.

Mile End was a pleasant bosky village a little way east of the City, being gradually built up with handsome terraced houses. The two-wheeled barouche which took them there had no difficulty in finding the farm, more a smallholding, in which fowl – geese and chicken – paced splay-footedly in the mud and where, at the back, half a dozen pigs could be seen enjoying the morning air.

—She ain't 'ere, said a labouring man leaning on a fork.

The arrival of strangers was enough to attract a gaggle of the curious. There was a group of what at first seemed to be three children. Then they realized that it was two children, of about eight and ten, and a dwarfish woman – perhaps an aunt or grandmother – no taller than four feet.

—Perhaps if we wait, proffered George.

—If she is to return.

—Is he Russian? asked one of the children, pointing at Humboldt.

—We are happy to wait until she returns.

—Only, said the labourer, it's the Orkses now.

—Orkses?

—Mr and Mrs Hawks, said the dwarf. They're the proprietors of Mile End Farm now. I say, are you lawyers?

—One of 'em's Russian.

—'E didn't say so.

—No but 'e wouldn't would 'e, fat-ed.

Four more women had approached, excited by the knowledge that lawyers had been sent all the way from Russia to see the Widow Cook.

—Got ideas, she did, said the bonneted dwarf.

So, Mrs Cook had moved, and after inquiries, they found her new address, in Surrey. Their driver believed he could effect the journey to Clapham in half an hour. In the fly, Alexander asked,

—What is hoity toity?

—Snobbish.

—And these *ideas* Mrs Cook has. They are scientific ideas? Philosophical ideas?

—It's possible. I think they meant that, since her husband's fame, she considers herself a little grand.

Their driver was a helpful young man. When they reached Clapham, a well-built village with a new church on a piece of common land just south of the River Thames, inquiries were made at the inn, and they were soon pulling the bell-rope outside a handsome double-fronted house, some ten years old, with a trellis of roses – still in bud – framing a garden gate, and a neat path edged with box. The shiny new door was opened by a shiny new footman, and when they had left cards, and a note, on his salver, and waited in the hall, attending the reaction of their hostess, they were eventually ushered into her pretty drawing room, to find Mrs Cook, wearing a crimped bonnet of creamy lace and with a waisted black dress. When George had explained his identity, and that of his companion, Mrs Cook said,

—You'd be the younger of the German gentlemen.

—No, no. I am considerably older than Mr Humboldt.

—But the younger of the German gentlemen who sailed with Captain Cook.

—Oh, yes indeed, ma'am.

—And your father, he yet lives?

—Yes, ma'am. He is a Professor in Halle.

Mrs Cook had a small straight mouth like a rat-trap, which now closed, indicating that further mention of Reinhold would not be desirable.

—And your sons, ma'am. You have three sons, I believe? They are all at sea?

The silence which followed reminded George of the Captain's silences.

—Nathaniel, my second boy, was serving on the *Thunderer* in Jamaica – ten year ago now – '80. The whole ship went down in a hurricane. At least his father did not have to know of it.

The frosty silence almost forbade inquiring about the other boys, but she eventually conceded that James, the eldest, was a Lieutenant, and Hugh, still a schoolboy, hoping for Cambridge.

Resolution

(What, asked Humboldt in the fly as they came away, was he hoping for Cambridge?)

—I almost wondered, when I gave her *Cook the Discoverer*, whether she would have preferred not to see the book.

—How could she not be pleased with it?

—Alexander. Memory is a strange thing. It is more than ten years since I was in England. Before, I saw it with young eyes, but also with my father's eyes. Only when I was with Mrs Cook did I remember how angry it made everyone, my writing *A Voyage*. I had blotted all this from my mind. I remembered only the voyage itself – and then arriving – and the book – and how popular it was. But the other things I had either forgotten or put from my mind – that I had only written the book because the Admiralty forbade Vati from writing it. They said Captain Cook should be the first to go into print over the matter. That it was owing to him – the kudos, the money. It now amazes me that we had the gall, the sheer cheek, Vati and I, to write my *Voyage* book. I wrote it fast. We finished it before Cook. It sold well – only now do I quite see how angry, how justifiably angry, the Captain must have been! I'd done more than jump the gun. I'd violated him – the man I most admired in the world. In spite of the row caused by my book, the Admiralty allowed me and Vati to publish another, a botanical book about the voyage. It was an expensive book to produce. I had to do the drawings, and copper-plate engravings had to be made, and although they reimbursed us, it was not enough. Vati got into terrible debt in London . . . they were frightening times . . . Vati was threatened with the Debtor's Prison, the Marshalsea. Where was the money to come from? He found a job as a humble secretary to the Prussian Ambassador. Without diplomatic immunity he would have gone to prison. That was when he wrote the *Letter* . . .

—What *Letter?*

—It seems so utterly crazy to me now. His written English was good, but not good enough, so I had had to write it for him. We borrowed money and had it printed and bound . . . a letter to Lord Sandwich at the Admiralty, at the way we had been treated.

—But you had been wrongly treated?

—Yes, but to go into print, Alexander, with petty complaints about how much money we had spent on sketch-books and scientific instruments . . . and to end by saying we *detested* England.

—You wrote this?

—I wrote this paragraph in which I described the Forsters running away from Oliver Cromwell because of their loyalty to the King . . . And then I said, Vati 'returned to England, from a natural predilection to it, as a mother country. If he is not yet entirely weaned of this prejudice, it is not your lordship's fault; you have done your endeavours to make him detest this country' . . .

—George, you wrote that?

—And then Wales – you know, the astronomer – wrote another pamphlet, attacking Vati – and, really, I think, making everyone hate us.

—What happened to Mr Wales?

—What happens to anyone? He became a teacher.

The little two-wheeler had crossed the river once more and was making its way to Plumtree Street, Newgate, where Humboldt was lodging with a German wigmaker. There wasn't room for him at Bloomsbury, where George was staying with his sister Victoria, whom he scarcely knew, who was married to a tedious clergyman.

—I can walk to my sister's from here, he said, as the barouche came to a halt at the little wigmaker's establishment near Newgate Prison. We could dine together?

—Or, my friend, you have had enough of me, perhaps, for one day?

—I could never have enough of you.

—Barty might show me the sights a little. We thought we might see the Vauxhall Pleasure Gardens.

—Watch out for the women there! They are after your purse more than your . . .

Even as he heard himself looking, first at Alexander's mildly blushing face, and then at the much more knowing smile of Barty, the coachman, George felt foolish. Barty was a thin man in his twenties, with laughing blue eyes and mousy hair tied back with a black ribbon. Perhaps the women were not to be a temptation.

—Thought I'd show Mr 'Umboldt the docks – go down to Wapping, meet some of the men coming off the big ships – coming in from the Indies.

There was slightly too much hesitation – was he catching the habit from Mrs Cook and the late Captain? – before George answered,

—A very good idea.

—If 'e wants to be a great traveller, he's going to want to meet some sailors, said Barty with a proprietorial finality.

Walking back to Bloomsbury alone, more and more of those final weeks in London, with Reinhold and the family in '78, returned to him, and, inevitably, he thought of poor Nally.

So they saw England as strangers see it. Before their arrival, his mind having mysteriously blotted out the *Letter to Lord Sandwich* and its impassioned, intemperate words, George had supposed that it would be a month of glad reunions. The frostiness of Mrs

Cook was, however, a harbinger of cold weather to come. An audience between Forster the world-encircler and the Prince of Wales had been petitioned for, pre-booked and arranged. When George and Humboldt arrived at St James's Palace at the appointed hour, however, they were told that His Royal Highness was not, after all, available. They did visit Mr Dalrymple at the Admiralty – Mr Alexander Dalrymple, the hydrographer who had accompanied Cook on the first voyage to Tahiti to observe the transit of Venus in '69, and who was an employee of the East India Company much of his life, an organization with which he had a stormy relationship. In a breezy way, Dalrymple was friendly enough, gave the two men dinner and spoke incessantly, in part, which was of absorbing interest to them both, of astronomy, and in part, which was a little baffling to them, of the trial of Warren Hastings which had been taking place, with long intervals, over the last couple of years in Westminster Hall. Hastings, the Governor General of India, had been brought home and impeached, subjected to furious denunciations by Edmund Burke, accused of personal corruption and maladministration. Dalrymple, a plump fifty-something man whose tongue and teeth appeared too large for his mouth, poured out scorn for the Council of the East India Company, recounted how badly they had behaved towards himself ever since he'd arrived in Madras in '52. Neither Forster nor Humboldt could fathom the interstices of legal argument; nor, next day, when they went to Westminster Hall to witness the cross-examination of 'Lord' Hastings as they wrongly supposed him to be named, did they feel much the wiser, though the spectacle was an absorbing one – the Lord Chancellor in his wig and robes, the Speaker of the Lower House, also in a wig, the heralds in bright tabards, emblazoned with heraldic arms, resembling the Knave of Hearts on playing cards. A ruddy-faced man with sharp nose, ironical mouth and dark eyes was addressing the assembled Parliamentarians on the cruelties perpetrated upon the natives of Bengal. It was Burke himself, the famous radical orator, who had called for the abolition of slavery, defended the American colonists' right to independence, and now denounced the cruelties and corruptions of the English in India. Alexander, who could read English with fluency, could not really understand it when spoken, and it was faith alone rather than judgement which acceded to George's excited assurance that Burke was the great orator of the age.

—The accent I could detect – is that Cockney? Scottish?

—He is an Irishman – ah, Nally! – which is what gives him his total independence of outlook! How I long to hear him speak on the French Revolution! What prose poems would pour forth on the destruction of the Bastille!

They were thorough in what they sought out, and saw, but they could only do so as tourists. They went to the theatre and saw Mrs Siddons in a play called *The Crusade*. They went to Mr Townley's Museum of Classical Sculptures and gasped at his busts of Emperors, his mutilated marble bearded Bacchuses and chipped Apollos. They saw the Castle at Windsor. More excitingly, they saw Herschel's telescope at Slough. They journeyed to Bath and saw the Roman spa and the beautiful new Crescents and Circus. They went to Birmingham and saw Matthew Boulton's factory – and a farce at the theatre called *The Romp*. (Humboldt, who did not really understand it, laughed because he thought it was called *The Rump*.) They went to Buxton Spa, swooned at the Peak District, exclaimed at the palatial Chatsworth, visited Oxford and dined with the Keeper of the Botanic Garden, but never once felt they had completely understood the country through which they had passed. In London, particularly – where Banks was eventually gracious enough to give them dinner and to show Humboldt a multitude of botanical specimens – they were fascinated by the freedom: while, for example, in coffee shops, the French Revolution was ecstatically celebrated, this did not prevent them from politely serving French refugees.

George was more saddened than dispirited by the English journey, although he was delighted by so much of the landscape and architecture. He had never before seen so clearly how badly 'the tactless philosopher' had blundered, when the *Resolution* had come home and Cook had been celebrated as a National Hero. Never before did he see how close they had been to acceptance by the British, but how capriciously they had thrown all that away: as though there was some compulsion to make them queer their own pitch: as though they were natural nomads, never destined to grow roots. Reinhold probably felt, in each of the quarrels he picked, that right was on his side, and perhaps it was. Perhaps another truth was that they were all the products of Great Creating Nature and must behave as She dictates; that the Forsters, father and son, were no more destined to stay in one place than migrant birds.

So they left England – Humboldt had chiefly enjoyed the Herschel telescope and the Botanic Garden. He also appeared excessively to have enjoyed his visits to Wapping to sit in taverns with sailors and hear of their adventures and travels. George felt an instinctive unwillingness to inquire too closely about Humboldt and the sailors. There was quite enough, without this, to remind him of poor Nally. So forcefully did the English tour remind him of the Nally *débâcle*, that when Humboldt one day said —Show me the house where you lived – it was near the British Museum, no? – George pretended he could not remember its exact location, and, even when he had engineered one of their walks so that they walked down Percy Street, and looked across from what had been their front door to the open rolling country to the north, and the hills of Hampstead a few miles distant, he could not bring himself to share with Humboldt even the most trivial of the memories which overpowered him. Poor Nally. Poor, poor Nally. That was worse than any of the other memories, worse than Reinhold's nearly being arrested for debt, worse than George realizing, by writing his popular *Voyage*, that he had made his hero, Captain Cook, into an enemy, worse than the realization – some of which was invisible to his twenty-year-old self and had only become clear to the thirty-five-year-old tourist – that his clever father was a fool.

They spent their last night in England at a Dover inn and George's description of the moonlight on 'Shakespeare's Cliff', on 28th June 1790, was destined to become one of the set-pieces of German Romantic prose, anthologized to this day. Looking back at the huge chalk cliffs next morning, from the deck of the Channel ferry, George found himself weeping uncontrollably. Humboldt either did not notice, or politely pretended not to notice. He smiled sweetly, girlishly, at George. Then, the strange smile faltered and he began to point at the sea. Five miles out from England, the ship of human beings was joined by other creatures, and Humboldt was not alone in his excitement. Men clutching their round-brimmed straw hats, women in tied bonnets ran to the railings to see the shoal of dolphins which surrounded the boat, leaping from the water with apparently smiling faces. Normally, the appearance of dolphins like this heralded a storm – or so said the sailors aboard. But there was no storm as they sailed towards France on a blue sea, and the dolphins seemed, rather, to be harbingers of euphoria.

Humboldt was not really a political man and, in so far as he was political, he was one of Nature's conservatives. Even he, however, could not but respond to the atmosphere of France on that bright June day. In the inn at Calais, in the coach to Paris, in the streets of the capital, there existed an atmosphere of rapture. The weather turned. George recognized in himself the symptoms which led him to become a devotee of the Rosicrucian enthusiasm. Even before they witnessed the celebrations for the anniversary of the storming of the Bastille, he knew that his enthusiasm for the Revolution had moved far from that liberal sympathy, expressed in some of the London coffee shops, for the ending of old hierarchies and the extension of privilege. He was tingling. The excitement was uncontrollable, beyond reason.

They were up early, determined to find a place in the Field of Mars, but already, when they arrived there after a hasty breakfast, thousands had gathered in the rain. Once wedged there, there would be no escape: and as the hours passed by, the free citizens of France were in no mood to lose their places in the giant amphitheatre merely to answer the calls of nature. By midday, with the rain still pelting down, it was difficult, in their particular patch, to distinguish between the mud and the shit on their boots. Some said there were as many as a hundred and fifty thousand people there, to see the hastily constructed wooden Triumphal Arches, and the great amphitheatre which had been dug out by 'volunteers'. Duchesses, abbots, even the King himself, had been along in the previous week, to advertise their enthusiasm for the new ways by digging for an hour or so in the mud. The result resembled a sodden farmyard of puddles. Humboldt just saw mud, but all George saw were Fields of Glory. He saw the huge military procession which squelched into this rain-soaked scene, fifty thousand National Guard, as an angelic host, and the procession which followed as an epiphany of freedom and light: the ancient bearded regular veterans, greeted by workers holding aloft pickaxes, and banners proclaiming the King to be their 'father, their brother, their friend'. Women with trays of pies and sweetmeats slithered through the mud to offer the old soldiers food. Below, the towering wooden arches swayed slightly in the wind and reminded dispassionate observers of those 'flats' in the theatre which represent woodland or castle wall but without conviction, as though on the verge of collapse. In the centre of the Field was the Altar of the Fatherland, again wooden, but painted to resemble marble and adorned with symbols – a female figure representing the Constitution and then came the procession – the Estates, the clergy, the King, and taking up the rear, flanked by the revolutionaries who had stormed the Bastille – now clad in the helmets and togas of ancient Roman republicans – was the cynical old fraud Talleyrand, in mitre and cope, the Archbishop who proceeded to celebrate a High Mass, as the crowd applauded, and as the driving rain put out his altar-candles and made the burning incense fizzle and hiss. The ceremony ended with a pledge that the Revolution would bring 'Peace to the World'. Alexander looked at his companion's face. Tears rolled down George's pock-marked cheeks. His eyes glowed with zany fervour.

Three days later, he found that the little Rosebud, his Rosechen, had grown several inches. She clung to the doll on which he'd spent his last few Thaler, coming home through Strassburg.

—He's such a fool, a china doll, can you imagine! And in two minutes she'll have smashed its face.

Caroline met his gaze; saw these words of Therese's lacerate him, while the little group – Therese's 'admirers' – clustered around her. Rosechen pulled at his dark blue coat.

—But what shall we *call* her, Daddy?

Homecoming made him shy. He was stepping from the freedoms of the road, of meals at inns where no one noticed his mood (for Humboldt cared little for this) to an atmosphere where all his statements seemed to be blunders, and were put on trial, all his reactions were agreed to be laughable. Therese held Wilhelm von Humboldt's arm while she emphasized the absurdity of the doll-purchase.

—And all this revolutionary fervour? My dear – she stroked Alexander's upper arm – when the Bastille was stormed we were dancing for joy – you remember. What did Schiller do?

This last question was shouted across the room to young Huber, to whom George was showing a number of English books.

—I thought we might make an attempt to translate some of these together, George was saying.

—Schiller wrote an Ode to the Revolution, didn't he? persisted Therese's voice.

—I'm not sure about this.

Huber's high colour deepened. He was now the lodger, occupying a room next to the nursery. He looked even younger than five months ago when George had last seen him. His formal manners had become stiffer, even a little pompous.

—George, if I remember, he said, was of the view that the Revolution in German lands will come about by the rulers reforming themselves: and we surely have an example of this in our Archbishop Elector. After all – Huber bowed, as if about to present George with a medal at a public dinner – he has appointed a Protestant librarian. He drove out the monks and nuns to provide buildings for the new University. He is, so to say, an Enlightenment man!

Resolution

—At Tübingen they planted a Liberty Tree – Schelling, Hölderlin, Hegel, Therese called.

—I . . .

—You were too *busy* to notice the Revolution. Too busy writing books about the world to *see* it!

This made the roomful of guests laugh, while Huber said,

—Some of these English books, they look really interesting . . .

and Rosechen said,

—Papa, Vati, tell me a name to give her!

—Call her Freedom! said the father.

—You see! said his wife. He has gone mad.

Caroline, her dark curls on her shoulders, her eyes glossy, her breath carrying on it a mixture of the gravy and dumplings they'd eaten for dinner – this smell being by no means disagreeable, actually quickening his sense of her physicality, her sexual being – came close to him, with her back to her best friend Therese, and said,

—I want to know more of the ceremony in Paris. I want every detail.

Later, in bed, Therese amazed him by allowing him to make love. By their perfunctory standards, it was even halfway towards being a decent fuck. After it, lying back in the darkness, she said what she rightly calculated to be the kindest thing she could say.

—Rosechen really missed you.

In the dark, holding her hand, he squeezed it gently.

—And she loves her doll.

He squeezed her fingers again and stroked her hand.

—It's good to be home, he said. A little speech came to his lips. Let us *learn* to love one another, let us be kind, let us cherish our children – but the speech died, and instead, they lay there in silence.

Some weeks later, when she had again allowed him to make love – but once, and with no repeats – they were lying once again in the dark, and she was continuing to let him hold her hand.

—Listen, George. There's something you must know. I am pregnant.

He withdrew his hand from hers and placed it on her shoulder, trying to enfold her.

—Oh but this is wonderful.

—I'm going to have a child.

—Oh, darling Therese.

There followed a very long silence. Before it, when an upsurge of love for her made him try to hug her, there had been a moment of post-coital irrationality. The silence brought thoughts which caused stabs of pain.

—It is my baby, he said aloud to the darkness. As far as I am concerned, as far as the world will be concerned, it is my baby . . . we . . .

Again he'd hoped for a few sentences in which he said, it is more important to hold our family together, to learn to love one another, than to cause scandal. But these words died. Instead, he said,

—After all these months with Alexander, our friendship with the Humboldts has become . . . very dear . . . perhaps . . . to us both.

It was difficult to say these words but he felt rather grand saying them.

—Wilhelm will go on being a friend, he said, and wondered, as thirty seconds became two minutes, and then a quarter of an hour of silence. Is anything stiller or darker than a man and a woman, lying together in the dark, unable to speak, having made love, but not being in love?

—Wilhelm, said Therese's voice into the darkness, is not the father of the child.

PART FOUR

Devouring

Are those her ribs through which the Sun
Did peer, as through a grate?
And is that Woman all her crew?
Is that a DEATH? and are there two?
Is DEATH that woman's mate?

I

1773

OEDIDDEE, OR ODIDDY, AS THE CAPTAIN CALLED HIM, WAS
a South Sea Islander taken on board at Raiatea in September. 'He
may be of use to us if we should fall in with and touch at any isles
in our rout to the west which was my only montive [sic] for takeing
him on board,' as Cook wrote in his *Journal*. He was an amiable
young man, perhaps a little younger than George – eighteen, say.
(He didn't, probably couldn't, say.) He replaced a Tahitian (Porio)
who had gone ashore in pursuit of girls.

When they had been moored several days in Cape Terawhiti,
Cook was leaning on the rail of the quarter-deck. The rain spat-
tered into his tobacco-pipe.

—It is too wet for me to go on an expedition, Kapitän, not this
morning.

—For once in a way, Dr Forster, I agree with you. Ee ay. It's
miserable.

It was the persistent, grey, soaking rain which got into your
clothes, however many layers you were wearing, and which made

work impossible. The previous day they had started boot-topping the starboard side of the *Resolution* but this morning that was impossible. Some of the crew – the sail-makers and coopers – were able to work on shore in the gigantic tents which had been erected for the repair and construction of equipment.

—They can get on wi' things – we can do nowt! said Cook with a bitter laugh. Leastways they can work wi'out you putting your head round the flap o' their tents and giving 'em Horace.

Though they'd only been there three days, they had all tired of *trahuntque siccas machinae carinas* ('tackles are hauling dry hulls towards the beach') and today, nothing could be less appropriate than the epithet *siccas*.

This was almost friendly. The Captain's banter. He suggested that Reinhold joined him in the cabin for a glass of Madeira. When the servant had departed, leaving them with the decanter and two glasses, Cook leaned forward. Reinhold should have known the Captain did not appear to do anything without a purpose. He was not the man, even on a filthy, grey, rain-sodden morning, to go indoors to chew the cud over his wine-table just for no reason.

—How's Nally? he asked.

—Our servant.

—Nally.

The tone implied, reasonably enough, that after sixteen months, the name of Reinhold's servant might be familiar to him.

—He slops my shaving water. I say, there might be a swell, a list, so to say, but fill the bowl less full – just look, I say, at the water slipping off. Somewhen will he learn this, I think.

—Happen. But there's been no trouble?

—Do you mean does he steal? Irish are like children, but I see nothing missing. Now these New Zealand savages – *they* will steal.

—I didn't mean stealing. Well, I may as well be plain with you, Dr Forster. Nally's made a bit of a nuisance of hee-sel' with Odiddy. He's a boy who takes things to heart. He was crying.

—Nally hit him?

—No – not that. Odiddy said – he's quite expressive, is our Odiddy, seeing he only has a hundred words of our language. He says – *Nally try make me lady boy and I no his lady. I man.*

—I don't understand you, said Reinhold.

The Captain drained his glass.

—Ay, you're right there. But let me know if there's trouble, like. I'd hate your George to be bothered. He's a good lad, your George.

The next day the weather cleared. A number of natives came out to the *Resolution* in canoes. There was the usual exchange of sex, or fresh fruit, for nails and buttons. Taking Odiddy and the two Forsters, the Captain went ashore in the pinnace. They took picnics, sketch-books and measuring instruments, intent upon making a day of it. It was a relatively crowded boat, since they took with them four hogs, three sows and one boar, two hens and three cocks and carried them to the very bottom of the bay, leaving them with ten days' worth of food. Together with the Forsters and Odiddy they tramped half a mile or so inland through gentle green brushwood to visit the settlement where, on his last visit, Cook had left various farm animals. Alas, as far as they could make out, no breeding had taken place. The goats and fowls had been eaten, and one rather scrawny old sow limped about in the mud.

—Ask 'em what happened to the boar, said Cook.

—No get.

—Ask 'em. Man-pig. Is man-pig alive?

It seemed on investigation that the boar had been taken to a different part of the island – news which made the Captain smite the middle of his forehead with the palm of his hand. George even wondered if exasperation would make Cook dance one of his *heevas*.

—How's they going to breed if they're on opposite sides of the . . . ye Gods! – but he was laughing at the folly of it.

Hodges and George both sketched some of the hut-dwellers, while Wales and Reinhold went botanizing, returning with two new specimens – *Dracaena*, and a new plant they could not identify. It was several hours since they had left the shore when Pickersgill, one of the young Lieutenants, burst through the undergrowth shouting,

—Captain, Captain!

The Captain, still in a mood between exasperation and good humour, was deep in a conversation with two of the Maoris, about how to keep the new hog and the sows together in order to produce piglets. Odiddy had to convey most of this message by sign language, so that Cook's forthright pieces of advice about the breeding of livestock turned into a charade which made everyone, Europeans and New Zealanders, laugh.

Pickersgill's facial expression, and the anguish of his bellowing, made smiles die.

—Captain.

—Mr Pickersgill – what's the matter?

—The beach – we must – all – go – to – the beach.

The words came out in tragic gulps. George waited with Hodges, who took the longest to disassemble his equipment, a small portable easel, and they ran through the bushes to the bay. By the time George and the painter had caught up with the others, it was clear enough what they had discovered. Pickersgill and Clerke, strolling idly about the beach, had come upon the remains of a boy on the sand. His head had been stuck on a forked stick. Part of the skull had been broken, and some of the lower part of the face had been torn away, but it was clearly that of a fourteen- or fifteen-year-old lad. The heart had also been pronged on a primitive wooden fork – but this was sticking up as a sort of mast or totem pole in the canoe which was pulled up on the sand. Other parts of the boy's body could be seen in the prow of the canoe.

George could never completely account for what happened next. Years later, when he read Captain Cook's strange sentences about the matter, he realized that Cook wished to establish before witnesses that the New Zealanders were cannibals. For he commanded the Maoris to bring the remains of the boy back to the *Resolution*.

There were as many as fifty Maoris clustered either about the sloop in their canoes, or actually on deck, and the arrival of the beach party with their gruesome load caused every man aboard to stop what they were doing and stare. For it was obvious why the parts of this boy had been skewered on forks. He had already been partially cooked in readiness for consumption. Was it, George asked himself in after years, Cook's simple prudence which kept him so calm? Did he judge that a violent reaction to this terrible sight, of the half-cooked boy, might occasion a massacre of his entire crew? After all the whole of the *Adventure* had gone missing, and so far, Odiddy could get no coherent message from any New Zealander about the ship's fate – though one or two Maoris had nodded that there had been 'big boat' – two moons since. Or was there a vein in Cook of pure, pitiless curiosity? Did he observe these people's behaviour with – inner revulsion, yes – but also with a sort of cold interest, as he might in Nature observe any other predatory animal feasting on its prey? The sentences which he wrote about the incident, and which chilled George's soul, were:

I concealed my indignation and ordered a piece of the flesh to be broiled and brought on the quarter-deck where one of these Cannibals eat it with a seeming good relish before the whole ship's Company which had such effect on some of them as to cause them to vomit.

Odiddy was in tears – great convulsive sobs. Nally had crossed himself – as had several of the Irish or Scottish sailors.

After the obscene feasting was over, Captain Cook asked the cannibals to leave the vessel. They seemed to be in jocund humour, perhaps not aware of the enormity they had committed. They, and their fellow New Zealanders, clambered down the rope ladders and into their canoes with no more awkwardness than if they had been eating plum duff.

It was a perfect spring day. The blue water was calm, as the cannibals and their women left in their canoes. Afterwards, that evening, or perhaps the next day, Odiddy told Cook and the gentlemen that there had been a war of some kind and there was a custom among the New Zealanders that those killed in battle were eaten by their victors.

—I had to see it, Cook said quietly. There'd been so much debate – with Mr Banks and others – as to the likelihood of New Zealanders being cannibals. I had to see it wi' me own eyes.

A shocked silence had descended on the *Resolution*, broken only by the half-hourly ringing of the bells. The men returned to their work and duties, but there was none of the usual roaring, swearing, banter, jokes or songs. At six o'clock in the evening, the view of the shore from the quarter-deck was of shimmering spring foliage, of birds – oyster-catchers and curlews wheeling overhead, shags gliding with yellow-eyed, dark-feathered innocence over calm waters which now seemed polluted. Spontaneous church services were usually a cause of grumbling, even if they only took ten minutes. This evening, the men came to the quarter-deck not merely with willingness but with the positive need of some purgation, some cleansing – to hear the Captain pray.

—O *Eternal Lord God, who alone spreadest out the heavens, and rulest the raging of the sea; who hast compassed the waters with bounds until day and night come to an end: Be pleased to receive into thy Almighty and most gracious protection the persons of us thy servants, and the Fleet in which we serve* . . .

The next day, the gentlest of spring days, with bright sun catching the tree-tops and streaming upon the distant hills, they unmoored. Several Maoris came out in their canoes to wave a smiling farewell.

As the little sloop made its way northwards in increasingly blustery conditions, all minds were on the officers, crew and gentlemen of the *Adventure* – where were they, and what had befallen them? There was no chance of the *Adventure* being stranded on the coast, round most of which the *Resolution* had sailed before casting anchor.

—I am convinced – the Captain told the crew the next evening when they assembled in choppy weather on the quarter-deck – that no ill has befallen the *Adventure*. Rather, for reasons known to Captain Furneaux, I believe they have left for home. But we came forth on our journey for a purpose. To find the Southern Continent. You are the most heroic bunch of men with whom it was ever my privilege to serve. I know what you endured when we last went into the icy hell, but I am determined, with your approval, that we should make another attempt. It can only be done with common consent, common courage. Are you with me?

A roar of agreement. A raising of arms. Had the high wind allowed it, there would no doubt have been the throwing of hats, but had such an exuberant gesture been tried, the tars' hats would have blown southwards with the speed of leaves blown from autumn trees or a flock of starlings borne across a sky at evening.

—We have hardship ahead. We have ice and snow ahead. But we will face them like men. And if we are permitted by God's grace to descry new lands, future humanity will thank us. Not just thank James Cook. Not just thank Mr Gilbert—

There was laughter.

—Not just thank our learned gentlemen – Dr Forster and Mr Wales.

This really broke the sombre mood and led to outright guffaws.

—No. Humanity itself will bless *you* – the brave boys of the *Resolution*! So God bless you. And God bless His blessed Majesty King George III! And to put us in the mood for a hard voyage, my lads, we'll double today's ration of grog!

A tumultuous roar greeted the announcement – with the bo'sun leading hip-hip-hip-hoorahs for King George, the Captain and just about everyone else, and the men went to work in the blowy sails and flailing ropes and rigging to the airs led by the shanty-man – they sang 'Hearts of Oak' and an alphabet song:

> *A is for Anchor as everyone knows, and*
> *B is the sharp bit that we call the bows . . .*
> *So hi derry, do derry, hi derry dee,*
> *No man on the land's like a sailor at sea*
> *So turn the glass, ring the bell, keep sailing along.*
> *When it's time for our grog then it's time for this song.*
> *E is for Ensign – at the stern it's now seen – and*

Resolution

F is for fo'rard there to liberty clean – and
G is for gangway to shoreward we goes – and
H is for Harlot, whose body we'll know.

—I wonder at their coarseness, said Dr Reinhold Forster. Songs, yes, by all means, but is it really requisite that they should— but his voice was drowned by

I is for inches, she's going to get fed
And J is the jouncing we'll do on her bed

as the sloop *Resolution*, without its chaperone the *Adventure*, bounced and heaved its way towards the icy south. They sang of drink. They sang of buying boys' bottoms for sixpence and pretty boys for half a crown. They sang of Good King George – as the southern skies grew colder and the curlews circled. Snow fell in the middle of December, and as they altered course eastwards, and floating ice came into view, they were once more issued with their protective winter clothing. There were no more birds in the sky.

II

1791

—*IN ORDER TO ENSURE PUBLIC TRANQUILLITY, TWO HUNDRED thousand heads must be cut off.* It seems a little — what should one say? Intemperate.

Sömmerring was holding a French paper, *L'Ami du Peuple*.

—It's obvious, said Brand, their English visitor. France is descending into chaos. Lafayette lost control when he started firing on the crowds in Paris.

—How else would you control a mob? It's anarchy . . .

—Thank God that the baby has stopped crying, said Therese.

They were all too ill — Therese, George, Rosechen, Clara, the baby Luisa — to have one of their evenings. They had been passing round a heavy cold — hacking cough, unstoppable catarrh — for what felt like weeks, and it would have been more sensible to put up the shutters and to instruct Mattias and Inge, their invaluable 'treasures', to tell their friends that Frau Forster was not At Home. They had the English visitor — Mr Brand — to entertain. He was the son of a former Prime Minster, Lord North: *en route* to Greece. Mainz was a stopping place on his Grand Tour. They felt obliged, since he had stopped to meet the Circumnavigator, to parade their more intellectual friends. Filling the apartment with company, moreover, was a remedy against the demons who inhabited it if they were there simply *en famille*. None of the friends, not even Caroline, guessed the full truth until the marriage was decidedly over. Even Caroline, who had known Therese since childhood, accepted that the pink-cheeked, boring Huber was no more than the lodger, and entered in to Therese's brittle jokes that Huber was the latest of George's crushes. The two men spent the best part of each morning together on their translation work. Together they had done Beaumarchais's *Mariage de Figaro*, Mrs Piozzi's *Anecdotes of Dr Johnson*, Sir William Jones's translation of the Indian drama *Sakontala*. They had just received two more English books from Voss, their publisher in Berlin: Captain Bligh's account of the Mutiny on the *Bounty*, and Burke's *Reflections on the French Revolution*.

—You should be in bed, Caroline said to the four-month pregnant Therese, who stood beside the fire-screen honking with bronchitis.

—They are all in their way stories of Revolution, George was saying to Sömmerring. Christian and his men rose up against the tyranny of Bligh; Figaro the servant is wiser than his masters – I've yet to read Burke, but I am sure that he who lambasted the brutality of the British in India and who defended the American colonists—

—That's where you're wrong, said Huber who had been at work on Burke's first few pages. He is a counter-revolutionary.

—Read on, read on! said George, with a tremendous sniff, his own version of the cold turning more to sinusitis – at this stage at any rate – than to the chest.

—We are all just exhausted, Therese was saying. Poor little Luisa has been awake two nights running, and although Inge is a saint and Karin is a good nurserymaid – a mother *wakes*. This is the first time the child has slept in – oh, I can't count the days.

—Dearest, said Caroline, should we all just *go*?

—If being a Jacobin means believing that the Revolution cannot be held back, must go *on* until Justice and Freedom are extended throughout France – throughout *Europe* – then yes, I am a Jacobin. But believe me, reason will prevail. The huge majority of the Assembly are moderates – the Feuillants.

—And if two hundred thousand don't want freedom and equality, said Sömmerring, you'll be brotherly enough to cut their heads off?

—It won't *come* to that, spluttered George from behind a handkerchief. He swigged some schnapps. That paper, *L'Ami du Peuple* – it was written by a man we know. When my father was lucky enough to secure our position on the *Resolution*, he had to leave his teaching post. Dr Marat succeeded him at Warrington as the language master. Do you really think Mr Wedgwood and Mr Priestley would have engaged a homicidal maniac to teach the good Protestant boys of Northern England? No. Dr Marat is an *enthusiast*, but of course . . . he doesn't mean—

A giant sneeze interrupted him.

Someone else was saying,

—The Girondins now call for open war against any of France's neighbours who harbour refugees. That rather puts us in the firing line. There's not a boarding house in Mainz – not an inn, not a monastery – that is not filled with French *marquises* and *abbés*.

—The Royal Family made a cardinal error trying to escape.

Resolution

—The Queen was trying to cross the border – to get to her brother the Emperor in Vienna.

—It played into the revolutionaries' hands. Of course, after that, they suspended the monarchy. She and Ludwig were making themselves the enemies of France. There's a Republic now.

—Such rumours are rubbish, said George. Ludwig and Marie-Antoinette accept their destiny. They have accepted the Revolution. They will stay now and eventually – you'll see – they'll become constitutional monarchs, like George III in England. Trust me – we saw it, Alexander von Humboldt and I with our own eyes – we saw Lafayette and the King in the Field of Mars – accepting the sovereignty of the people: accepting that the King only exercises power with the consent of the people. He is their tenant, not the other way about.

—That is precisely the view of politics which Burke rejects, said Huber rather abruptly. Then adding —Excuse me if I go to look at the child.

Only about a year later did Caroline, who overheard this, consider it odd that Huber, not the child-obsessed George, went to look at the baby.

The hum of voices, fuelled by schnapps or wine, filled that room, continued to fuel it, making a murmurous music in which none of the conversations, from the corridor, could be distinguished or understood. Karin and Inge were outside the nursery.

—O mein Herr, said the elder woman.

—To hide it from the little ones – Karin was saying through her tears – the little ones are asleep – O Rosechen, O Clara—

—She was breathing, said Inge. Half an hour ago when Karin lifted her to change her, she was breathing.

—Inge, said Huber desperately. What are you saying?

Returning to the music-murmur of voices in the fuggy room, his ears could now, technically speaking, make out the words spoken. Here, a declaration that a war was imminent. There, praising a felicitous *mot* of Beaumarchais. But none of the sounds any longer connoted meaning. Therese's gaunt, sleep-deprived, fevered face turned to him, as he said,

—It is the baby.

And George, catching at once what had happened, cried,

—Oh God, oh God!

And all the room became silent.

She gave birth to another baby five months later. They called it Georg. That one also died.

—Huber's babies don't have a very good survival rate, George remarked bitterly to Caroline. It was the first time she saw the truth of the whole situation.

In April '92, the month of baby Georg's birth, the French National Assembly declared war on Austria; not long afterwards, Prussia came into the war on the Austrian side. The Austrian and Prussian courts were open in their hatred of the Revolution and in their support of the émigrés, priests and aristocrats, who called upon their fellow Europeans to save France from what they feared would be bloody anarchy. For the revolutionaries, with whom George now fervently sympathized, a metaphysical conflict was in evidence. As one of the more messianic of the *Deputés* had declared in Paris,

—Here is the crisis of the universe. God disentangled the primitive chaos: the French will unravel the feudal chaos . . . for free men are God's representatives on earth. Kings will make impious war on us with slave soldiers and exhorted money; we will make a holy war with free soldiers and patriotic contributions.

French troops invaded Brabant.

Mainz was put on alert. The city's battlements were strengthened. Ditches around the city were filled with water. Two years' supply of corn were bought up and stored by the Archbishop Elector for public consumption in the event of siege. The Prussian army, marching down through Koblenz, needed to be fed – they consumed fourteen thousand pounds of meat a day. The price of food become prohibitively high. In Paris, the mob seemed poised to topple the established order, and in German lands, despite the fervour of intellectuals like George, there seemed a dogged determination to hold anarchy at bay, and to maintain the *status quo*. Nothing could demonstrate this with more ritual insistence than the coronation of the Holy Roman Emperor at Frankfurt in July. Brand, the indefatigable young English sightseer, insisted on going to the ceremony, and – ignorant of the tensions all around him in the Forsters' apartment – upon taking George and Huber as his companions. There was actually something very comforting about Brand's friendly, breezy presence. With Brand around, they all had to act a part, and there was no possibility of explicit discussion of the fact that Therese and Huber were lovers.

During the Imperial coronation, Brand kept up continuous conversation. The coronation of his King had taken place years before his own birth, but this did not prevent him saying,

—I say, d'you think they did that in Westminster Abbey, to old Farmer George? What d'ye think they're up to now – rubbing oil on him, what?

And the end of it all was that the twenty-four-year-old Francis, a brocaded doll in white tights and buckled shoes and a bejewelled medieval crown, was led by mitred bishops and coroneted electors, to the chancel steps to be shown to his people, to the fanfare of trumpets and the chorus of *Vivat Imperator Romanorum!*

While Huber tried to point out the names of famous princes, and while Brand said —Beats a night at the opera, eh? – Forster, the only committed republican of the three, felt tears flowing at the passing of things.

The Duke of Weimar, Karl August, rallied to the cry of the Duke of Braunschweig and the King of Prussia to rescue France from the sacrilegious hands of sans-cullotism. Loyal to his Duke, his young friend, the *Geheimrat* (Privy Councillor) of Weimar, marched with the ducal armies, and let it be known that he would be passing through Mainz in August. It was just a month after the death of baby Georg. Therese was in no state to host two conversazioni with *Geheimrat* Goethe, so he was entertained at Sömmerring's apartment. They all – the intelligentsia of Mainz – were there – even Therese; Caroline Böhmer, who had moved to Mainz to be near the Forsters, Zimmerman, Sömmerring provided beer, not wine, which perhaps accounted for the rather stiff conversation.

In after months, George remembered Goethe's range, his self-confidence, his sheer spiritual energy, even though he was plainly exhausted by a week of marching with a hungry army. Sömmerring, the foremost anatomist of his day, was plainly thunderstruck by Goethe's momentous anatomical discovery. Hitherto, it had always been maintained that the human race was distinct from the other mammals because it lacked an intermaxillary bone. Until this very decade, even anatomists of Sömmerring's calibre had accepted this as a doctrine, handed down from Aristotle and

Galen. This is the bone which contains the incisor teeth. Man has incisor teeth. In 1784 Goethe had demonstrated the existence of the bone in a human skull.

—Our sense that the ape is almost human! Goethe's face gleamed – and George remembered Nally saying almost the same thing on board the *Resolution*, the day he painted the monkey.

—My theory of plants, declaimed the *Geheimrat*, is that they all derive and stem from a single source. What if it could be shown that all Nature, all living beings, are kindred?

He was thin, sallow and, though not as pock-marked as George, his skin bore the marks of smallpox suffered in youth. The celebrated features, the bright brown eyes, darting from person to person, the asymmetrical and enormous forehead, were all there on display, but Therese and Caroline felt crushing disappointment. They had hoped for fervour and passion in his talk, and they found the polite courtier, who praised the neo-classical splendours of the Deanery, which had just been finished, and where the pagan poet had evidently enjoyed being feted by the Catholic clergy. Although his figure was lean, Goethe's face, according to Huber, was flaccid, inclining towards the double chin. Therese wanted him to talk of *Werther* and the novelist said he had left it all behind him. Caroline asked —Was it really true that the book had inspired copy-cat Werthers, young men in blue coats who had killed themselves for love? – and someone else had tried to start a conversation which Goethe quite evidently did not wish to have – about suicide – and George, who even more evidently did not wish to have it, asked the poet-scientist to explain his refutation of Newton's colour theory – and this did not go well because Sömmerring, with no intention of impoliteness but simply with the instinctive reaction of a scientist, interrupted Goethe's flow by saying,

A. N. Wilson

—But sir, you have misunderstood what Newton's colour theory is. You are refuting something Newton never wrote.

And to cover the awkwardness someone asked Goethe about the campaign and the Revolution, and they heard of hardship on the road, mud-spattered, hungry troops, a collective fear. He appeared to have small sympathy with the Royalists . . .

—A revolution must be the fault of the Government, not of the revolutionaries . . .

Which made George tap the table in excited agreement; but he was aghast then to hear Goethe denouncing the Revolution's core principles: questioned what it even meant to say that all men were equal when it was so clear that in every capacity – bodily strength, intellect, wealth – they were not. He ridiculed the idea of government by the people – said it was a contradiction in terms, and deplored the violence of the Paris mob. Who but a strong Government – a King – could protect the Many from the Many?

Perhaps it was the effort of being on best behaviour for Goethe, perhaps it was the strain of the last weeks, in which neither Therese nor George had discussed their painful situation, the dead baby, his paternity, the continued presence of Huber in both their lives – but after they came home from the Goethe evening, they had one of the most painful rows of their entire marriage.

Sometimes one, sometimes the other, said an unpardonable thing. Sometimes, seeing a word thrust home, causing intense pain, awoke in the perpetrator a pity which felt like love. But on they rowed – that afternoon – that evening – through the next day.

—You could see I was in no condition to go out – but you'd rather go and lick Goethe's—

—No, oh no. It was *you* who wanted to go to meet him—

—You care more about tuft-hunting than your own family. Even at a time like this—

—You think I don't care – you think I don't care about what it did to Rosechen – to little Rose – to see the dead . . . what it did to Clara – to see – oh God.

—You don't *care* about Georg being dead – any more than you cared when Luisa—

—All right, all RIGHT. He suddenly lost control. He felt his lower lip trembling, as he shouted through tears,

—Can't we be candid – isn't it better they're dead – *his* children? If we're to have any hope of a future together . . . as a family . . .

But he was moving at a different pace from hers and very slowly she opened her mouth in shock and said in a broken staccato,

—What did you say?

He stared at her. He hated her very much, but the pain in her face was wrenching his heart.

—You said it was *better* that two of my children were . . . were—

—Yes. YOUR children – your accursed children. Not mine – not mine, Therese – can you wonder that . . .

And he had left the bedroom. She had thrown herself on the bed and sobbed. He had left the apartment and paced through Mainz. The bells of churches and monasteries clanged a meaningless carillon in his head. Pacing and pacing he had no consciousness of place, walked past Schöborner Hof and down to Stefansplatz, indifferent to their Renaissance magnificence, heaved and gulped with anger and pain – her pain, his pain, the child's pain. At a smoky hostelry near the Carmelite church he drank schnapps – quite a lot of it, and hatred of his wife turned to pity, pity to lust, as he lurched homewards, determined to bring all this pain to an end, to be reconciled with her.

—We ate without you, she said with cold fury. Where were you? Rose was crying – the maids were asking . . .

—I needed to clear my mind.

—You smell like an alehouse.

—Please, Therese . . .

Huber, who was present, said,

—I think Therese wants to be alone.

—*You* think! *You* tell me what my wife wants. Oh, God, God . . .

And a door was slammed.

Huber had the decency to keep to his own room that night. Waking on the cold day-bed in his study in the small hours, George burst into Therese's room.

—George, if I don't sleep, I shall go mad.

—My darling girl—

—I'm not your darling. Please. Please, George, go away.

—What I said was unpardonable. About your babies. About your adorable lost children. But Therese. Let us make more children. Our children. Let us make – a future. Let us make—

—Go away, George. Go and put your head under a tap.

—You BITCH!

The morning was silent. No speaking at all, not at breakfast, not when Therese said she was going out to visit Caroline. Later, over Second Breakfast, Karin, bringing in a tray of warm rolls which she had lately baked, said,

—The flour is running low. There is no more to be had in the market.

And Huber, who found a newspaper, said,

—The Prussian army was checked at Valmy. They are in retreat. It is only a matter of time before the French arrive here . . .

Resolution

—Isn't it what you want? said Therese bitterly to her husband. Your Jacobin friends taking us over? Oh what are we to do?

—Sömmerring has already left town – he has gone to Vienna. He thinks we should all do the same, said Huber. We are not fighting men. There will be no virtue in remaining, to be murdered in our beds by the *sans-culottes*. I am going to Frankfurt tonight.

Therese half rose in shock, as if electrocuted.

—But you can't, she said.

—Maybe I should not have stayed, said Huber. Maybe you two should—

—Don't tell me what I should do, she flared. I don't want to stay here. I don't want to stay with George – you know that, Ludwig.

George heard himself say, almost as in a trance,

—Perhaps we all became used to it – perhaps it is what we all . . . *want* – Ludwig and you together – but not leaving me, not leaving the children. If we all stayed together . . . I'd allow . . . It is in order – it is all right. If you *need* one another . . .

—Oh, said Therese furiously, what are you TALKING ABOUT?

Huber left that afternoon for Frankfurt.

The army of General Adam-Philippe Custine reached Worms on 4th October.

The majority of the cathedral clergy, and many of the religious – nuns as well as monks – fled Mainz. Horses and carriages were in short supply.

—I don't want to stay here and be raped – I don't want to watch French soldiers raping our children.

—They're an army of liberation, darling – they are not going to rape anyone.

—Don't call me darling. Look, Huber can keep us safe, me and the girls.

—I can keep you safe. I am your husband.

When the French army finally reached Mainz, depleted by disease, unwashed, tipsy, they seemed as if they would fulfil neither Therese's fears nor George's hopes. The soldiers, vaguely sinister figures in huge plumed judge's hats, their faces smudged with the moustaches which were the badges of their revolutionary serious-ness, did not make the bosom thrill with political optimism. Nor did they inflict much violence on the population. Huber, writing from Frankfurt, said he'd seen the crowd set upon a French soldier and hang him from a lamp-post, an horrific event which made Huber all the more anxious to get well away from the scenes of occupation.

The plans kept changing. Some days Therese spoke of returning to live with her father. Sometimes Huber wrote that he could take her and the children to France. Sometimes George protested that he did not want her to go away with Huber.

One of the consequences of the visit of Goethe was a re-awakening in George's mind of all the areas of intellectual interest which the unhappy domestic scenes made impossible to pursue. He wanted to consult Humboldt about mineralogy. On his desk was a half-finished paper on the botany of Tahiti. He wanted to pursue more translating work. Translating *Sakontala*, from Sir William Jones's English, made him want to learn Sanskrit, Hindustani, and other Indian languages: but the quarrels, and the need to earn money, had distracted him from any work which engaged his brain and his imagination. Now, the political events made it seem even less likely that he would resume his work before Christmas.

Therese and Caroline both urged him to be careful.

—What if the Prussian army arrives next week? asked Caroline. These soldiers – this French rag-bag – won't put up a fight. They'll be driven back over the border.

Resolution

—I believe in the Revolution. Don't you?

—Belief, fiddlesticks, said Therese. You'll look a fool if the Prussian troops *are* victorious.

—The Old Man – Caroline meant Archbishop von Erthal – will come back and he's not going to look very kindly on his librarian wearing that ridiculous cockade.

—It isn't ridiculous. It's a badge of Liberty – of solidarity.

—You look like a Christmas tree.

—Therese is right, George. It is irresponsible to take risks. Think of your children.

He did think of the children. They were frightened, and came to sleep in the big bed with their mummy and daddy. George loved feeling Rosechen's hot, even breath against his face as she slept. In the morning, when she woke, he would tell her fairy stories as she lay in the crook of his shoulder.

—You could travel with Brand. He's going on to Athens. You could make one of your books about it, said Caroline.

—You could go back to England, said Therese.

He had been thinking of this. The *Letter to Lord Sandwich* had to some degree queered his pitch, but he would still find work.

—Would you join me in England?

—George. We would have to talk about it. Let us not deceive one another. My life is with Huber now.

—I can't accept that. Go on having him as your lover if you must, but do not take my children from me – do not be as cruel as that. Therese. *Please.*

There was such contempt in her expression, such refusal to listen. Both seethed with anger against one another. Both, with some part of themselves, actually dreaded a separation.

George was one of the founder-members of the Mainz Jacobin Club. To his father-in-law, Heyne, he wrote —The Revolution has been brought to pass by Philosophy. The Republic of twenty-four million people will do more to change Europe than the mad English despot George III and his slave-subjects.

Heyne wrote back that he deemed Jacobins to be the murderous scum of the earth.

—Are you surprised that he should write those words, asked Therese furiously. She held out a Strassburg newspaper. Have you seen what they did – fifteen hundred men and women put on a so-called trial and then simply massacred? Is that Liberty and Fraternity?

George and his fellow German Jacobins – and there were disappointingly few of them in Mainz – met the commander of the invading army in the Baroque Deanery so much admired by Goethe. Count Adam-Philippe Custine, with his thick shock of white hair and very pronounced arched dark eyebrows, would have been a handsome man had not the bushy mustachios, symbols of his revolutionary fervour, not given his aristocratic features the look of an amateur-dramatics version of a bandit, perhaps a minor role in Schiller's *The Robbers*. George had perfect French, so there was no question of their conversing in the language of the defeated.

—. . . pleasure in offering you both the position of *Deputé* in the Provisional Revolutionary Government of Mainz, said Custine. It was a remark which he addressed to exquisitely manicured finger-nails, though presumably addressed to George and to a lumpen fellow called Adam Lux, whose presence was disconcerting. Had one of George's close friends at the University stood beside him as a 'Mainz revolutionary', his resolution would not have wavered. As it was, Lux, who smelt of underarm sweat, was not a reassuring presence. George knew Lux slightly – the man came to the library to consult an impressive range of books. The son of a local farmer, he had written a doctorate on 'Enthusiasm'. For a while he had worked as a private tutor in the town: then a fortunate marriage had enabled him to buy a small farm, and to live the life of a private scholar.

—I'm sure, Lux was saying, that it has come to your attention, Citizen Custine, that some of your troops have been appropriating sheep, pigs, pulleys . . .

—Pulleys.

—He means chickens, translated George.

—. . . without payment. We appreciate that the army has to eat and has to sleep. But we would respectfully ask that you should ask permission . . . For instance, one of your sergeants authorized his troops to stable horses in the Carmelite hat. I cannot endorse superstition, of course not, but the hat is a place where our fellow human beings have experienced the sacred . . .

—He means a chapel, said George, to the General's puzzled face.

Even at the moment of joining the Rosicrucians at Kassel, George had experienced a sense of sinking, an awareness that this was a step too far. As Lux and Custine discussed points of administration, water supply, accommodation, hours of curfew, George was beginning to ask himself how he could escape. He would take Therese and the children to follow Brand. That was what they would do. Caroline's idea had been a good one – *A Journey to Greece*, by the author of *Through the Lower Rhine, Cook the Discoverer* and *A Voyage Round the World* . . .

When he returned to the apartment, he found that Therese had left, taking with her Karin, the nurserymaid, and their two children.

Her short letter asked him not to follow her, but since she did not tell him where she was going, this was scarcely possible. The single piece of paper which contained this news had been propped, on his writing table, against a Hindustani grammar and his copy of Linnaeus. It would have been hard to assess how long he sat there, staring at his wife's handwriting. Once or twice he rang the little hand-bell on the writing table, an instinctive gesture, though Inge and Mattias had presumably deserted. Then, somewhere in the region of the kitchen corridors, he heard a movement, and believed he had done his two remaining servants an injustice. He rang the bell again. Moments later, the door opened. It was Caroline, carrying a *papier-mâché* florally decorated tray on which tinkled two glasses and a decanter of Riesling. Her thick chestnut curls fell on to her creamy shoulders. She was completely naked.

PART FIVE

The Roaring Breakers

And now the STORM-BLAST came, and he
Was tyrannous and strong

I

1774

—ROUND THE BACK, SOBACHKA, ROUND THE BACK!

In their winter clothes, strange mummified Resolutions, they all looked very much alike; from Captain Cook to the youngest midshipman, they were all tubby, semi-comical dolls. All, that is, but Nally who, even in his thick woollen leggings, managed to pirouette and wiggle his hips in balletic twists and by moving first one buttock, then another, provoked the dog to dance about like something at the circus. Sobachka was George's dog, but it was Nally who taught her tricks, running behind his calves, and performing figures of eight around him before sitting in front of him and opening her mouth for a reward. When she had learnt the tricks, Sobachka could hope for pieces of meat or cheese, biscuits or fish-tails. Supplies were now running low and she was lucky if, in reward for her dance round Nally's writhing legs, she got more than a 'There's a darling' and a pat on the head.

Sobachka had come from Bora Bora, one of the Society Islands, which they had visited the previous September. A dog-loving race, the inhabitants. Many of the women, as would have been the case in the higher reaches of society in London, petted over their dogs, devoting to them an excess of physical affection which, if shown to their children, or to a man, would have been considered distasteful. The Bora-Boran ladies, however, went further. When George had first set eyes upon Sobachka, her human minder was holding the puppy to her breast, wiggling a rubbery pink nipple at the dog's tongue and mouthing chuckled endearments.

Sobachka was a white and brown, round-headed dog, who, in the four months since becoming George's pet, had grown wiry fur. Her eyes were small, her ears upright. She could never be described as beautiful, but her arrival had changed George's ship life. Although the midshipmen openly despised her ('Hello, shitter' was Pickersgill's usual way of greeting her), she was much liked by the men, and owed her slightly barrel-like shape to the treats they threw to her.

Nally and she had a number of tricks, apart from 'round the back'. She held up her right paw whenever he said, 'How d'ye do?' She could balance bread pellets on her nose and feign death by lying on her back. Nally surreptitiously gathered up her knotted, stony little turds whenever he found them on the deck.

—We don't want you suffering the fate of the monkeys, eh, Sobachka, do we now?

And George would lay down brush or pencil and remember the poor monkeys, those early casualties of the voyage out. Sobachka shivering on his lap made bearable the other circumstances of life as the thermometer sank from the early forties to the thirties: the scurvy, which began to affect some of the men, the fact that everyone was hungry, everyone had a cold. She also numbed his irritation with Reinhold, in particular his father's ability to quote an apt line from Horace or Virgil to cover any eventuality, from a storm at sea to a case of constipation.

His love for her was tactile, the whole relationship based on her nuzzling him, licking him, butting him, his being able to reach her, stroke her, pat her. Twenty years later, stubbornly wakeful, though exhausted in the marriage bed, knowing that he lay beside a woman who hated him – knowing this because she said so – George would think fondly of Sobachka. Presumably those who had the knack of matrimony were able to lie together and receive the same consolations from one another which the ugly little island dog and the lonely, spotty boy symbiotically enjoyed.

They had been at sea for two long months, the harshest months of the voyage. The Captain was determined to see if they could find the Southern Continent. The *Resolution* took a westerly course S60˚15 and sailed through severe gales, fog and snow until they once more had met the ice. For over a month, the sloop simply froze. The ropes were wires of ice. The sails became like huge sheets of metal, heavy and hard. The shivers froze fast in the blocks, so it became all but impossible to hoist the topsail up or down. Moreover, supplies were running low. Most of the bread brought from New Zealand and packed in green casks had begun to go off.

—The casks were not sufficiently cleaned. Normally I would hold my tongue, but, Mr Gilbert, there are moments when a man must speak out.

George had heard Mr Gilbert, the master, tell Captain Cook that it would be the grace of God alone which saved him from the gallows, since he could not envisage getting back to England before his patience with 'the tactless philosopher' snapped.

—You see, even the good bread, the twice baked, so to say, has touched the sides of the casks. This is most unfortunate because it has become rotten. It is for this reason all the men are now hungry.

The master said nothing.

Battening on to the surgeon, Reinhold said,

—Mr Patten, the Kapitän has put the men on a two-thirds allowance. This will undoubtedly lead to sickness.

—Very likely, Dr Forster.

—You must speak to him, you are responsible for the health of the ship. I'm here on this ship now nineteen months and already I am finding it astonishing that you cannot be responsible for the health. To my point of view this is astonishing. You should tell the Kapitän it was a mistake, this attempt again to find the *Terra Australis*, a land, by the way, which plainly does not exist. It is ice, ice and again ice. There is no Southern Continent. Of this you can be sure.

—It is to establish the truth or falsehood of that proposition, Dr Forster, that we all set forth.

—Why will the Kapitän not listen to me? Is not mine the voice of reason? Are my rheumaticks worse or better? They are worse. My son's legs, they have begun to swell. His teeth are falling out. He has scurvy, Mr Patten. Scurvy. My son. His face was a mass of spots before this, I own. Now it is nothing more than a blotch. And this is my reward for accompanying this voyage. My reward.

—I like the way your son never complains, sir. He holds the pencil in his mittens. In ice and snow, he keeps drawing, drawing. Hello, hello – what's that?

And the surgeon pointed to what seemed to be a whale, surfacing in the foggy middle distance, beyond the floating ice. In the silver-white air a few petrels swooped, but there were very few birds in evidence.

Resolution

George and his father were too depleted, too depressed, too ill to make observations on Natural History. In their separate little cabins they lay in their bunks and George's only consolation – for much of the time, he was too sad even to read, too stiff-fingered to draw (in spite of what the doctor said), he lay there under a damp blanket, shivering, with aching gums, and blotchy skin and swollen legs and a dizzy sick headache – was to clutch Sobachka, whose large black sad eyes stared at his. Was she imploring him to get well? Was she praying to him, her Deity, for warmer weather? Or did she want him to come out and play on the frozen decks?

Once again, they failed to find the Southern Continent. When the Captain deemed that everyone on board had suffered enough, they turned from the freezing waters. The wind suddenly picked up. With the greatest run since leaving England, the *Resolution* crossed three degrees latitude in a single day – the thermometer in Reinhold's cabin began to climb – to 48° by 9th February, to 58° by 15th February. Bird life resumed. Shearwaters hovered, portents of better days in the fresh breeze. Mr Cooper, First Lieutenant, shot two grampuses with musket balls. Albatrosses swooped and flapped. The sea, from being iron-cold and life-destroying expanses of dark blue black, became a shook silk bedspread of vibrant green. Porpoises leapt from its surface.

Then, as the temperature rose through the sixties, very many on board, having suffered minor colds, cramps, rheumaticks and constipation, got truly ill. Nally began to double up with intolerable colic. Reinhold, distrustful of a simple Irishman's capacity to explain his own condition with scientific accuracy to the surgeon, insisted upon forming his own diagnosis.

—I have questioned him in great detail, Mr Patten. Nally has coagulated, bilious faeces. Without a purge, there is no hope for him. He will die.

Similar pains began to afflict the Captain. These, however, were much more severe than Nally's, indeed incapacitating.

—Kapitän Cook, I must enter.

This was Reinhold at the door of the Captain's cabin. He could hear light groaning within, punctuated by yelps of frantic hiccoughs. Cooper, who had been to consult the Captain about essential navigational matters, said,

—I entreat you, sir, our beloved Captain is in such pain, he can scarcely speak. I am doing my best to navigate us towards Easter Island.

—This is a mistake. None of us can wait so long. Easter Island, it is too far. You should aim for Davis Island.

—Which the Captain believes to be one and the same place.

—If Kapitän Cook dies, proclaimed Reinhold in his carrying voice, I do not reckon much to any of our chances of returning to New Zealand alive: let alone to England.

He pushed past the First Lieutenant and stood beside Cook's truckle. The body upon it, wracked with agony, hiccoughed convulsively.

—I would suggest, Kapitän, that this hiccoughing is continuing now for several days, and if it continues much longer you will be dead. You have coagulated faeces in your gut, sir. I have consulted Mr Patten, who informs me that you have not responded to the purges he administered.

Cook, on quivering elbows, raised himself from the narrow bed and gasped,

—Bowl!

His servant had a metal pail to hand in which Cook vomited copiously.

Resolution

—This is good, said Reinhold. This is the first stage.

—If you don't mind, sir, I'd like to clear up, said Willis, the servant. There's no room for three in this space, sir.

A few hours later, the Captain passed motions for the first time in over a week. The hiccoughing, however, continued. The coming and going of the attentive Willis, and the almost constant attendance of the surgeon in Cook's small sleeping-quarters, did not keep Reinhold away.

—Mr Patten, you must not be afraid, sir, of the vomitings. The purging should continue. Camomile tea and a glyster, these would be my remedies. Then, perhaps, a warm bath and a plaster of Theriac on the stomach itself.

The crisis was past, but Cook was still too weak to rise from his bed. He was able to sit upright and to take a little nourishment. Mr Patten agreed with Reinhold that strength would only fully return when they reached land and found fresh vegetables and fruit. In the meantime, however, the Captain was not going to gain strength from salt pork and biscuit.

—There is no fresh meat to be had, sir – these were Patten's fateful words. The last sheep died of scurvy. *There is no fresh meat.*

Moments later, Reinhold lurched off down the swaying, heaving deck in search of his son. With the warmer temperatures, George and Sobachka had sought out a sunny spot on deck. In the middle distance, a flock of greyish tern flew in the bright sky. George was sketching them, while Sobachka, weaving in and out of Nally's gyrating knees, performed an elaborate version of her 'round the back' trick.

—Now, this one is for George, Sobachka. George – George, now, have a look at this one.

—I have told you before, not to address my son by his first name.

—Vati, it's all right. I don't mind it.

—Watch this, George.

In common with the entire crew, Nally now appeared unresponsive to most of the instructions emanating from Reinhold's brain, though he continued to be an efficient and unobtrusive valet and man of all works to both father and son.

—On your back, Sobachka! You're dead! Bang! Bang!

She obliged him by lying on her back with paws in the air. It seemed as if she was laughing.

—*Dira necessitas! Dira necessitas!* intoned Reinhold.

He had picked up Sobachka before either George or Nally realized what he was doing, and, in so far as it is possible to *bustle* on a swaying deck, he had bustled away with the wiry creature wriggling in his arm. George, still intent on the grey tern, did not immediately take in what was being said, something about the Captain's health being more important to all of them than the life of a dog.

—No sir! Nally was calling out. Jesus Christ, I beg you . . .

George never brought himself to ask his father, neither at the time, nor afterwards when he wrote up *A Voyage Round the World*, whether Reinhold himself or Pattinson, the ship's cook, put Sobachka to death, nor how the execution was effected.

The Captain himself later remarked,

—I received nourishment and strength from food which would have made most people in Europe sick, so true it is that necessity is governed by no law.

George tried to persuade himself that Captain Cook had not known, until after Sobachka's death, what Reinhold and the surgeon had in hand. No man aboard, apart from the Captain, partook of the dish.

Resolution

A week passed. Before a coastline came into sight, there were harbingers that land was near. One day, they caught four albacores in a net – 'very acceptable', in the Captain's opinion. George found the fish so rich, after weeks of an austere and near-starvation diet, that he almost vomited on the first mouthful; but he kept it down, and after only a few hours, he could feel the food giving him strength. Day by day, there were ever more birds circling the *Resolution*, always a signal of land – man-of-war birds, noddies, tern, petrels. Cook was now sufficiently restored to have resumed control of navigation. With a gentle breeze and in pleasant weather, the sloop scudded through the waves, easterly in the course W2'S. On Friday 11th March they covered sixty miles. Shortly after midnight, one of the Lieutenants, Charles Clerke, believed that he'd sighted land, and with dawn on the 12th, this belief was confirmed. Trees, sand, semi-naked people appeared in the spyglass. In confirmation of Cook's belief that this was Easter Island, the telescope also revealed a number of the enormous stones for which the place is famous.

After breakfast on board the *Resolution* two separate landing parties set off for the shore in jolly boats. Reinhold and Dr Sparrman carried bags for plant specimens, Hodges took his collapsible easel, his sketch-blocks and colour-boxes. With Lieutenants Pickersgill and Edgecumbe they intended, despite the intense heat, to pass the day exploring the interior. Cook and George, still incapacitated by illness, went in the other boat with Odiddy the interpreter. By the time the Captain's party came ashore, the first group had already set out into the cinder-strewn, ashy island.

The pain in George's swollen legs had not gone away. There was no possibility of his walking far. By the time their boat had been pulled on to the black shingle, over a hundred natives, most of them males, had assembled to meet them. Barratt, one of the oarsmen, let out a guffaw at the sight of them: brown, all but naked save for little loincloths made of what appeared to be mulberry bark, many of them heavily tattoo'd. Some of their faces were painted with yellow turmeric stripes, some with a reddish dye. The cause of Barratt's mirth was that two of the three, with the red and yellow face-paints, also sported feathered, fringed tricorn hats, inconceivably battered, possibly of Spanish origin. One of the men had a red and white chequered cloth which he wore as a bandana, while a third man – this is what really made Barratt and the other oarsman, Smith, whoop – was wearing a wide-brimmed dark blue felt wideawake hat which was unmistakeably the property of Herr Doktor Forster.

—That bleeder's only gawn 'n' swiped Farty's 'at.

Even the Captain joined in the hilarity.

Peaceful and friendly as the islanders clearly were, they shrank from the sight of the Captain's pistol. It was obvious that they had seen European firearms before.

After the shock of seeing the Easter Islanders in European hats, the next remarkable fact was the fearlessness of the wild birds. One of the islanders, a tall man with a rugged, majestic, bony face, which burst into a grin as George approached him, had a noddy sitting on his shoulder, seemingly tame as a pet grey parrot. Nor was this an isolated knack achieved by one bird-loving individual. To George's huge delight, another noddy, spreading its dark plumed wings, flapped towards him and landed on his shoulders.

While Odiddy attempted to communicate with their new friends (it appeared their languages, though cognate, were not interchange-able, as different, George decided, as Dutch and German), the Captain ordered Barratt, Smith and the two oarsmen from the other jolly boat to set up the stall. This was ever his custom upon arrival in a new place (if inhabited). A row of upturned crates served as his counter and, with Odiddy's help, it was explained that the islanders were welcome to help themselves to these gifts – coconut shells, medals of King George III made by Mr Boulton, pieces of Tahitian cloth, nails, a few glass beads. Nobody wanted beads, but there was some healthy bickering when the coconut shells ran out.

The islanders offered in return what George craved more than anything: fruit, yams and bananas. George, Odiddy and the Captain engaged the man wearing Reinhold's hat in conversation. In the interval of ravenous sucking on yams and gobbling of bananas, they indicated a wish to see some of the famous gigantic statues.

The hat man gave his name, something like Maroowahai.

—*Ahu, Ahu . . . Mo'ai?*

After a few repetitions of these syllables, it was clear they were all discussing the same things. Captain Cook, not hitherto conspicuous as a play-actor, did rather a convincing rendition of an Easter Island statue, and George thought, in his deep set eyes and marked cheek-bones, that there were resemblances. Maroowahai led them round the corner of the bay, a short walk, but for George's swollen legs, a difficult one. Maroowahai spoke earnestly and sadly, pointing to the far distance inland and gesturing wildly, sometimes with both hands at his throat – miming a throttling – sometimes waving his fist.

Odiddy said,

—Some months ago, fierce fighting between West of Island people here and East people. West high people, East – Smith and Barratt.

—So the West are the aristocracy, said the Captain bluntly, and they were attacked by the plebeians.

—Pleb Eeen, but very good fighter, explained Odiddy. They kill many West men. Take West women. Fuck many.

—Steady the buffs, there, Odiddy, said the Captain. Our George . . .

He jerked his head sideways to indicate that the final words were unsuitable for one so young. It was a strange piece of delicacy from a man who swore so freely when speaking to sailors; George wondered if Cook did not quite know how much he swore.

—They kill the great-grandfathers, great-great-grandfathers. Kill long-ago people.

—Kill their ancestors.

Odiddy smiled enthusiastically at his promising pupils.

—The statues. They are the statues of their aristocratic ancestors?

—This true. Statues their many-time-ago fathers. Statues their gods. Power in the statues. Power to Aha . . . Mo'ai.

Maroowahai nodded his head. Then, with a sweeping gesture of his long brown arm he pointed to one of the saddest sights which had ever appeared to George's eyes. Across a barren, scrubby stretch of land where underfoot there was no grass, just grey-black cinders, was a row of pillared statues, some fifteen feet in height. Morning sun, not yet high, cast long shadows behind these massive structures. Only two were standing. Their heads appeared to be leaning slightly backwards, an attitude in part defiant, in part hurt, as if, having just heard bad news, they were determined to bear their misfortune stoically. The strong light cast the sculpted faces into deep shadows, the beetling brow, which was of a reddish stone, contrasted to the huge grey of the pillar-bodies. Beneath the semi-circle of brow, the eye sockets were shaded pits, the deep nostrils and pronounced lips seemed pursed in pride so badly wounded that nothing could ever be sufficient reparation. The glory was departed. The two figures who remained standing mourned over the mutilated ancestors lately toppled – toppled, decapitated, deprived of spiritual power.

Maroowahai stood beside one detached giant head, raised aloft his arms, and wept. He let out moans of grief. Instinct made the Europeans freeze at the display of emotion. George removed his hat, the only mark of respect he could think of. Maroowahai continued to wear Reinhold's hat, to keen and to sway. Unnecessarily, Odiddy said,

—He weep for grandmother. Great fathers of old, old people, family people many year ago. He weep for old days no more. He weep for aristocracy no more. All power in head. Pleb people take power from head.

—Ask him *why* there was a war. Why did East come attacking the West? Was it becoss they were hungry?

Cook's practical mind looked at first for simple explanations.

Odiddy put the question as posed. Maroowahai was silent. He was trying to master his emotions, that much was evident. George felt instinctively that it had not been a food war, but that the answer lay at their feet, the huge toppled grey granite, the detached red sandstone heads on the cindery ground.

He spoke. Odiddy translated.

—Hungry for spirit of the old days. Not hungry for yams. They take the spirit of the grandfathers. The power of the Western gods. Eastern people no spirit. They envy spirit of old gods. No heads, no power. Eastern people make the Western people like them – take their spirit, their power.

Maroowahai, who, from the first, had recognized the Captain as the Chief of the *Resolution* party, took Cook's elbow and led him up to one of the statues which lay on its side. He pointed in the stinking darkness beneath the angled granite. A truly intolerable smell emanated.

—*Eevee – eevee.*

—What's he saying, lad?

—Bones, Captain – this was George who spoke. (By the end of the first day he had a hundred words of the Easter Island language and was beginning to master the sentence structures.)

Odiddy said,

—Mother bones.

—His own mother? There was real horror in the Captain's voice.

—They seem to have the same word for wife and mother, said George.

The Captain allowed himself a little pleasantry.

—Rather Greek of them.

—They come from East, said Odiddy. Fuck mother. Kill her. Put bones everywhere. Maroowahai he gather bones, gather her flesh, bury her near the head of old gods, maybe some little power left near one god's head. But he weep. No power any more. The old gods lost power.

It was a relief, a great delight, to be rowed back to the *Resolution* in the sunshine of late afternoon in a boat laden with provisions. The islanders gave them chickens ready dressed – they were cooked in holes in the ground, wrapped in stones and straw. There were sweet potatoes, and more bananas. Though it was hours past dinner time, every man aboard had a rich supper that day. Before eating, however, there was a surprise in store.

—Ee oop! said the Captain. Look who's swam out to see us!

Two or three male islanders were sitting on the main deck in the sunshine trying with smiles and sign language to offer fish to the men. They also brought little wooden totems and fetishes which were miniature versions of the melancholy stone giants so lately despoiled. As well as these enterprising male entrepreneurs, some ten women had swum out to the *Resolution*. Several of the shore party had remarked, in the morning, on the scarcity of women. The huge preponderance of islanders awaiting the visitors were men. Cook had said,

—It's a case of lock up your daughters when sailors come to visit.

Clearly, any woman with a care for modesty or chastity had remained concealed in one of the low-lying huts visible from the boat. The women who'd come aboard the *Resolution* were – in a phrase which George took some pride when he wrote about it in *A Voyage* – *carrying on a particular traffic of their own. These women were neither reserved nor chaste and for the trifling consideration of a small piece of cloth, some of our sailors obtained the gratification of their desires.* Even by South Seas standards, these girls were flagrant.

—Don't stare, lad, just come along o' me and I'll gi' thee a glass o' brandy and water, was Cook's only comment as George watched transfixed, as the women knelt in front of the sailors, gobbling their private parts. Other groupings, in various stages of undress, recalled the writhing statue of Laocoön rescuing his two sons as they were strangled by sea serpents.

The women were still entertaining the men of the *Resolution* when the second rowing boat came aside bearing officers and the resident naturalist.

—He led us through banana groves. Through scrub, Mr Pickersgill. I told him – yes you, sir, I told you. We were going in quite the wrong direction. We saw almost no tree but banana and mimosa. We marched to an elevated place in the midday heat and I had no hat. I assure you, no hat. Did Mr Pickersgill complain to the savage who stole my hat? I put it as a question. And now, Kapitän Cook, we climb up the ladder on to the quarter-deck, and what do we see? Those women! Do they know I am a minister of the Church? That I am a Doctor of Civil Law at the University of Oxford?

The late supper of roasted chicken, sweet potatoes, followed by a banana duff laced with one of Pattinson's very finest egg custards, put most of the human beings on board in a very good humour. Even Reinhold seemed much happier after the meal as he smoked a pipe over his brandy and water, positively gloating in his discovery, which happened to be wrong, that the heads of the great statues were made of wood, not stone.

—Ja, ja, Mr Wales. You would see if you examined them more closely they are a species of petrified wood. I imagine they fell down quite of their own accord — not erected with sufficient foundations.

From Easter Island, which they left on 17 March, they sailed northwest, then west, to the Marquesas, and from there began their second South Pacific Island Sweep. Cook's purpose was less to give his crew a six-month sunshine cruise than to map the coastlines of the islands, to give the astronomer and the naturalists more time to investigate trees, plants, birds and beasts, and, by the way, to settle other incidental matters, weighing on his orderly, if somewhat inscrutable, mind. He wanted to eat no more dogs. In the Marquesas, he managed to acquire, in exchange for some six-inch nails, no fewer than eighteen pigs, so that the quarter-deck of the *Resolution* came to resemble the farm in Mile End, which it was to be presumed often occupied the thoughts of that silent and family-loving man. Reinhold was torn between unexpressed thankful acknowledgement that pork dinners were in prospect for the foreseeable future, and a wish to draw everyone's attention to the noise and the smell. He and the Captain had other things on their minds beside pigs, and one of these matters was the future of Odiddy.

Much of May and June was spent in Tahiti and Raiatea. Reinhold took a shine to a twelve-year-old boy called Noona, who followed him about on his botanizing expeditions, and carried his plant-bag. George liked the boy, too, conversed with him in primitive phrases and, together with Odiddy, began to teach him English. At nineteen and a half, George had begun to feel very old. Watching his father's tenderness towards Noona – holding the boy's hand as they nego- tiated the seawater swamps, taking note of the multifarious plants, trees and ducks – George remembered his boyhood journey down the Volga, and his pleasure in Reinhold's companionship. Although it was obvious (without their so often saying it) that Mr Gilbert and Mr Wales felt tempted to murder Reinhold, he was kind – perhaps at his best with child-friends. Noona was soon expressing a wish to come 'home' with the Forsters to Britannia, and to meet Reinhold's 'friend' the King. Odiddy told them that he too would accom- pany them, just as Omai, Captain Furneaux's companion on the *Adventure* (who had been taken back to England by Mr Banks after the Captain's first voyage), had delighted London, been painted by Sir Joshua, and achieved celebrity.

Clearly Captain Cook was divided. His libertarian instinct warred with wisdom; his fondness for Odiddy's company warred with a desire to spare him the horror and hardship of another visit to Antarctica; his respect for his officers, all of whom opposed adopting islanders, warred with the fact that Reinhold had begun to educate, hence, to improve, these boys. Odiddy and Noona could say the Lord's Prayer and sing 'God Save the King'. These things moved Cook.

After several days' silence upon the question, however, Cook acted, with the same forthrightness and expedition which George had so often seen, feared and admired. He chose to invite Odiddy, Noona, George, Reinhold and two officers – Clerke and Pickersgill – into his cabin after dinner.

—Now, Odiddy. I'm having to speak to you, lad, becoss you know English better 'n Noona. But these words are for you both. If you stayed wi' us, you might never get to England, never see the King – *becoss* – no, let me speak, please, Dr Forster – *becoss* – we might all perish. In some months' time, I am going to ask my gallant comrades to accompany me just one last time into a land of ice and snow and wind and more ice. We'll have no other ship besides us to help us if we freeze solid in the ice. No other ship to rescue us if we are destroyed in gales and hurricanes. But let me suppose you are brave enough lads to stay wi' us. And you're good lads. I know that. But even if you survive and even if you come back wi' us to England, you'll be homesick. You'll miss your own kind. I'm homesick every day of my life – but I'm in a ship full of Englishmen. And that's why I've decided – no buts, Dr Forster – no protests – this is my decision – you must go home.

Odiddy, who had deduced what the Captain was saying before the speech was done, openly sobbed, and Reinhold's cheeks were moist.

—We'd all like you to stay till the King's Birthday – we celebrate it in style – and then – it's worth your tears lad, but a life at sea is punctuated wi' the tears o' farewell.

Some weeks earlier there had been another unscheduled farewell. As the ship was leaving Tonga, the gunner's mate, an Irishman by the name of John Marra, dived over the edge and swam to a native canoe. Two of the ratings, accompanied by Mr Midshipman Elliott, went after him in a rowing boat. He told them he had only come aboard the *Resolution* as a student. He wished to write an anthropological study. Now all he asked was a house and a pretty wife. Cook had entrusted the midshipman with a message. He had deserted His Majesty's ship. If he returned to it without a struggle, he would avoid a flogging. The Captain was as good as his word. As they approached Raiatea, however, Marra had made another attempt at desertion. He was not flogged but he was put in irons.

They kept the 4th of June, the King's Birthday, moored off. It was a day given over to drunkenness. Some of the hogs collected in the Marquesas were roasted, and two or three gallons of brandy were consumed. Odiddy, his last hours on board, gave a tearful toast to His Majesty and tried to join in a rendition of 'Hearts of Oak' before being helped into a jolly boat. Marra, who had been released from his chains in honour of His Majesty, and who had also been applying himself liberally to the grog, somehow managed to lurch up to Nally, himself far from sober, to ask whether, as an Irishman, he wished to serve in an English ship.

—I'm a scholar, Marra kept saying. Anthropo – anthropo – researcher – anthropo—

—And no one ever denied it, Mr Marra.

—A pretty wife. A bit o' land. Is it too much to ask?

—It's not for me to say, Mr Marra, though I'm sure—

—A bit o' land. Is it too much? I said to the Captain, a pretty wife. Anthropological.

It had reached the stage of the afternoon when it would have been difficult to tell the difference between the natural heave of the ship at sea and the undulations of vision occasioned by the brandy. Everyone saw a world in motion, some of it double, some of it misty. Neither Nally nor Marra could necessarily distinguish between dream and reality, and if Captain Cook was not as drunk as they were, he had nonetheless found himself wandering from deck to deck – in part to show his face to every member of the crew, lest discipline broke down altogether, and in part because a journey to the privy had turned, without much planning, into a random ramble.

Two midshipmen and a Lieutenant being by, the Captain called them to witness.

—Mr Marra thinks hissel' entitled to a pretty wife and a bit of land.

—Only a pretty wife, said Marra.

—They seem reasonable enough requests, said Cook. When did I pick you up, Marra? When did you come aboard – on my first voyage – on board the *Endeavour*?

—Batani, sir.

—You are right, sir. Batani. You're a good sailor, Marra. Sailed in both the English and the Dutch Service.

—Yes, sir.

The atmosphere had suddenly sobered, and those who heard it knew that this conversation could end with the Captain arraigning Marra for desertion, an offence for which he could be hanged.

—You tried to desert at Deptford before you came aboard the *Resolution*?

—Ay, ay . . .

—And now you think I've been interrupting your anthropological researches by asking you to perform the tasks of a common sailor . . . Speak, man – is that what you've been saying?

—Anthrop – well, sir, I . . .

Resolution

—Soon I'm going to ask a lot of these men, Mr Marra. As much as I've ever asked of any man. I don't want to force any man to serve against his will. Now it's His Majesty's birthday and in His Majesty's name I give you leave. Go with Odiddy. Look after the boy. Find your pretty wife.

Marra's mouth moved but words did not come – until Nally threw his straw hat into the air and cried —God save His Majesty! God save our Captain – and a cheer went up, which was repeated when the crew, by the light of late afternoon, waved goodbye to Odiddy, Noona and Marra the gunner's mate, as they clambered into a native canoe and paddled towards the Raiatean shore.

George did not see Rai again, though the dream of doing so wove ineffectually out of the onanistic miasma in which he passed those southern winter months. Islands came towards the ship, and drifted away again. His pocket knife, with automatic precision, sharpened his diminishing pencil collection – sketch-books were filled with ever more competent likenesses of reeds, birds, seals, fish. The sun rose on turquoise waters. The moon threw shimmering confetti on purple murmuring waters. Brown faces smiled as the Captain performed his courtly routines of bowing to feathered chieftains, and accepting indigestible dispensations served on leaves or nutshells. The ship pursued its brave course, through choppy waters, grey as the North, through gales, through salty cataracts of sea-rage, through azure brightnesses. The sun beat on scorched heads when they became becalmed. Rain came as blessing after such days, as curse when it pelted and stung the face. Mr Wales and the Captain peered through their instruments, calculated distances, measured coasts, descried the starry firmament. Midshipmen kept up their interminably tedious banter. Nally was always at George's side except when washing or pressing his clothes, and preparing favourite dishes. Reinhold continued his alternative narration of the experiences, noting new species and marine phenomena, mostly with keen observation, sometimes with wild inaccuracy, punctuating his observations with complaints about damp and rheumaticks. But all these phenomena were experienced as if through a hot tropical mist of George's own inner preoccupations. For hardly a moment, even when asleep, did he cease to be painfully conscious of his skin, which had never recovered from the attack of scurvy. Though the disease had cleared, through the consumption of fruit on Easter Island, the skin had not, and to the pits and rashes of scurvy itself were added fresh onsets of acne so that for some days, it seemed as if his whole head had been blotched and covered with shining red blemishes. Half his teeth had gone. His gums were soft and his breath smelt. When Nally spoke gently to him, or the Captain praised his drawings, he sometimes responded with a curtness like anger, because he could not imagine there was disinterest in their kind words: they were patronizing him, trying to compensate for the fact that he had become a thing accursed.

Reading the Psalms with his father, he felt that Reinhold had wilfully selected the self-hating passage – *Meine Wunden stinken und eitern vor meiner Thorheit. Ich gehe krumm und sehr gebücket; den ganzen Tag gehe ich traurig.*

Moreover, the Devil had George firmly in his talons, and though, day and night, he knelt with earthly Father and prayed to the Heavenly, the overpowering temptation would not go away. The little 'o's for *Onanie* were written guiltily in his pocket-calendar, day after day, sometimes – o, o, O! rising to a four- or five-fold cry for release from carnal compulsion.

And so the brave little ship went on, and, as Reinhold liked to repeat (*Aeneid* III. 548) —we pointed the horns of our sail-clad yarns . . . We mount up to heaven on the arched billow and again, with the receding wave, sink down to the depths of hell. . . . And new lands were found – Palmerston Island in June, New Caledonia at the very beginning of September. As they all peered at the coastline of this *terra incognita*, they saw what at first appeared to be tall stone pillars.

—They will be found, Reinhold was already excitedly saying, to be structures erected in celebration of a great victory – as in Rome with the pillar of Trajan. Ja, ja, this is something of which I mean to write when we return to England, the kinship, so to say, between the primitive world and that depicted in the heroic verses of antiquity, it will be found.

Loyalty, and the adolescent miasma, made George keep silent, even though his younger eyes could see evergreen foliage sprouting from the height of these 'pillars'.

Taking one more squint through his spyglass, Captain Cook said,

—They are trees, sir.

—You are right, said Mr Wales, who had reached the stage of his relations with Reinhold where he would have said anything to contradict him.

—Sure, they'll turn out to be pillars, sir, you'll see, no doubt at all of it, said Nally, in Reinhold's cabin, bringing in to Reinhold's cabin some of the whitest, best-pressed shirts ever seen, and his brown breeches all but invisibly darned and mended.

Even as he uttered these brave words, however, a landing party had identified a hitherto undiscovered species – *Araucaria columnaris* – Cook's Pine.

—Just think of the masts they'd make! exclaimed the Captain.

Reinhold, not thinking, with Mr Wales beside him, it was the moment to admit directly to error, quoted:

to equal which the tallest Pine
Hewn on Norwegian hills, to be the Mast
Of some great Ammiral, were but a wand . . .

And Cook, magnanimous in victory, said,

—Quite so, sir, quite so! ignoring Wales's churlish

—He didn't even think they *were* trees this morning!

From New Caledonia they continued to sail southerly. On 10th October another undiscovered island, named by Cook as Norfolk Island, came into view. It was uninhabited. Hodges did a beautiful oil painting of it in the few days of fine weather before the choppy seas became stormy and storm turned to gale. Cook was heading for the familiar waters of Queen Charlotte Sound.

—There to refresh my people and to put the ship in a condition to cross this great ocean in a high latitude once more . . .

Elliott, one of the midshipmen, wrote in his diary —*every way we stood for an Hour, the Roaring of Breakers was heard . . . a most anxious perilous Night . . . at last Daylight appeared.*

Steering the sloop into Queen Charlotte Sound in very strong westerly gales and cloudy weather was no easy task. Hauling round Point Jackson, Cook privately believed – as he later admitted – that the *Resolution* might actually capsize. The next day, however, the very high winds continuing, he managed to steer them into Ship Cove, and moored a cable. Everyone was hungry but it was not fishing weather and the best they could offer the men were scrawny old shags which two of the Lieutenants managed to shoot as they came towards shore. In foul weather they struck and unrigged the fore and mainmasts. It was a miracle that one of the masts at least had not snapped in two during the storm. Brave boys rowed ashore and set up tents in driving rain, and beneath the sodden canvas there began the work of repairing the rigging and, more importantly, cooking some wholesome food. Even the most hardened carnivores among the Resolutions eagerly devoured what Pattinson prepared – vegetable and oatmeal soup for breakfast and peas and vegetables for dinner. After two days during which the rain pelted unceasingly, the wind turned to southerly. They woke, on Sunday 23rd October, to light air and pleasant sunshine. All, even the papists, joined the Captain in his hearty prayers of Thanksgiving, after which, most unusually for him, Cook declared a day of total rest. He put his large brown hand round George's shoulder and squeezed him. George thought —My father has never hugged me.

—Bathe in the sea, lad. Run about in the sunshine. It'll do thee good.

All, in that moment, felt New Zealand to be their refuge, their saving place, their second home.

II

1793

THERESE DID NOT BREAK HIS HEART BY LEAVING HIM. His grief at her departure, his wrenching anguish at the loss of the children all fuelled the anger he had felt with her, the uncontrollable anger, which had been part of their relationship from the beginning. And anger, as warriors know, is an anti-dote to heart-break. It was Caroline who broke his heart, by her kindness.

Not in Easter Island only did the souls of the ancestors, and the statues which contained them, topple. The huge equestrian statue of Louis XV in what was now the Place de la Révolution in Paris was pulled down to make place for that human instrument of pun-ishment, the guillotine. On a cold January day in 1793, with his hair cropped, Louis XVI was led out and decapitated in the presence of eighty thousand armed men who cheered. People ran forward to dip pieces of paper and handkerchiefs in the blood. Some even dipped their fingers and licked, with the quip —*Il est bougrement salé* – it is well salted.

A letter came to Mainz from Brand to say that he had abandoned his Grand Tour and was heading back to England. Some feared England would now declare war on France. Others, said Brand, feared an English Revolution. He told George that he would always be welcome in England – that if he came to London, Brand would see him right. The news about Therese came as a postscript. —*You will have heard that your wife and children have gone to Switzerland.*

George, in Mainz, had burnt his boats. He knew that. By consenting to be a *Deputé* in General Custine's Provisional Revolutionary Government in Mainz he had nailed his colours to the mast. Surely, he thought, on the days when optimism prevailed in his heart, the Revolution will *settle*. Having won Liberty, men and women will live at Peace. On pessimistic days, however, he was less sure. The 'revolutionaries' of Mainz consisted of, at most, a few hundred people. Some were disgruntled peasants; most were intellectuals like himself. The population at large – the lawyers, the merchants, the shopkeepers, the clergy – were sullen and grudgingly accepting of the Occupation – for they could not fight. They in no sense endorsed the Revolution. Most of George's administrative work – and that of Lux, who presided over the small French staff – consisted in fielding complaints: that French troops had stolen wine, committed acts of indecency, occupied buildings which the citizens of Mainz believed to be their own. You could not, George reflected sadly, *force* people to accept Liberty in such circumstances.

Custine seemed to like George. He asked him, inevitably, about Captain Cook, about New Zealand and its landscape, about the Forsters' view of Bougainville.

For the most part, the General tolerated the fact that George was doing very little work, and spent most of his time in his apartment with Frau Böhmer. He even helped George with his servant problem, supplying one of the batmen from the officers' mess to cook and valet – Martin Dupin – who had a gift for finding food in the increasingly scanty market and who converted the few bits of sausage available into a more than palatable *cassoulet*.

Those winter days, while the world was absorbing the news of the French King's death, were the days of George's deepest intimacy with Caroline. As so often happens to lovers, the place turned into a mere backdrop to their drama. The Baroque terraces of the former monastery gardens of St Alban became 'their' garden. Walking beside the riverbank and gazing at the great cold confluence of the Main and the Rhine became 'their' view. Flecks of snow dotted pearly grey skies behind cathedral towers and church spires.

Indoors, no matter the time of day, they continued what seemed an unstoppable, deep conversation, in which it would have been impossible to know whether the talk punctuated the love-making or the other way round. Kind, peachy-bottomed, quick-witted, thick-tressed, chestnut-haired, Hellenophile, erotomane, Kant-and-Herder-read, large-breasted, poetic, bright-eyed, hilarious, rubber-nippled, conversational, aesthetic, intuitive, good, generous-thighed woman, Caroline Böhmer, born Michaelis, was George's saviour. In her arms his strange bony pock-marked body became gloriously beautiful, an instrument which made her writhe, gasp, gyrate, cry out. On her soft bosom he could lay his toothless spotty face and speak of the whole past, as he had never spoken before. She told of her girlhood, her dull marriage to Böhmer, her long, complicated friendship with his Therese. Largely, however, she let him talk for what seemed like a month – of his mother and father, of Reinhold's escape from an unhappy marriage into friendship with the boy, of their journey down the Volga, their times in Warrington, of Mr Priestley's chemical experiments, of London and its galaxy of scientific excellence. He spoke of Therese – not bitterly – at last, not bitterly – but with absolute candour – of their lack of spiritual sympathy, of the sexual incompatibility, of their pointless, self-protective need to differ about even the most trivial matters, of their joint ability to find cause for dispute in absolutely every area of life.

—We even quarrelled about *The Sorrows of Young Werther* but then . . .

There was a long silence, as she wound some of his hair round the fingers of her left hand and stroked his naked stomach with the other.

—I did not tell her the truth.

—About *Werther?*

She let out a bright laugh.

—What is the truth about *Werther?*

—I told her I'd read it in Percy Street.

—Was that not true?

—No, no, *that* was true. I told her the love interest in the book left me cold – that I could not imagine *feeling* what Werther feels for Lotte, and of course that made Therese angry. But then everything I said made her angry.

—And what was the real truth?

After a silence, George said,

—It was true I had not felt . . . I never had felt . . . until now, I . . .

—Sh, sh, sh.

She disentangled her finger from his hair and touched his lips.

—We are too old for pretty speeches, she said.

—I'm not.

—Go on about *Werther*.

—When she began talking about it, that was when I knew she could never be my friend, still less my life-companion and only love. I could not share with her my memory of poor Nally.

—And you can . . . with me?

He turned, rose on one elbow, and kissed her lips.

—I loved reading *Werther*. I was just the right age for it. The first half, I read in a single afternoon, and I remember putting it in my pocket and walking up to Hampstead, and finishing it as I sat on a little hill looking down on London. I suppose we'd been back in London about a month.

—From the voyage?

—From the voyage. We were all living in the house in Percy Street – all my brothers and sisters – my mother, who was an absolute stranger to me, Vati, who was out much of the time – as I now see, he was both attempting to further his career, and managing to damn himself with every blunder. So, there was the Family Forster – and a couple of maids who slept in boxes in the scullery – and there was Nally.

—He'd followed you from the ship.

—Vati told him we could not afford to pay him, but he had asked if he could come to live with us as a servant until he found another position. What of his position at sea? Vati had asked. But this was not a question Nally addressed. Mother liked him – was in positive raptures about the condition of everyone's clothes after Nally had been through the wardrobes. Lace was white, and neatly pressed, for the first time in years. Sheets were crisp and spot-less; shirts odourless, or rather smelling gently of what seemed like meadow flowers. The few pieces of family silver shone. Books were not only dusted but their leather spines gleamed – he had somehow polished them. Everyone's shoes were as bright as the ebony on the fortepiano. When we were at sea, Nally had needed to hide his cleverness. From the other sailors. I mean – living with us – he could sit in the scullery in Percy Street reading a little volume of Alexander Pope. His favourite was 'Elegy to the Memory of an Unfortunate Lady'.

—Oh my poor darling. You are weeping.

She pressed his face to her bosom. Then he continued,

—I should have seen it all – seen it all, all. He used to quote these lines:

Is there no bright reversion in the sky,

For those who greatly think or bravely die?

And then he'd whistle gently to himself as he was polishing a shoe or a candlestick. Oh, Caroline.

—Are you saying you . . . you *loved* Nally?

—Of course I was devoted to him – but no, it was the other way round, and I never saw it. Vati came home one day. Perhaps he knew. Perhaps he knew and decided it must stop. Or perhaps he was just being quite casually and unthinkingly brutal, as when he got Pattinson to cook my dog Sobachka . . . he came home one day and told Nally that there was no room for him in the house, that they could not afford him, that he must go . . . 'But . . . but Dr Forster. *Where* am I to go?' 'I will write a good character for you. There should be no difficulty about finding a position. Or – surely you could go back to sea?'

This conversation happened at the bottom of the stairs in the little hallway. My father and Nally stood opposite one another beside the hall table. I overheard them because I was halfway down the stairs. I was coming down to report to Vati, as soon as he came home, about my progress with the day's writing. I had got the *Resolution* as far as the Cape. Nally's face altered. There was normally something inscrutable and humorous about his features but now his mouth formed a long oval; he might have been about to scream. His eyes were those of a man facing a torturer or an executioner. —No – no – NO! he said. George – stop him – don't make him do this – George. I beg you. —How many times must I insist you call my son *Mister* George? I am sorry I must ask you to pack your belongings and leave. Leave this house. —And where am I to go? —Vati, surely he does not have to leave today? Surely he can stay with us until he finds a position? —Ja, ja, very well. But a week. I do not think it is unreasonable to suggest, Nally, that you are gone in a week?

Later that day, when I was alone in my room, there was a knock at the door. It was Nally. He said he'd come to say goodbye. He said he knew he had probably gone too far – upset my father by going too far . . . And I was saying – oh God! How could I have been *so* insensitive – What, Nally? Go too far for what? And he just turned to me and said —I love you, George. I've always loved you since you first came aboard the *Resolution*.

Oh Caroline.

—What did you say?

—I laughed.

She momentarily stopped stroking his stomach. Then after a silence,

—You were very young.

—I laughed, damn it. He walked out of the room. It was simply beyond anything I had ever experienced. Here I was, emotionally much younger than twenty, and I had just read the greatest

love-novel ever written – and here was my servant casting himself
as Werther and myself as Lotte . . . So I laughed – and I did not
know there was so much truth in the parallel between Nally and
Werther. A few hours later, there was a terrible shriek. The maids
had been upstairs, seeing to the children – but one had gone down
to the kitchen to boil a kettle. They found Nally. He had hanged
himself from one of the meat-hooks in the scullery.

—Oh my poor dear.

After a very long silence,

—Did you . . . see him?

—I knew, Caroline. When I heard the shriek, I knew that something had happened to Nally. I ran downstairs. Luckily neither my
mother nor the children saw him. His face was a terrible colour
– blue. I stood on a chair, cut the piece of rope – but he was
dead. Of course he was. Men have died and worms have eaten
them, but not for love – well, that isn't true. That's what *Werther* is
about.

George was doing his best, both in that moment and during
those weeks, not to die of love, but this was not how Caroline
saw things. When 'all this' was over – the French Revolution, the
war – then 'all this' – their love affair – would be over too – or
if not quite over, then part of the background of her friendship
with Therese. She tried to make George see that Therese had suffered too, that Therese needed love too, that Therese had found
in Huber things which George had been unable to give her. There
was no need to make old Professor Heyne unhappy by making
his daughter an object of scandal. As far as Heyne, and the academic world, and the French authorities, were concerned – as far
as Reinhold was concerned in Halle – George had sent Therese
and the children, with the maid and their English guest as escort,

into safekeeping in Strassburg. There was no need for them to advertise their unhappiness.

—It hardly suggests, monsieur, a wholehearted belief in the Revolution, if you sent your wife into safekeeping to avoid it.

So, Custine. And when the French General had so spoken, it became impossible to decline his request to go to Paris, with smelly Lux, as *Deputés* of the Mainz Revolution, to report to the National Assembly.

—It will only be three weeks, George told Caroline.

Both feared this was untrue, although it was the timescale proposed by General Custine.

Before he got into the diligence, George assumed, in front of Lux, and the other dignitaries, that Caroline would observe the proprieties; but she flung her arms around him and said,

—My dear, dear boy.

—You have saved me – you know that. I thought I would live my whole life without—

—Sh, sh. Come back safe. Your babies don't want you to die in Paris.

Even as they left, the French army was spreading out to occupy the countryside surrounding Mainz while the Prussian and Austrian forces positioned themselves to attack. Mainz had become not merely an occupied town, but a war zone.

Their diligence trundled westwards. Metz–Verdun–Reims. It was almost impossible to take in the change which he had undergone. Days before, he had been naked in bed with Caroline, dwelling in an enchantment. Now, cold, intensely bored by Lux, and very uncomfortable, Deputé Forster was rattling towards Paris. Only when the luggage was stowed, the border crossed, did the reality of it all impinge on his brain: that there could be no turning back.

Resolution

His other friends and contemporaries, who had escaped before the French army arrived, could continue to keep open their options. He no longer had this privilege.

PART SIX

A Lonesome Road

Like one, that on a lonesome road
Doth walk in fear and dread,
And having once turned round, walks on,
And turns no more his head;
Because he knows, a frightful fiend
Doth close behind him tread.

I

1774

THEY WEIGHED ANCHOR ON THE TENTH DAY OF NOVEMBER, and that was the last time George saw New Zealand. The *Resolution* headed eastward in a steady gale, at a speed which terrified most men aboard.

—In the last twenty-four hours, roared Cook into the wind, we have run the greatest distance we ever reached in this ship, Dr Forster. One hundred and eighty-three miles!

The statistics seemed more than facts, more than numbers; the journey into cloud and ice once more a cosmic metaphysical struggle between the intellectual courage of the Captain and the scarcely tractable waters, winds, temperatures. He made no attempt to pass the Strait of Magellan when they reached the southernmost tip of South America, taking the south side of Tierra del Fuego and coming through the Strait La Maire, a hazardous passage, during which Cook barely spoke, other than to bellow orders. One small mistake could have wrecked the ship or stranded her aground rocks and ice where the entire crew would certainly have perished. They were punctiliously following sea charts based on Spanish discoveries of the 1580s; and then again, when they changed their course northward, Dr Harley's Cartography of 1700. By 8th December, the number of petrels, albatrosses and seals visible from the sloop told them they were near land and on the 14th, having passed a flock of penguins, the officer of the watch told the Captain that an island of ice had come into sight. The glimmering light of morning revealed vast mountains of ice covered in snow: a new land. To the south of this newly discovered land were small rocky islands of a dull black. They passed coal-coloured cliffs where thousands of shags were nesting, and where porpoises and seals bobbed in the water. Wherever they went, they gave the islets and coves names – Cumberland Bay, Royal Bay, Cape Charlotte – as though the invoking of those distant German royalties could domesticate the hard black rocks, the winking black waters, the sprouts of coarse grass on guano-splashed black cliffs, the walls of ice and snow. After careful circumnavigation they found the new land to be an island, and Reinhold spoke for all when he suggested to the Captain,

—It would be proper to name this land after the monarch who set on foot our expedition – and whose name ought therefore, so to say, to be celebrated in both hemispheres – *tua sectus orbis nomina ducet*.

—King's Land? New Georgia? South Georgia? Ay, sir, it's proper.

And Captain Cook, on Christmas Day, planted a pole displaying the British flag, formally took possession of those barren rocks – 'in the name of his Britannic Majesty, and his heirs for ever'.

Of all their three Christmases together, this was the happiest for the Resolutions. In the waters they named Christmas Sound they found enough sustenance to give a splendid feast to every man aboard: mussels, with wild celery which grew abundantly on the rocks, duck, shag, and many upland geese which found themselves boiled, roasted and encased in Pattinson's excellent short pastry before the dawning of the Nativity. The absence of any human habitation, the impossibility of imagining human beings here, made many of them, not merely George, feel weirdly like the last people left on the planet. As they yelled AMEN to the Christmas collect there was an awesome sadness about the absence of their families. Never had the exclusively male nature of the company felt more truncated, more half finished, more inadequate. When Captain Cook boomed —We pray for our loved ones at home . . . for our wives, our bairns, our sweethearts — a desolation howled in the winds towards the ice-mountains.

It was actually very difficult, as they continued their voyage through the frozen waters of the South Atlantic, to know the difference between ice-bound land and frozen ice. South from South Georgia, in latitude 58°15′S longitude 21°34′W they found a group of islands which Cook named Sandwich Land, an inhospitable ice-bound pack of rocks which could, he believed, be a promontory of the *Terra Australis*, the Southern Continent which was the grand object of their exploring. Thick fog and intense cold made further investigation impossible. Snow fell in huge flakes as they sailed eastward in a vain attempt to find the Cape de la Circoncision discovered by Bouvet in 1739.

—It's a strange thought, said Nally, that the only bodily part of Our Saviour left on this earth He came to redeem is the Saint Prépuce revered in the holy chapel in Paris, La Sainte-Chapelle.

—I'd never really thought about it, said George. Relics mean less to us Protestants than they do to you.

—To the Papists, you mean? Nally laughed. All the same, it's a strange thought, he said. The little babbie's toodle-ri-ree. It's there sure enough bang in the middle of Par-ee.

George felt it impolite to inquire if Nally – that strange mixture of the submissive and the rebellious – actually believed that the relic in question was genuine. Nally himself perhaps felt the subject was exhausted, because he said,

—They stand to attention like a row of dragoons.

Misty as it was, on an icy stretch of rock quarter of a mile distant from the *Resolution*, they could see a row of penguins erect in a perfectly straight line.

—I didn't at all mind the penguin we had for dinner on Monday, said Nally, who, while he spoke, was rubbing, half caressing, a pair of George's boots which did not really need cleaning every single day. But Mr Gilbert went to Pattinson and said they'd mutiny, the lads, if they were asked to eat much more of it.

—I thought it was revolting, said George.

—Ah, but you always need to watch what you eat, young George, and that's the truth.

Further south, they came to Thule, where Cook named one piece of coast Forster Bay.

As February drifted into March, the Captain began to fear another outbreak of scurvy, and insisted, in his daily harangues, that they try to eat what was set before them. Not only, he insisted, did Pattinson attempt to dress all his dishes in as appetizing a way as possible (a declaration which drew forth satirical groans) but they themselves, every man of them, could take pride in the fact that no ship in the history of seafaring had been out as long as the *Resolution* with no deaths from scurvy.

—A few weeks, and we shall be at the Cape, and our voyage together will be all but over. I'm proud of you, lads. We have still a few barrels of the *Sauer Kraut*. Keep eating!

By the beginning of March, the wind came more aft, allowing

them to steer a north north-west course directly in the direction of the Cape of Good Hope. On 16th March, in very choppy weather, they saw two vessels flying Dutch colours. They were Indiamen from Bengal. Cook sent officers over in a boat to find news.

The Dutchmen had news of Captain Furneaux and the *Adventure*. Far from being lost, the other English sloop, with its Captain, had arrived at Cape Town twelve months before with a tale of woe. Furneaux had lost a whole jolly-boat full of his men, who had gone ashore in New Zealand and had been eaten by Maoris. Cook found it difficult to credit, though the Dutch Captain, Cornelius Bosch, was plainly an honest friendly man who came over himself to the *Resolution* with sugar and Arrack. Cook told his *Journal*:

> I shall make no reflections on this Melancholy affair untill I hear more about it. I must however observe in favour of the New Zealanders that I have allways found them of a Brave, Noble, Open and benevolent disposition . . .

Next morning, after a few calm hours, a westerly wind blew up, and another English ship, which was to windward, bore down on the *Resolution*. She was a merchant ship that had sailed from China, and her commanding officer, Captain Broadly, came aboard, bringing piles of old newspapers, and taking away with him, when he left, letters from Cook to the Admiralty, announcing their safe arrival in the Cape, and an anxious communication from Reinhold to his wife. The prospect of safety, and the home run, had suddenly filled his mind with anxieties. For years, they had heard nothing of his wife and other children: a series of putative calamities, all the things he might have been worrying about during earlier parts of the voyage, suddenly overcame him.

George could see that the grown-ups were preoccupied, as they prepared to drop anchor at the Cape. He was unable to enter into their preoccupations. He was simply excited to be returning to the Cape, last seen in November '72, two and a half years earlier. Here, as he remembered, were vast numbers of small petrels, shearwaters, Cape pigeons or pintadas, and two types of albatross – the great white *Diomedea exulans*, and a large reddish one, which he had not spotted on his previous visit. He longed to be ashore, but there was a day or two, as they approached the coast, before it became possible to haul in for the land.

Before they did so, another English ship, this time an East India Company vessel, came alongside, and Captain Cook gave to Captain Newte, its commanding officer, the greater part of George's drawings in a portfolio, together with a copy of his own journal and all the log-books.

—And you, Dr Forster – you've kept a journal.

—A private journal, Kapitän.

—If it remains private, well and good.

Only later, when they returned to England, did George remember this exchange between the Captain and his father, and reflect upon its import. When they had gone ashore at the Cape, Cook had been horrified to be presented with a copy of Dr John Hawkesworth's printed account of the first great voyage – with His Majesty's Bark *Endeavour*. Hawkesworth had not even been on the voyage, and yet, here he was, stealing Cook's thunder. Stealing it most certainly was. Cook had stood to make a huge fortune from his account of sailing to Tahiti with Banks to watch the passage of Venus, and his discovery of Botany Bay and New Zealand. Reinhold – when they returned to London – would try to play the same trick, but he would be prevented by the contract he had signed with the Admiralty. This was why George, basing his account on his father's journals, would write the prodigiously successful *A Voyage Round the World in His Britannic Majesty's Sloop, the Resolution*.

By the time he reached his thirties, his father's cheek, and his own collusion in it, had become incomprehensible to George. Cook was their hero, their deliverer. Why could they not have been content to be his naturalists and illustrators, and to take pride in having played a small role in the great voyage? By the time he wrote his second book on the subject, *Cook the Discoverer*, he had felt himself to be indulging in pure hero-worship. Nothing, however, about the writing life is pure, and he would be shocked to hear Therese refer to this exercise as 'not content to cash in once, he's cashed in twice on his God!'

All that, however, when the young George, who had just turned twenty, arrived at the Cape, lay in the far, the tainted, future. As they glided past the low land of Penguin, or Robben (as the Dutch called it), Island the Captain took his bearings from the Table Mountain which loomed above the coast, and which, by night, was lit with fires. When they had landed, and established themselves in the port, George discovered these fires were lit by shepherds, burning grass, and not, as so many sailors aboard the *Resolution* had believed, out of kindliness to approaching vessels.

Oh, but it was good to arrive in the Cape and to feast on oranges, and every imaginable variety of fresh fruit! The shore was fronted by forts and warehouses. Behind these, the domestic buildings were arranged in streets on a grid pattern. Reinhold and George were each assigned a bedroom in a comfortable lodging house run by a kind Dutch family. Fresh bread! Chocolate to drink! Exquisite sausages.

—Please, not too much to my son who is inclined always to looseness! urged Reinhold as their plates were heaped with food.

The first day, after a night of deep, comfortable, uninterrupted sleep, George took his sketch-book and a picnic and clambered halfway up the Table Mountain. Sitting on a tuft of grass in his shirtsleeves amid a clump of various brightly coloured fynbos – Karoo, Peninsula Sandstone and others – he was joined by two friendly dassies who stared out of their furry faces with puzzlement at the boy and his sketch-book. That morning on Table Mountain, in radiant sunshine – the slopes beneath were thick with pink and orange flowers, the sea was the deepest blue, the air so pure – was one of undiluted euphoria. The happiness was so intense that he even forgot his usual compulsion when out, and alone. He was, indeed, literally ecstatic, standing outside himself and lost in a visual beauty, and an atmosphere, which were celestial. Later in life, when he had lost his faith in an actual Heaven, the recollection of Table Mountain in summer weather made a plausible substitute, and returned to comfort him during those lonely, dismal days, nearly two decades later, in France.

II

1793

Heaven be praised that your wife and children are safe in Switzerland. They at least are away from the madness. It is beyond my comprehension how you could have been carried away by this lunacy. Let us hope, when you have seen for yourself what this Revolution has done – with its massacres of innocents, its obscene Guillotines – that you will come to your senses!

THE LETTER FROM HIS FATHER LAY UPSIDE DOWN ON THE table in front of George, opposite whom sat Citizen Guénot, the representative of the Committee for General Security who saw it as his duty to '*surveiller*' the German visitors and to read their private correspondence. George hoped that Guénot's German was not good enough to understand Reinhold's more tactless apostrophes.

—It would seem, Citizen Forster, as if your revolutionary fervour is not shared by all your friends.

—My father is entitled to his opinions, though they do not happen to be mine.

—Perhaps you would be so good as to translate this paragraph here. It contains Citizen Marat's name.

—May I? George said, and, retrieving the letter decided to take a gamble.

—It is, I assume, the celebrated Citizen Marat to whom your correspondent refers?

—Let me see.

Reinhold's words, wise some twenty years after the event, claimed to have seen something untrustworthy in the face of Dr Marat when he had come to take up his appointment as the languages master at Warrington. When Reinhold had been so fortuitously selected to replace Mr Banks as the naturalist aboard the *Resolution* in '72, Mr Priestley and Mr Wedgwood had been warm in their congratulations, but somewhat at a loss as to how to find a replacement teacher at such short notice.

—To find a gentleman possessed of a scientific temper *and* who can help the brats wi' their languages – their French and their German above all . . .

Mr Wedgwood's voice had died, for the sentence, short of a miracle, could no more be finished than the right man be found. Then, on his way south from Edinburgh, the young French doctor, anxious to pick the brains of Priestley on his theories of dephlogisticated air, had paused at Warrington. Their meeting had been a success. Marat was almost absurdly overqualified to teach schoolboys language and science; but then, so had been his two predecessors, Reinhold and Priestley. He had needed the money, and he had stayed.

Luckily for George, his father, while excoriating Dr Marat's extreme Jacobin views, had expressed an interest in news of the man.

—My father says—

—Oh, so you admit that this letter is from your father.

—Well, it cannot be denied. France itself is full of families divided politically.

—Is that so?

—Anyway, my father says he hopes that I shall find time, while in Paris, to discover M. Marat's address, and to pay him a visit, for old times' sake. M. Marat had many theories, as a young man – about electricity, aeronautics, optics. Mr Priestley, who ran the school at Warrington with which my father was also associated, is an eminent man of science. Your own M. Lavoisier owes much, I am told, to his theory of dephlogisticated air.

There was an awkward silence.

—Lavoisier is a traitor to the Republic.

—But the foremost chemist of the age.

—The Revolution has no need of chemistry, citizen. But it has a very definite need of Citizen Marat.

George had the opportunity to speak to Marat in the Lobby at the National Convention, which the German delegates were required to attend three times a week.

—You are scarcely recognizable, said the doctor coolly looking George up and down, and taking in his scrubby hair, near tooth-lessness and pock-marks. Time had not, however, been kind to Marat either. A pungent rotting smell came from his person, and his eyes and neck were covered with the suppurating blotches of psoriasis.

—I distinctly remember your father, said Marat, his book on *British Insects*.

—He subsequently sailed with Captain Cook, sir, and made many important additions to the taxonomy of Linnaeus.

Marat's smile was unreadable. Had he misheard? Or was it inappropriate to praise a man who had sailed in a ship of the Royal Navy? France was now at war with England, the Netherlands, Spain, Sardinia, Naples, Portugal, the Holy See and the Holy Roman Empire.

—I live in the rue des Cordelières, said Marat. I work day and night. If I turn you away it will be because of busy-ness. I am glad to have made your acquaintance again.

Lux, George's (increasingly unsympathetic) fellow *Deputé* from Mainz, expressed surprise.

—I thought that must have been Marat. I am shocked that you could speak to such a man.

—We've declared for the Revolution. I must believe it, said George.

—But they are killing citizens without fair trial, said Lux. Paris has become an abattoir and, now Marat has had all his Girondin opponents locked up, it is only a matter of time before he has them beheaded. In many of the French towns outside Paris there is *revulsion* against the Jacobins – in Toulon, Bordeaux, Lyon . . .

—Lux, the Revolution has to protect itself. The whole of Europe is at war with us. Consider what Mr Priestley has had to suffer in England – simply for defending the Revolution: his laboratories in Birmingham destroyed by the mob, his church burnt down and then, when he escaped to London, more riots, more looting.

—Looting by an ignorant mob is not to be compared with a sovereign government authorizing mass slaughter.

—Defensive violence is different from aggressive violence.

Burke – Burke, save the mark! – has attacked Priestley and said that even his *science* is anarchy!

—The other day you told me that the mad policeman told you the Revolution has no need of chemistry!

—Well, *touché*. But Guénot is an oaf and Burke should know better. We would have been able to welcome the Priestleys to France . . .

—His son became a French citizen when the Revolution broke out.

—Indeed – but now England and France are at war, and Priestley's son has become an alien in *both* countries. No wonder they have both gone to live in America. The war goes on!

—From what I read, Priestley has begun to preach that the world is coming to an end, that the Revolution heralds the second coming of Christ, said Lux with ponderous scepticism. I know which Revolution I should rather have, the law-based republicanism of the Girondins, rather than this bloodbath, this *tyranny!*

—The Girondins are traitors to the Republic, said George.

—You know that's rubbish. Are you saying the citizens of Lyon, of Toulon, of Caen – who supported Mirabeau and all the ideals of '89 – at the risk of their own lives – are traitors?

Some days later, before George had the chance to take up Citizen Marat's offer of hospitality in the rue des Cordelières, the doctor received another visitor, a handsome young patriot from Caen by the name of Charlotte Corday: a woman who shared Lux's view of the Jacobins. Marat was in his hip-bath, rigged up as a desk with a board across it. Here he had his daily soak to ease the pain and dissolve the odour of his disgusting dermatological condition. He was reluctant, at first, to be disturbed by his young visitor, but eventually acceded to her importunate requests for an interview, and her feigned offer to provide him with the names of 'dangerous' Girondins in Caen. The fanatic eagerly noted the names which she spoke – those of her friends. When he promised that they would all be beheaded in a fortnight, Corday produced the large sheath-knife (which she had bought for the purpose in the Palais Royal) and plunged it into Marat's heart.

David was brought in to sanctify the Jacobin martyr, painting one of the most memorable icons of the Revolution. Corday behaved with unapologetic, classical dignity all the way to the guillotine; but she too had her artistic champion. Adam Lux wrote an Ode in her praise, comparing her to the noble Brutus who was prepared to stab Caesar in order to preserve the purity of the Republic. Citizen Robespierre and friends were not impressed.

George was thunderstruck. It was not a very good poem, but Lux had gone to a printer and had two hundred copies run off to distribute to anyone foolhardy enough, in that Paris riddled with soldiers and spies, to take one. It was impossible not to admire Lux's pluck. After he'd read it, he felt, for the first time, a warmth for Lux.

They were both lodging at the rue des Moulins, housed at La Maison des Patriots Hollandais, between the Tuileries and the Palais Royal. It was a frowsty, draughty, smelly accommodation, with panelled walls which had, long ago, been painted the colour of mud. Their bedrooms were tiny. No one had changed the bedding since they arrived in March, and, in preference to laying their heads on the grey, moist pillows where, it would seem, many a Dutch patriot had already lain a dandruffy skull, they tended to sit in the small coffee-room on the ground floor, the room in which meals were served, and round whose table there were a number of knobbly, uncomfortable chairs.

Resolution

The table was covered with a cloth of the same degree of cleanliness as their bed-linen; a greyish linen, perhaps once white, heavily soiled with many a brown circle where coffee-pots had been slammed down, many a purplish-black splodge where sour wine had been spilled, many a greasy spot where soups and ragouts had slopped from their plates. The smell of rancid grease competed with the other smells – coffee, farts, cheese – competed and won. Lux and George conversed in low voices over a pot of coffee which had been brought them by a surprisingly amiable maid, an Ardennoise named Clothilde. The coffee was made largely with acorns, but because it had been skilfully made, it packed a certain punch.

—All I want is to return to my wife, my farm, my children, said Lux.

—I've burnt my boats. I have nowhere to go, said George.

—They told us we would be here for three weeks at the most – at the beginning of April. Three *months* have passed.

—Have you news from Germany?

Lux shrugged and there was something very eloquent about his smile.

—We are utterly routed, he eventually said.

He looked as though he would say more, but at that moment, two moustachioed *sans-culottes* entered the house, without ringing the bell. They peered into the darkness of the eating-room and sniffed.

—We are searching for Monsieur Lux.

—In that event, said Lux, your search is an easy one.

Never having addressed Adam Lux other than as 'you' and 'Lux', George suddenly said,

—Adam, my dear, thou needst not go with them.

A. N. Wilson

—There is a warrant for Citizen Lux's arrest, said one of the moustaches.

—No, said George.

—Whoever you may be, said a moustache.

—Citizen, come with us at once, said the other, with his hand on Lux's shoulder.

—I'm coming with you, said George.

—There is no point in our both being killed, said Lux. I suppose I am dying for Charlotte Corday.

A strange smile lit up his face.

And they took him away. George obeyed him and did not follow him to the prison. After a summary 'trial' – in effect little more than a denunciation – Lux was given the punishment of sleeping in an overcrowded, shitty cell with some ten other prisoners. The next day his head was removed by a guillotine. News of the death reached the House of Dutch Patriots within the hour.

It was not a surprise to George, not quite. It was, however, shocking – the execution of a foreign visitor, simply for likening a girl, herself beheaded, to Brutus. George was – only the French word quite described it – *bouleversé*. He was shattered. He felt his whole personality fly into smithereens. All the events of the previous two or three years – the Revolution of '89 which they had all – the Mainz intellectuals – greeted with joy, the collapse of his marriage, the journey with Humboldt, the discovery of Therese's affair with Huber, the coming, and death, of two babies, the departure of his wife, and of his two beloved children. The disruption to his work, the French invasion, his wild enthusiasm, a revisiting of the mad Rosicrucian phase, his affair with Caroline, his journey to Paris – had all led . . . to what? To this seemingly pointless gesture of State violence against a decent-hearted, rather dull farmer of whom George, in the last week or so of his life, had suddenly grown strangely fond.

In the course of 'normal life', the multiplicity of our relationships, occupations, lines of intellectual inquiry, reading, lusts, thoughts and memories are held in a wonderful order – wonderful because there is no obvious reason why they should. Only when a body is seriously diseased does the patient become aware that blood, heart, liver, digestive organs, lungs are all interdependent and, with the absolute collapse of one, all others are affected. In similar fashion, when the shock of Lux's death, the manner of his death, clanged its deafening tocsin in George's skull, all the preoccupations of his soul came jangling to life, making him momentarily 'out of his mind'.

It was a hot day. He had no need of hat or cloak. He paced out of the House of Dutch Patriots into Paris. All that he needed to do was to walk, and he did so without design or a decided direction. His last visit to Berlin, when he had met Reinhold and Sömmerring, had made him feel he was visiting a barracks, with every third figure one passed in uniform. That, however, was some-what to be expected, so soon after the death of Frederick the Great. The military were orderly, unthreatening.

In Paris, that sweltering summer day in '93, they said as many as a hundred thousand were under arms – horse, foot, artillery, bewhiskered sappers. The Tuileries were solid with soldiers. The Bois was a vast military encampment. The proclamation of Year One (otherwise known as 1793) in a new earth, a new chapter of history – the beginning of an age of Liberty – required a mili-tary presence larger than the population of most European cities. The new era of brotherhood required mechanical bloodletting on a scale without parallel. Squares, *allées*, cobbled yards smelling of urine, old courtyards thick with geraniums, locked churches – for Catholicism had been abolished – empty food shops – for every vegetable and cheese and sausage had been eaten by troops – passed him as he walked along. Sometimes he took conscious notice of what he saw – where once stood the statue of Louis XV in the Place de la Révolution, a giant statue, still of plaster, though it was intended to cast it in metal – the Statue of Liberty, holding her torch into the air. As if very drunk, though he had never been more sober, George saw the huge statue and felt her to be shaking her fist at him, threatening him. He even broke into a run to put her behind him, and as he hurried northwards he felt Liberty on his heels, threatening to pound him with her plaster torch.

And now he was on a bridge, the Pont St-Michel, thick with wobbly-gabled houses, some looking down at the cathedral where, so recently, an actress had been made a *tableau vivant* of Reason to replace the God of the Catholics. Again like an inebriate, but uninebriated, George saw it all in a haze – his eyes taking in some scrawny cats, an old woman shredding string beans, two boys joshing, on the verge of a fight, some moustachioed figures with tricolours in their hats quarrelling with a whore about her price – but though he took in these sights with his optic nerves, his mind was pounding, sometimes with different thoughts and worries – where *was* Therese? How were the children? Would he ever see Reinhold again? Was he, George, going to die in this madhouse like Lux? Sometimes – and at these times he had the terrifying sensation that he might indeed be losing his reason, descending into complete madness – all these thoughts and impressions came at once. His beloved daughters, Clara and Rosechen, waved to him from the mansard roofs of the old houses on the Pont St-Michel. Reinhold, borrowing Liberty's plaster torch, came running after him, Lux's last hours came thumping at the same time into his head, and Custine, wiping his moustaches on the back of his hand, and telling him he was to go to Paris, as the Mainz Revolutionary *Deputé*. (Custine had fallen foul of the system and been guillotined.)

Leaning on a parapet between two old wooden houses and looking down at the sludgy Seine, George took a deep breath and some of the more alarming symptoms of his brainstorm began to recede. He breathed deeply. Perhaps the association, while he slowly inhaled and exhaled, of looking downwards at the brown river awakened conscious memory of shipboard, but for whatever reason his mind found Captain Cook. At once, an immense calm descended. In his mind's eye, he saw that large honest face, presumably descended from the Viking settlers of North Yorkshire.

Robespierre and Marat and their colleagues were intent upon 'changing the world' by ideas – by inventing new calendars and imposing upon the intractable nature of things their own version of the world. Cook, in every sense a humbler man, had been patient enough to discover the world as it is, and because of his discoveries he made the world a larger place for everybody. In the case of Cook, everything grew out of practical intelligence and empirical knowledge. He had chosen to explore in small sloops, which could hug coastlines – ideal for the cartographer – rather than the hulking warships recommended by the Royal Navy. He had paid attention to every small detail – for example, naval wisdom strengthened planks with copper plates to prevent woodworm, but copper deters fish, the essential source of food on a long trip. So, Cook did not use copper nails but iron nails with big heads. Within a few weeks of wet weather, rust spread over the lower part of the woodwork of the *Resolution* and the *Adventure*, just as effective against woodworm as copper. The man who discovered New Zealand and Australia was not a dreamer. It was the coal-haulier, the practical man who knew how to *pack* a ship. Every storeroom on the *Resolution* was crammed with things – he personally supervised the packing: Cook and the stevedores at Sheerness made the voyages possible. Once the voyages had been made, the world became larger – it had more lands in it, a greater variety of men and women, birds and animals and plants than had ever been known. George's friend Humboldt was alive to this and would embark on journeys equally stupendous. Breathing deeply and staring at the water, George saw with absolute clarity why Goethe, that evening at Mainz, had expressed contempt for the Revolution and its 'ideas'.

Reinhold came into his son's head as he stared at the murky summer Seine. Of the three Warrington schoolmasters – one had been stabbed in his bath, the other had had his laboratory destroyed by a baying mob – it looked as though Reinhold had done something right by becoming a Professor at Halle. I will arise . . . *ich will mich aufmachen und zu meinem Vater gehen* . . .

The dirty waters mocked him, called to him. George did not feel suicidal, so much as fatalistically aware that his own life had fallen out of control. Had he, a year ago, been asked the central purpose of his existence, he would have said simply, his work and his children. The unravelling of life's ordinary daily complexion meant the one was impossible, the others were separated from him . . . His everlasting wanderings since childhood had now become a norm. *Ich will mich aufmachen* – the Prodigal Son in the parable, feeding the swine in a strange country, realized that if he were to return to his father, he would have a better life even if he were only a household servant. The figure who now stood on the Pont St-Michel, staring with panic, real fear, at the river-water, was in a more pitiful state than Werther; he was homesick but had no home to be sick for. Home was not Mainz any more: but nor was it his birthplace in East Prussia . . . He had no home. His links with his family were all but broken. His wife was in the bed of another man – and such a boring man at that.

The inhalations and exhalations on the bridge were an attempt to make his thoughts have some kind of order – for the impressions, memories, voices which danced about in his skull made a phantasmagoria of confusion, in which his wife and children, Lux, his father, Captain Cook, General Custine and the lugubrious police chief, Guénot, skipped a *danse macabre*, and in which the brown waters of the Seine appeared like those of the Tiber in the Sibyl's vision at the mouth of Virgil's hell, foaming with blood.

Guénot, the investigator, among all the participants of the *danse*, now brought the music to a close. The kaleidoscope settled. He began to breathe normally. George realized that the one saving fact of his time in Paris had been his own instinctive lack of candour *on paper*. In his letters to Heyne, to Reinhold, as to Therese or to Huber, he had not acknowledged that his marriage was over. He wrote as if she had taken the children into safekeeping, but that one day soon they would be reunited.

Nor had he written any word of criticism of the Jacobins and their regime. It soon had become clear to him that all letters, written and received, were subject to censorship. It was not pure cynicism, however, which had made him continue to profess his belief in the Revolution. He genuinely did so.

Now, standing on the Pont St-Michel, he felt within himself the unmistakeable symptoms of disillusion. After the heady few hours of champagne comes the mild headache, the sense of slight depression. After six months of Rosicrucianism in Kassel, enthusiasm in which even the sober-minded Sömmerring had shared, came the cold grey of dawn, the shame at his own capacity to be deluded, the thrill of freedom. (*I don't have to believe all this stuff!*) How could the execution of Lux not, quite literally at a stroke, have destroyed his faith in the Revolution? Yet whereas the loss of faith in Rosicrucianism humiliated him, made him feel weak in his own eyes, as well as the eyes of the world, the present moment of enlightenment gave him a quiet strength. He felt, quite simply, Resolution.

If he could not return to Mainz, then his best bet was to remain in Paris, until the chance came of an escape . . . to England. He had made friends in Paris with a Scottish family named Christie, and with Mary Wollstonecraft and her circle of radical friends. Already one of them had suggested he returned with them to London to help set up a radical press . . . If he were patient, if he were careful . . . He was not going to allow Therese to destroy all his peace of mind and to take his children, any more than he could allow Robespierre and Guénot and the other cut-throat self-righteous maniacs to destroy his belief in . . . whatever it was which had led him to belief in the Enlightenment. And herein was the difference between this loss of faith and the loss of faith in Rosicrucianism. Awaking from the Rosicrucian nightmare he had felt merely that he had been a colossal chump. Present feelings were different. He had not been a fool to delight in the end of superstition and tyranny. He had not been a fool to believe that, in pre-Revolutionary France, a man of humble birth, such as Captain Cook, would have found it all but impossible to rise to eminence . . .

Nevertheless, the all-too-familiar sensation of losing his faith swept through him as he paced on from the bridge, up the river, down the river, until tiredness overcame him and he returned to the patriotic Dutchmen.

Resolution

When he had reached his little room, which was near the eaves and was very hot, he sat down at his writing table. His brain had cleared and he wrote a letter to Therese. It was both truthful, in what it included, disingenuous in what it omitted. He said nothing of Lux, nothing of his fears, nothing of his doubts. He wrote of his heart-broken yearning to see his children and begged her to come and live with him in Paris. He said nothing of his conviction that Huber was too lily-livered to consider living in Paris. In one masterly letter, he had demonstrated to the censors his loyalty to the Revolution (for who but a true revolutionary would beg his wife to come to Paris in July '93 – or rather, Thermidor in Year One?) In the marital war, he was now on record as being reasonable, generous even, reconciliatory. As a father he genuinely yearned to see the children.

For a few weeks after this, he spent most of his time with the British exiles: with Miss Wollstonecraft, and the Christies. To escape the stultifying heat of Paris, he stayed near Lucienne, near the Comtesse de Barry's Pavilion. The Christies had befriended a rich banker called Lecoulteux: he had offered two million livres to the Government to spare the King's life. It was a refreshing time. They took walks over to Versailles. The royal palace had been taken over by *sans-culottes*. Some appeared to be living there. Others were simply mooching about. On one of their walks they watched a woman casually smashing a window and bursting into laughter. Not long after this the Christies left for England, repeating their offer to find work for George, as a writer and publisher, if he were able to escape.

On their last night in Paris, the Christies took George and Miss Wollstonecraft to *Iphigénie en Tauride* by Gluck. They had dinner and drank a lot of wine. Upon his return to the Dutch Patriots, he found a letter from Therese. She told him she was in Switzerland (Neuchâtel) with Huber and the children. It was not clear whether she had received his last, carefully worded letter, or not.

She had written to George to tell him that she was writing a novel, but she did not confess its subject. It was in fact the first novel ever written with an Australian background, and by the time she admitted its existence to George, its first episode was serialized in the women's magazine *Flora*. It was an epistolary novel, in which George, renamed Rudolph, was on a ship bound for Australia, writing back to his two 'friends', Berthold and Reinette: a thinly disguised Huber and Therese. It included his visit to Norfolk Island, which Therese had planted with coconut palms – which would not be found there – and Rousseau-esque 'noble savages'. George's essays on the penal colonies were infused with an 'enlightened' belief that they would turn their vices into virtues and be redeemed by the practice of enlightened activism. She replaced all this with a crude 'primitivism' with 'honest Hottentots' and a blind old Arab happily playing with his grandsons in the shade of a camel. She did not admit to George that some phrases in the letters of 'Rudolph', for instance speaking of India as 'the cradle of mankind', had simply been lifted from the letters he had written to her from Paris. She described George's interview with the Emperor Joseph.

—And what will you do when you are finally tired of roving?

—Then I shall go home and grow cabbages.

Joseph put his hand on his shoulder and asked earnestly,

—Why don't you start doing that today?

As 'Rudolph' wrote to 'Berthold and Reinette', he was by nature a wanderer . . . —There is *another* kind of happiness and *another* philosophy, which is perhaps not generally useful but is most bracing for anyone who is driven by Fate to adopt it . . .

Reinhold was shocked by her acts of fiction, when his wife read them in *Flora*. George, had he ever read them, would have been more indulgent. While his family considered Therese turning him into a character in fiction to be the ultimate act of gratuitous exploitation, he would have seen that Therese, who had always been an addict of sentimental fiction, was actually unable to respond to George in any other way. As soon as she had parted from him, she had been liberated to become what she had always been in her heart: a novelist. George would have remembered their quarrel about *Werther*. In part he could not speak to her fully about it, because its story of a man who commits suicide having been driven mad by love too painfully recalled Nally. But another reason for their acrimonious difference was that he had been genuinely unable to *inhabit* Werther, which revealed far more than a simple difference in literary *taste*. It showed they were looking at the same world and seeing two quite different things. They were a pair of misplaced library books. She was more capable than he was of seeing that both of them, for as long as they had tried to be married, were on the wrong shelf. He had wanted her catalogued as *Travel* with himself. She belonged with *Fiction*. He was with Pausanias and Hakluyt, while she was moving from Richardson's *Clarissa* to Rousseau's *Emile*. Linnaeus and Reinhold thought that you had told the truth about the world by making it into a series of life forms listed in categories: she felt such life forms – animal, plant or human – made no sense until they had been interpreted and *shaped*. George's *Voyage* was as much a work of interpretation as a novel. Did anyone suppose that Mr Hodges's demurely picturesque depictions of aboriginal life, or his South Sea islands, as brightly decorated as flats in the Imperial Theatre at Mainz, provided a neutral or accurate picture of the seas and landscapes explored by Captain Cook? And were not George's letters a projection, a version of himself, which was halfway to being a novel?

With the still, considered creativity of a mind soused in a bottle of red Burgundy, George wrote to his wife one of his finest letters. He urged her to bring Huber and the children to Paris. He continued to regard Huber as a friend – they could continue with their translating work. He did not reproach Therese. Some form of living together could be found. It must. His heart was broken by not seeing Rosechen. As for *where* they all were – surely this made no difference?

> I have no homeland, no fatherland. I no longer really have friendships, not really. Everything which seemed certain has become contingent. Everything to which I clung has forsaken me. I have found a new life, independent, liberated . . .

He was not sure quite what it meant, as he powdered the wet ink of the words and sealed the wax on the back of the letter with his ring. One of her letters crossed with this profession. It was quite short, and asked him for a divorce, to allow her to marry Huber.

It was not long after he received this letter, when he was sitting at the dining table of the Dutch Patriots, and spreading a newspaper over the crumbs and wine-stains of the greying linen cloth, when the lugubrious Guénot again appeared.

—I came here rather than summoning you to the *Préfecture*, citizen.

—I shall ring for wine—

—Thank you, coffee is all I require.

—It is some weeks since we were served coffee, citizen, and even that was made of acorns.

Clothilde brought out a jug of coarse red wine and two glasses.

—Walls have ears, said Guénot in a low gravelly voice when she was gone. It is from Citizen Robespierre himself that I have come. The English in the north have taken many prisoners. We in turn have some three or four hundred of theirs. We believe, Citizen Robespierre believes, we could negotiate an exchange.

—You want me to negotiate?

—You have perfect English, haven't you? Besides, in Citizen Robespierre's home town . . .

—Arras . . .

— . . . but of course . . .

Guénot was impatient. The birthplace of the Saviour of France was surely such common knowledge as to be unworthy of remark.

—Arras, he continued, is in an . . . interesting situation. There are . . . enemies of the Revolution.

By now Guénot was murmuring so low that his words were scarcely audible. Something about an inn: something about an English officer, Major Manson, who would be the man with whom the negotiations would begin. That evening, George did some packing – put notebooks into a portmanteau. He wanted to continue with his translations of the Indian tales. He was also at work on an *Essay on the Relationship between Happiness and Politics*. The money offered for his mission was rather good, twice the eighteen livres a day which he claimed as a *Deputé*. After a breakfast of very watery chocolate and some slices of yesterday's loaf, George climbed into the diligence, bound for Arras.

PART SEVEN

Sailing Home

Oh! dream of joy! is this indeed
The light-house top I see?
Is this the hill? is this the kirk?
Is this mine own countree?

I

1775

—AND IT SEEMS I HAVE A NICKNAME AMONG THE YOUNG midshipmen, said Reinhold.

He and George were climbing a hill together on the island of St Helena. They stood for a while and looked back at the Governor's house (where they were being entertained) at the avenue of banyan trees (*Ficus religiosa Linn*), at the zigzagging road which led out of the town, at the ships and boats in the harbour, and, inland, beyond barren, rocky terrain, well-cultivated orchards and plantations, at wooded slopes, down which rivulets cascaded, shaded by the snowy blossoms of *Calla Æthiopica*. It was a fine clear May day, excellent for botanizing.

—It would be better, probably, if you did not know the nickname, said Reinhold. It is disrespectful. I should prefer, however, that you heard it from me, than that you picked it up – for example, from one of the midshipmen – and that you were hurt by it. I must say, I find it *is* a hurtful name.

Hearing George address his father, as many Germans do, as

Vati, the midshipmen, followed by the crew, had instantly labelled Reinhold the all-but homophonous *Farty*. George had noticed it, probably, back in July '72, before they had even left Plymouth. Now, very nearly three years later, it had reached his father's attention.

—I am considering, went on Reinhold, writing a short letter to Kapitän Cook about the matter. It is very bad for the discipline of a ship if the midshipmen are allowed to be disrespectful to their elders.

—They did not use the name to your face, Vati.

Reinhold paused.

—Of course not. That would have been a court martial matter, I should guess.

—All the English go in for nicknames, Vati – especially on a ship or in a school. Think of the Academy at Warrington. All the boys revered Mr Priestley but they called him 'Loony P'.

—I took this to be a reference to the Lunar Society, said Reinhold. The learned society to which Mr Wedgwood also belonged. It met at full moon and so was named Lunar. From this you get the play on words, Lunar – Loony.

—They called Dr Marat 'Dr Tintacks' – for no reason at all.

—That I took to be a reference to the celebrated character, Dr Syntax . . .

—I got the reference, Vati. It's just there was no particular *meaning* behind the name. It is just a play on words.

—My name – they copy you, you see, and call me Vati. At first this seemed affectionate, for I am like a father to them, perhaps. Then I saw they meant to call me Farty. I am sorry to tell you this.

—It's a joke. It's their *facetiousness*. He spoke the word in English, though they were conversing in German. You see, we are so not *facetious* that we do not even have an equivalent word in our language – *frech?* No. *Witzig?* No. For the English *facetiousness* is a whole habit of mind. A *Weltanschauung.*

—It may be so. But to accuse me of flatulence . . . in the course of three years, I suppose there must have been occasions, for example when we lived too much on *Sauer Kraut,* that *some* digestive dysfunction could be discerned; bowel gases could have built up, but no more I find in me than among the average. Yet it is *me* they call *Farty.* This I find very difficult to understand.

—I should not worry about it.

—Perhaps if you called me *Father* in future, and not Vati, it would be Step One in the elimination of this unfortunate development. Meanwhile I shall, I think, have a word in Kapitän Cook's ear.

They had a good morning of botanizing, noting how the imported European furze (*Ulex europaeus*) over-ran the native plants in any less fertile spot. Among the trees they especially admired a large American willow beard live oak. When they came down the hill, hot from their walk, they approached a spot on the harbour-edge, outside the fort, where the midshipmen were displaying themselves on the greensward. The half-dozen boys, nearly all two or three years George's junior, made an impressive sight in their royal blue frock coats, with white lining and cuffs, velvet collars, brass buttons, highly polished black buckled shoes, and, on their heads, three-cornered hats trimmed with gold. In all three years of the voyage, George, who got along, in a superficial way, with these near contemporaries, had made friends with none of them. In all the long journey to find the never-known southern land, the *Terra Australis Nondum Cognita,* he had been aware of that other mystery-land, which spoke a cousin-language, which had adopted German kings, but which remained on some profound level untranslatable. George, on this occasion, could hear, and then

see, the midshipmen before the young men spotted him and his
father: and they were now young men – even Loggie and Maxwell
who had been girlish-faced little boys who, during the first gale
in the Bay of Biscay back in '72, had cried for their mothers, and
curled into Elliott's hammock to be hugged. Yet seeing them all
there, with their high colour and blond fluff gathered about lip
and ear, George felt less than them, he felt *put down* by their sense
of superiority to the rest of the world, a sense so ingrained that it
did not need to be expressed. George, whose ear had immediately
cocked itself to what they were saying, thought it was quite possible
that his father would not even know, if he were sitting at their feet,
who they were 'being'.

—I vil tell de Kingk of you.

—Tha shall do nah such thing, lad – becoss – and ah'll tell thee
wha – becoss . . .

The guffaws of the group drowned out the end of the sentence. By now their versions of Reinhold and of the Captain did
not even attempt accuracy, but it was always immediately obvious,
when they moved into these conversational routines, that their own
voices and personalities had been discarded and those of the naturalist and the navigator assumed, like fancy dress.

—Eye *tzink* I see trees ahead.

—Ah think if tha lukes a bit closer-lahk, tha'll find 'em tubby
masts, lahk.

It was too much. One of the young wags was laughing so much
that he actually bit through the stem of his pipe, and coughing was
added to the general mirth.

Reinhold, the real Reinhold's, cordial greeting, made the sillier
of them look away to continue their giggling, while Elliott, the most
mature, blushed with embarrassment, hastily looking from Forster

to Forster to see whether the 'imitations' had been overheard. The hasty way in which George's eyes darted in another direction, refusing Elliott's gaze, said everything.

—Good evening, Dr Forster, Elliott said.

—Good evening, Mr Elliott. We had a good day. George made an excellent watercolour.

—Excellent. Excellent!

—Well – after a pause – we must return to our quarters, said Reinhold, rubbing his hands, and hoisting to his shoulders his botany-bag, which he had momentarily laid down, in anticipation of a longer conversation.

On the other side of the harbour, they watched a party of slaves, chained from the neck, returning from a day in the plantations. Reinhold uttered a splutter of disgust.

Nearly ten years later, George found himself married to Therese Heyne, and in the first week of sharing a bedroom with his wife, he had knelt beside the bed before getting into it. She was already sitting upright against the pillows in that Polish inn on the way to Vilnius. They had been married a few days, but it was their first day without Assad, and he hoped that it might be possible for their union, his and the young bride, to become that of a man and woman.

—We have not prayed together yet, he said, from his knees, and looking into at least one of her confusing, scornful young eyes.

—Do you kneel to say your prayers? he asked her. Some, I know, pray in the sitting position. If you prefer – I can come to sit beside you.

Her lips curled into a smile of pure satire.

She said,

—Oh, *no* . . . and then giggled.

He did not immediately inquire whether this was, 'oh no, I sit to pray, I do not kneel' – or 'oh, no, I won't get out of bed'. He did not know these things because in the few seconds it took for her to giggle, and to utter the two monosyllables, 'oh no', he lost his faith. Not merely did he abandon a personal Divinity. Even the sort of Deistic moral arbiter propounded by Professor Dr Kant was dismissed by the laugh of this young woman. The universe was suddenly emptied of purpose. The angel choirs, the redeeming Christ, the seventeen hundred years of faith, the witnesses of Augustine, Thomas of Kempen, of Luther and Johann Sebastian Bach evaporated. The considered wisdom of every great mind in the Western world, from Ambrose of Milan to Dante, from Cyprian of Carthage to old Samuel Johnson, deferred to the knowing laughter of this conceited little girl.

When this loss of faith occurred, it was a shocking, and yet an almost familiar sensation, because of what had happened that afternoon, a decade earlier, in St Helena. The suppressed scorn of the midshipmen worked its devastating effect. By the time that Reinhold and George had returned to the Governor's lodge, the boy no longer believed in his father.

He felt, as, ten years later he would feel, upon the departure of his Creator, a poignant combination of emotions: hilarious relief, and an instantaneous stab of inconsolable mourning. Ever since consciousness dawned, he had seen the world through Reinhold's highly distinctive intelligence. From Vati he had learnt to speak – first German, then Latin. From Reinhold, as did the Apostles from the Holy Ghost on the Day of Pentecost, George received the gift of tongues, learning Russian, French, English, Polish. From

Reinhold, he learnt to name the plants and trees and birds. From Reinhold, he learnt love, in so far as we can learn love.

Wherever he had been with his father, his eyes had beheld the effect which this lanky scholar, both arrogant and vulnerable, had upon the rest of the human race. He had seen the bafflement of Russian customs officers and courtiers as Reinhold told them their business; witnessed the faces of English academicians as Reinhold laid bare for them their intellectual shortcomings. And on the *Resolution* he had seen the 'Reinhold effect' as it transpired that he was a better astronomer than Mr Wales, a more practical mariner than Mr Gilbert, even, on occasion, a better navigator than Captain Cook. At the beginning of the voyage George had possessed such total faith in Reinhold that he actually took his father at his own estimation. Later, as adolescence increased his capacity for embarrassment, George began to cringe when he noticed his father being proved wrong. His fundamental love of Reinhold, however, was unshaken: and he had remained proud of his father's prodigious range of accomplishments, the seventeen languages, the patiently acquired knowledge of chemistry, of botany, of astronomy, cartography, history, theology.

The split second loss of faith which occurred, as they left behind them the facetious group of midshipmen, did not deny Reinhold's cleverness, but it revealed him for what his son had always seen, but never allowed himself to see: preposterous. In the subsequent years in England, nothing came as a surprise. Reinhold's quarrel with the Admiralty, his urging on his son to write the *Voyage* – thereby insuring the enmity of the entire British establishment – his quarrel with Banks, his quarrel with Cook, his expectation of preferment – perhaps to the Directorship of the British Museum – his running-up of huge debts, his narrow escape from imprisonment as a debtor, only effected because he took a humble job as a clerk at the Prussian Embassy and could therefore claim diplomatic immunity – the whole ridiculous story, in which Reinhold threw away all his chances. His impossible character, which was what George, from infancy, had been programmed to love, made all his other accomplishments redundant.

Swinging past the gates of the Governor's lodge and up the front steps, they came through the wide front doors. Mr Skottowe, the Governor, was standing in the hall. He was a big bluff Yorkshireman. Without any embarrassment, Captain Cook had informed him that his own father, James Cook senior, had worked as a hand on a farm on Skottowe's estates in Great Ayton. Skottowe was a countryman, who knew all the birds, plants and fish of the island.

—More drawings? he asked eagerly. I say! What a gift you have, young sir! I was looking through this portfolio of yours.

George's recent drawings were spread out on the large, marble-topped round table in the hall of the Governor's lodgings.

—*Pentapetes erythroxylon! Solidago sparia* – you've got them to the life, sir!

Reinhold opened his mouth to speak, and for the first time, the new George, the faithless George, blotted out his father's words, even though they were anodyne, harmless, provoking from the Governor merely an

—Indeed, sir, indeed!

II

1793

IT WAS A TWO-DAY JOURNEY BY POST-CHAISE BEFORE GEORGE
reached the cobbled streets and Dutch gables of Arras. Building
work appeared to be in progress in the centre of town. The
cathedral, near his inn, the Lion d'Or, was surrounded by rubble,
but when he asked the head waiter what was on hand, the man
merely looked at him with dismay and shrugged. The next day,
when he had slept better than he had done in weeks, and when he
was breakfasting – again for the first time in an age – on fresh bread
and real chocolate – he heard from fellow travellers in the coffee-
room that the cathedral was being demolished.

—The new Mayor, the local *Controlleur* . . . M. LeBon – has
decreed it.

—A curious name for one who wants to do something so bad,
said his wife, who sat opposite him.

They were a couple in their fifties. The man dabbed his lips with
his napkin and said,

—Be careful, my dear, what you say.

They were all speaking in English. The couple, who were trying to get to one of the Channel ports, and so home, had been visiting the wife's sister in Amiens. The wife was evidently French, of the prosperous shopkeeping class. Her husband, in a buff coat and with high riding-boots, informed George that he was a brewer from Faversham in Kent.

—My wife's sister was widowed. Her husband, a most respected *parfumier*, was called to his maker a month ago. We were allowed to go to the funeral, in spite of the war. But it was before . . . all *this*.

All this was the atmosphere of Terror, which was palpable.

—I cannot take my wife out of the inn, sir. Not with those – those Instruments erected in the market square. Yet I wish to go to the *Mairie* to obtain permission to go on to Calais.

—I shall mention your case to the Mayor in person, said George. I have an appointment with the Mayor himself this morning at ten. Your name is?

—Mr Godfrey, Mr and Mrs Godfrey of Faversham, sir, Faversham, Kent – a brewer by trade, sir, one who travels in peace. We came only—

—Only to the funeral pomps, said his wife, briefly breaking into her own language. We wanted to see if we could help my sister – perhaps bring her to England to live with us for a while until she was stronger. Her son has taken over the running of the *parfumerie*.

—They cut five heads off in the market square only yesterday, said Mr Godfrey, who either could not speak French, or chose not to.

—And you sir, said Mrs Godfrey, what is your name?

—Argan, sir. M. Argan, said George.

He did not know what prompted him to choose the name of Molière's imaginary invalid, but it was a time when instinct prompted the use of aliases. His letters to Therese had become more and more gnomic and ciphered. Long since, when he was in the grip of his Rosicrucian madness in Kassel, George had taken the sobriquet 'Amadeus' as his name in the brotherhood of the Rosy Cross. Now he had taken to writing to his wife in his own person, but referring to Amadeus as if he were a third party.

The state of Amadeus's health gave some cause for anxiety but the doctors say this was to be expected in this summer heat. I think you know where he is spending the summer. I think he would like to meet you to discuss some of these matters, but you know that he might find it difficult to obtain permission.

George gave no hint to Therese of the reason for M. Amadeus to be in Arras.

Walking to the *Mairie* after his breakfast with the Godfreys was a distressing experience. Only the old women of the town were brave enough to make open protest against the destruction of their cathedral. They did so vociferously, tugging at the clothes of the soldiers and labourers who clumsily but effectively were busy with the destruction work.

—Out of our way, old hags, or you'll get rocks on your old *coifs*, yelled the foreman. They reckon the tower'll come down this morning and then the walls'll be child's play.

—Blasphemy!

—It's God's House, you fiend, that you destroy!

—That's what the *Abbé* said a week ago! called one of the workmen.

—He won't be saying it this week, laughed one of his colleagues, not unless his head can talk on its own in a basket.

And no sooner had he said it than a man on a farm cart, operating a large ball and chain on a winch and pulley, swung them with devastating effect to destroy a spindly flying buttress which supported one of the north side walls of the church.

—Away, away! he called, and there was a panic-stricken run, as workers and old ladies alike hurried from the quivering walls. A huge fissure appeared in the side wall. The pointed arches of two windows became detached at the top. Coloured glass cascaded outwards and the walls shook like rumpled blankets. A cloud of dust hid their fall.

Half an hour later, George sat opposite the man responsible for the destruction, the local *maire*, Citizen Joseph LeBon.

—What do you think of our little building project? Our clearance of rubbish, citizen?

He was a large man of twenty-eight, who stretched out long muscular legs from his office chair. Already, his cheeks and chins were fleshy, and he was vain enough to wish to disguise this with a flourish of white cravats at his throat.

—Citizen Robespierre, who wasted so many hours of his life in that building as a boy, was anxious to have the site cleared. Eh? said LeBon who had a drawly manner of speech and made even non-interrogatory sentences into questions. I should know, eh? Served enough damn masses, did I? Sent to seminary, was I? Ordained priest? Oh yes – a holy priest sits before you, citizen! Consecrated by no less a one than old Bishop Talleyrand, wasn't I? Priest of the Oratory in Paris? The Oratory? You know the Oratory?

—I don't actually.

—How is that, Citizen Argan?

—I am a Protestant.

LeBon looked momentarily discomposed, as if George had confessed to being a talking ape.

—Dangerous times, eh, citizen? Dangerous for all of us? Perhaps safer not to ask too much, know too much? But you are come to do delicate business, citizen? Of that I am informed. You will have our protection. You come highly recommended.

—Really?

Praise is always seductive.

—Citizen Guénot thinks highly of you. This surprises you, eh?

He ran stubby fingers through thick brown hair. There would be some women, George reflected, who would melt.

—Come to you, wouldn't you say? My guess? The English will make the first move, eh? But when they do, you'll have safe passage to the camp where they hold our prisoners. A straight swap, no deals? Their soldiers for our soldiers?

—That, I understand, is the deal.

George took this opportunity to tell LeBon about the Godfreys, the harmless couple staying at his inn. He explained about the death of the *parfumier*, of his sister-in-law coming to comfort her widowed sister, of their being marooned in Arras, uncertain of how safely they could get to Calais and find a boat home. LeBon seemed interested, wrote down their details.

—So may I tell them you will help them, citizen?

—Is it ever safe to tell anyone anything?

That afternoon the tower of the cathedral collapsed and by nightfall the whole building was a heap of rubble.

A couple of days later, two revolutionary soldiers arrived at the inn to inform the Godfreys that they were being offered safe passage to Calais. Mrs Godfrey was so effusive in her tearful thanks that George almost had to unclasp her from himself as they parted:

but he did feel quiet satisfaction that his interview with LeBon had had at least one happy consequence. Meanwhile, he waited at the inn for word from the British army. Three weeks passed. George started work on his essay on the relationship between politics and personal happiness. For the first time in months, despite a yearning for his children, he felt something like contentment. Even without its medieval cathedral, Arras was a fine old town, its squares and red-brick gabled houses beautifully planned and proportionate. The Lion d'Or was a pleasant inn, and he became fond of the servants, even the taciturn waiter, who had seemed cold and unfriendly upon arrival, gave him good white Bordeaux to drink in the afternoons, and took charge of his laundry with an efficiency which recalled the magic touch of Nally. These shirts, which had grown used to having grey cuffs and yellowing fronts, were now transfigured. An English midshipman would have worn them with pride. How these miracles were effected remained a mystery.

Guests came and went. Some engaged M. Argan in conversation, some kept to themselves. One who was quite obviously going to keep himself to himself was a bushy-browed traveller, with one of the new stove-pipe hats, white trousers and a green riding-coat, who never appeared to take his eyes from his newspaper as he ate his two cutlets and drank his red wine. Only when this ceremony had been conducted did he remark, in unaccented French,

—As good a claret as you could find in the cellar of Le Blanc's in the rue St-Jacques . . .

—In which city, sir? asked George.

—Why, à Londres, said the stranger, his voice sinking to a whisper. And there are those who find themselves stranded in the good land of France and would love to come home . . . if an arrangement, satisfactory . . .

Resolution

So this was Major Manson, who had come at last.

Once they were in the park which had once been the gardens of the (looted) bishop's palace, the Englishman reverted to his own language. When they were safely out of anyone's earshot the Major said,

—I won't mince my words, sir. It was a dirty trick. A dirty trick.

—You have the advantage of me, Major.

—The apprehension of Mr Godfrey, a harmless Kent brewer and his wife, who is of a nervous disposition. To have allowed them to get as far as Calais, and then to hold them in the barracks under armed guard.

—What is this?

—Either you are an actor, or they did not let you in on their little plan.

They walked in silence. George was indeed shocked.

—Well, you can tell the mad priest who has taken charge of this poor little town – if he thinks the Revolution will be helped by chopping off the head of an English brewer and his harmless little wife – good luck to him. I'm a gentleman and a Christian, but I'm not going to risk the life of one English soldier to save the sister of some French haberdasher—

—*Parfumier.*

—Does it matter? You can tell that to your pals. Chop off the little milliner's head – though you've no right to chop off the Kent brewer's. But if you do, you won't get back *any* of your prisoners. Understood?

George felt seriously aggrieved that he had been the instrument by which the harmless Mr and Mrs Godfrey had ended up being interned in a military camp at Calais. He said as much to LeBon.

—Was it not fair? Isn't Albion at war with France?

—Yes, but a *parfumier*! Why, M . . . whatever the name of the dead *parfumier* might be . . . he might have supplied Eau de Cologne for Citizen Robespierre's own handkerchiefs.

—Citizen Robespierre does not consider there is any need to lace his person with *eau de toilette*.

The next time they met, Major Manson informed George that the *parfumier*'s widow, Mme Martinet, had become ill. She was of too frail a disposition for it to be possible for her son, the *parfumier*, to disclose the fact that her sister, Mrs Godfrey, was now a prisoner of the Revolution. Humanity demanded that Mme Martinet be allowed to join her sister Mrs Godfrey and be taken to live in England with the worthy, dull, bourgeois Mr Godfrey of Faversham. If the authorities would not show compassion in this instance, there was no possibility of an exchange of prisoners of war.

—He won't *discuss* the exchange of prisoners unless we show compassion to a couple of shopkeepers?

M. LeBon looked at George with incredulity.

—We have four *hundred* English prisoners. They have – a few hundred of ours? They won't *discuss* – because of a baker's widow?

—Scent-maker's . . .

—Does it not strike you as odd, citizen, that an English Major, a *gentilhomme* who prides himself in his aristocratic friends, should care so much for a shopkeeper's widow? An old lady?

—Not really.

The negotiations started the next week. The *parfumier*'s widow, her sister and the Kent brewer were safely aboard their packet and bobbing on the waves of La Manche by the time Major Manson saw George next.

Walls have ears – that was what Guénot had said, afraid that their murmured conversation in the House of Dutch Patriots in the rue des Moulins might be overheard by the surely reliable Clothilde? Sure enough, George knew the postilions, ostlers, brushers, waiters, beggars, tramps have ears. He doubted his own suitability for espionage, though he had guessed, when he first saw Major Manson in the coffee-room of the Lion d'Or, that the man's interest in his newspaper was too intense to be feigned.

George had been entrusted by Citizen Robespierre with the task of negotiating an exchange of prisoners in Robespierre's home town. He knew that commissions from Robespierre were deadly and double-edged gifts. He had been entrusted with a task, but this did not mean that he, personally, was trusted. Superficially, all that the Committee of Public Safety required of Citizen Forster was to negotiate an exchange of prisoners between the Republic and the British. Were he successful in this aim, it might, just might, be enough to satisfy the Committee; then again, as he had realized from his first moment of receiving the commission and being dispatched to Arras, there was danger. The war with England, conducted at the same time as the war with Holland, Austria, Prussia, the Holy See and the Holy Roman Empire of the German Nation, was imposing insufferable burdens upon the Republic, whose money and manpower were insufficient to sustain war on so many fronts. Many Englishmen supported the aims of the Revolution – as witnessed by the election of Mr Paine to the Assembly, the presence of Miss Wollstonecraft in Paris and the Christies, who had told them that in Warrington the old Dissenting school was watched constantly by the police who believed Mr Wedgwood to be a Jacobin agent. But the Christies had left, and Citizen Robespierre had made clear that the adherence of these British madcaps was not always as slavish as the Republic might have liked. (Since George came to Arras, Paine had fallen from grace, and both he and Miss Wollstonecraft were in Paris prisons.)

George had been entrusted with a simple negotiation, but he was also – though the word 'truce' could not be used by LeBon – entrusted, by a nod and a wink, to see if the British were agreeable to a peace settlement.

—Your English, said Major Manson on their next meeting, it is too perfect to have been learnt in a French school.

—You are very kind. I assure you, I am a Frenchman.

—Ah yes, M. Argan. *Un français imaginaire, peut-être.* I think we all know that it was the death of the King which was what shocked the conscience of Europe.

—Yet we all know, said George, France was not the first country in Europe to behead its King. Yet France did not, I think, declare war on England when Charles I lost his head.

There was a silence. No need to fill it with reminiscences of a family in Yorkshire, named Forster, dispossessed for their loyalty to the Royal Martyr, fleeing into an exile which, in that moment one hundred and fifty years later, seemed to George as if it were eternal, like the expulsion of our first parents from Paradise. At the beginning of the silence, the Major had been the suppliant for the return of his prisoners. Now, mysteriously, the balance of the conversation shifted.

—The beheading in Whitehall was followed by shocked silence, said Major Manson. The beheading in the Place de la Révolution was followed by whoops of mass hysteria and a public bloodletting without parallel in history. You know that, sir.

Resolution

The Major came so close to George's face across the table that his thick bushy eyebrows almost touched George's brow.

—I once read an account, he said, of the longest sea-voyage ever undertaken by European man, M. Argan. I've concluded that the European who contemplated the life of the savages 'will acknowledge with a thankful heart, that incomprehensible goodness which has given him a distinguished superiority over so many of his fellow-creatures'. I wonder, M. Argan, if the young man who wrote these words were to visit France today, whether he would consider the barbarous murders which defile every town, the travesties of justice which splatter every court-room with blood, would not make him revise his judgement that we Europeans are always so superior to the race of savages.

George blushed, at the smugness of his own words aged twenty-three, and at the fact that, all along, Mr Manson had known his identity.

—Forgive me, I . . . I do not know what to say.

—The boy who sailed with Cook, the Captain's blue-eyed boy, arriving in Arras as the lickspittle of Robespierre? No doubt you were an idealistic fellow, believed in the whole bag of tricks, the brotherhood of this and equality of that. Look at where it has got you, man! Your wife in Neufchâtel . . . oh yes, don't look surprised . . . you here . . . and wanting, no doubt, the chance to visit her? Beg her to return to you?

—*How* do you know?

—We could get you all out. Get you to England. We would ask very little in return. A few addresses, a few names in Paris, that is all. Perhaps a very little attempt at burglary the next time you visit the *Préfecture*.

—You think I would risk my neck . . . for a British officer . . . forgive me, Major, whom I do not know.

—You have already risked your neck. Work with us and the secret of 'Mr Godfrey' and his friends is safe with us. Refuse us, and M. LeBon might be disappointed to remember how vociferously you argued with him. It was just a matter of humanity for you, wasn't it, M. Argan? That shows you in a very amiable light to me, but I fear the Revolution takes a much sterner view of things. You see, simple kindness made you question M. LeBon's view that there was something suspicious in my zeal, as a British officer, to rescue a Kentish brewer and some French shopkeepers before I would even begin negotiations. If you co-operate with us, M. Argan . . . come on, man, you're practically British. No one but you need ever be informed, what you must have already guessed – Mr Godfrey the brewer – oh he is a brewer, but also happens to be one of our finest agents in the field. His French wife—

—I met her.

—I think not.

Major Manson smiled.

—Mr Godfrey's wife is indeed a Frenchwoman, but she remains safe at home in Faversham. The homely little body to whom you were so courteous in the Lion d'Or is not his wife. 'She' is the Archbishop of Arras. And the *parfumier*'s widow, rescued purely, monsieur, because of your compassionate heart, was the Marquise de Liencourt. You have done good work, M. Argan, and, I do assure you, my dear fellow, your secret is safe. I know you to be a good fellow. Friend of Banks.

—Indeed, sir.

—He sends his best to you. Oh, and . . .

—Sir?

—I do *very much* admire your *Voyage* book.

*

Resolution

Their final meeting took place in a grubby little boarding house in the village of Travers on the Swiss border. He had come by post-chaise, put down in the village square, entered the inn, and been told that the young 'Madame', with her husband and two children, were over-yonder in the boarding house. So it was, there had been no noise of wheels to disturb their conversation when he walked through the front door, that moist, cold November day in '93. Therese's voice was saying,

—because he has been *manipulating* me all year – trying to – trying to make me agree to this *absurd* idea.

There was a murmur from Huber.

—You know it is absurd. It's *not* as it was when we were all in the flat at Mainz. It's *not!*

Her voice rose.

—Don't you *see* how this is calculated to make me *weaken*. That he should offer us so much? He says he will allow a divorce so long as we allow him to live with us and the girls. That he will become our lodger.

More murmuring.

—Of *course* it is an absurd idea. Don't you see, the most manipulative thing about George is his *stripped candour*, his lack of defences. That is why I should never have agreed to his coming to see us.

Murmur.

—Yes, they are his children, but he has not seen them in TEN MONTHS.

Rosechen, seven years old, ran out to meet him in the hall, and tears came to his eyes. Clara, not quite four, hung back, clinging to Therese's skirt. Rosechen had leapt up and he hugged her, while she put her arms round his neck and her legs round his waist.

—Oh, Daddy! Daddy! We were afraid you would not come. *How* did you come? Did you come on a horse?

George wanted to *answer* all the remarks he had overheard. He wanted to say, Therese, you know full well that I never intended to be apart from the children for more than a few weeks. It was *you* who ran away from *me*. The French said I'd be in Paris three weeks and they have kept me eight months.

He said none of these things.

He pushed open the door of the small parlour to see them there: Therese silhouetted against the window, through which could be seen larch trees, squirrels, a grey, pearly sky; and Huber, still in his travelling-cloak, looking so young, like a clumsy boy. With her elbow on the back of an upright chair and her tall hair-arrangement, brushed and combed, as it were sculpted into a ziggurat on top of her cranium. Therese looked poised, almost posed. George stepped forward into the room and, uncertain what his movement presaged, she drew the chair closer to her body as if to ward off an unwanted kiss, or act of violence.

A painful three days followed. George put up at the inn, and could not sleep for shivering cold. She and Huber stayed in the boarding house, with the children.

Therese had agreed to the meeting. Nevertheless she could make no secret of hating him for putting them all through the pathos of it. He must know she would never come back to him? He could have left them to make their new lives in Neufchâtel. He knew that if they came together again, they would destroy one another.

A week later, when she had returned to Neufchâtel with Huber and the children, she found a small heap of furious letters, denunciations by her father – denunciations of her intemperance, immorality, recklessness, lack of concern for his, the *Hofrat's*, reputation in Göttingen. She replied shortly that the meeting in Travers had been between three people who 'still honoured and loved one another'. She wrote the words because she wanted her father to believe them; or perhaps, more generally, because they looked good.

The three days at Travers developed a routine. While the children were awake, she left them with George, and with the maid, Ursula, while she and Huber took their watercolour boxes and their volumes of Schiller up misted autumnal mountain paths. George played pencil and paper games with the girls, and a simplified version of Skat, which little Clara could master but Ursula found baffling. He told them stories and they drew pictures.

The common table at the inn was the only place where the grown-ups could eat. The three of them could scarcely risk tears or raised voices in such a setting. To the relief of Therese and Huber, the intolerable situation between the three of them went undiscussed. Huber asked George about his continued interest in Indian literature. George asked Therese about her novel and received noncommittal replies. George – naming no names – spoke of his time at Arras: about the possibility of returning there, even, of going to Calais.

Regardless of the other diners at the table – two pedlars, a man in black who might or might not have been a Protestant pastor – George began to whisper intently.

—I think there is a chance of my being able, of *our* being able, to escape to England. We could live in London. I could make a living, writing in London. We could be *together*.

Arctic silence from Therese and Huber.

—Please, he repeated. Please consider it.

Later, she wondered whether the dishevelment of his appearance, his skeletal thinness, the oiliness of his unwashed hair, the greyness of the scurvy-scarred face, the brown sponginess of a more or less toothless mouth, the fraying of the cuffs, the holes in his stockings, the tears which spouted so often from his exhausted sleepless eyes were all part of his campaign to worm his way back into her life.

Next day, at breakfast, Rosechen said,

—Daddy, you *smell*.

Of course, Therese and Huber took the children back to Neufchâtel. Of course, though the squirming children allowed themselves to be kissed by his smelly mouth, he embraced neither his wife nor his friend. The heavy cold turned to flu on the first stage of his journey back to Paris. By the time he reached the city, and the Maison des Patriots Hollandais in the rue des Moulins, he had pneumonia.

Much correspondence awaited him. He had begun a series of essays or articles called *Parisian Outlines* – Voss, his Berlin publisher, wrote to say he was interested. He wanted to find out if there was any of his acquaintance left in Paris who had not either fled, or gone to prison, who could help him with it.

Sick as he was, he paced the unforgiving, ice-windy, sleety grey streets of the French capital. The cough had destroyed his appetite, but he would occasionally turn into tap-houses or bars for hot *marc* with lemon. Paris was a city of death, epicentre of a land of death. His 'aunt Cecile' wrote to him from Arras – George knew the aunt to be of the bushy-eyebrowed, male, English military variety – that Arras was now a scene of unrestrained butchery, hundreds of people in the departments of the Somme and the Pas-de-Calais having been decapitated in the presence of LeBon who, said Tante Cecile, imitated the convulsions of victims as they were dragged to the guillotine.

Resolution

In Paris, that merciful instrument was in constant use. Philippe Egalité, Marie-Jeanne Phlippon Roland, sublime with her waist-length hair, Bailly, first Mayor of Paris, were only a few of the thousands who were trundled that month to the guillotine. The Revolution which had begun with the storming of a prison, the Bastille, had made prisons out of the Luxembourg Palace, the Chantilly Palace . . . Twelve new prisons existed in Paris, forty-four thousand in France. In the churches, where vestments and treasuries had been burnt and plundered, strange mumbo-jumbo in the place of the old mumbo-jumbo was enacted: actresses posing as Reason before debauched, moustachioed, brandy-soaked buffoons.

Some of it George saw, some he heard of – he himself was drinking heavily and pneumonia creates its own intoxication. Impressions became ever fuzzier as the date of the former went. Christmas, now unobserved in Notre Dame, went unobserved; so did the Feast of Circumcision. Where was the Sacred Foreskin, which had so fascinated Nally, and which had once reposed in a reliquary in La Sainte-Chapelle? George was apparently asking the question when Clothilde said,

—Monsieur is not well. Monsieur should be in his bed.

And now Monsieur was in his bed. For something like a week in the year which he still regarded as 1794, though to the Revolution it was Year Three, he tossed and turned. Clothilde was in constant attendance. She put her red, coarse cheeks near his and he could see her very blue eyes as she said,

—We'll get you out of here. You'll be well. We'll get you to England.

—You are English, Clothilde?

—I am Dutch, monsieur.

Friends came and went. He recognized their names, but not their faces. One of them, leaning over him eagerly was surely . . . but no! Joy almost broke his heart as he said,

—Vati! But how did . . .

—Forster. It is I.

—But, Vati . . .

Clothilde's voice said, to the strange doctor, who was not his father,

—It is the fever, monsieur, the fever. His mind plays tricks.

—Do not go away. Clothilde . . . Clothilde.

—Yes, monsieur.

—Hold my hand.

She did so.

—Do you know the Our Father?

—In French, monsieur? No.

—In Dutch, then. You say it in Dutch to me. I'll . . .

His voice was weak, but as she said her very similar words, his lips mouthed,

—*dein Reich Komme, dein Wille geschehe* . . .

Someone else was speaking French, something about bleeding him, but he had weighed anchor. It was the firm Yorkshire voice of the Captain who bellowed out to the wind,

—*O send thy word of command to rebuke the raging winds, and the roaring sea* . . .

III

1775

—*AND THE ROARING SEA*, BELLOWED THE CAPTAIN, *THAT WE,
being delivered from this distress, may live to serve thee and to glorify
thy Name all the days of our life.*

Everyone shouted AMEN, but the wind was louder than over
a hundred human voices, as the little *Resolution* rose up and was
hurled down again. The day before, they had seen the last of the
Azores, and now, in late July, the ship had encountered a terrible swell from the west and the wind raged mightily. Shearwaters,
albatrosses and great skuas were blown across the sails and above
the masts like pieces of newspaper escaped in a gusty alley. After
three years of it, half those aboard were still unable to endure such
squalls and swells without vomiting, so that the swabbing of the
decks was all the more vigilant for a couple of days.

The breeze continued fresh, but seasickness became rarer, in
bright weather. George, sketching a shearwater which had alighted
on a coil of rope in the corner of the main deck, reflected sadly that

by the time this sketch-block was filled up, he would be drawing land-birds.

—So what I was thinking, Nally was saying, was that you could do with a hand about the house. The valeting of your clothes, sir. I mean, if you are going so much to court.

—This is true, but what arrangements Mrs Forster will have made in our absence . . . We shall have to see, Nally. We must . . .

—But she's not going to have engaged a valet, is she, sir?

—There is also the question of where you would sleep, Nally, where you would sleep.

—Land AHOY!

The voice, high in the rigging near the mainmast, broke through the complaints of Mr Wales, who was saying to the Captain,

—and he told me – *me* who brought all the chronometers and measuring equipment with me – apart from what you had collected from Greenwich – that he knew of an instrument maker in Berlin—

—Not now, Mr Wales.

Cook had applied his telescope to his sharp eye. That instrument, which had shown him the tall pines of Norfolk Island, the mountains of New Zealand, the statues of Easter Island and the limitless crags of ice on South Georgia, now revealed the Lizard. It was 28th July.

—Nally thinks I shall be much at court.

—Is that what you want, Vati?

—The King might insist upon it. He might well wish me to take on the running of the Botanical Gardens at Kew—

—Instead of running the British Museum.

—Both, I find, are likely. And for that, maybe Nally is right, maybe I *do* require a valet.

Resolution

—We'd miss Nally if he wasn't there.

Reinhold's face screwed into puzzlement.

—What do you mean? he said.

The next morning, the 29th, they scudded past the Lizard, and had begun to pass a large number of ships, plying to windward in order to get out of the Channel. The mood of the sailors was heady. Spontaneous outbursts of song accompanied all their tasks.

> *Come cheer up my lads, 'tis to glory we steer,*
> *To add something new to this wonderful year.*
> *To honour we call you, as freemen not slaves,*
> *For who are so free as the sons of the waves . . .*

—There's nothing beats a sense of homecoming, and sure that's a fact, said Nally.

—I suppose so. Only I'm not really coming home, am I, Nally?

—Oh, get off with you, George, wherever I am, there'll be home for you.

They passed Eddystone Lighthouse. As they sailed along, they could make out people on the shore, see the outlines of English trees and hedges and the bright green of fields. They anchored at Spithead on the 30th. A post-chaise was waiting to take Captain Cook to the Admiralty. It was Sunday morning, but George felt the church bells would have been ringing for them whenever they'd arrived.

—Well, Dr Forster, I am going to London, said Captain Cook. Is this where we part?

—No, no, said Reinhold firmly. There will be more than enough room for myself and my son, in the carriage with you, Kapitän.

—Well, I'm not so . . .

—Ja, ja. And Nally can go above – on top, *oben*.

—Nally? What the devil are you bringing Nally for? asked the Captain.

—Your luggage, Kapitän, can follow with ours, said Reinhold, with a lordly, sweeping gesture of his hand.

—Sure it can, said Nally.

AFTERWORD

TEN YEARS AFTER SHE PUBLISHED *ADVENTURES ON A JOURNEY to New Holland*, Therese Huber completed the short sequel, entitled *The Lonely Deathbed*. Both were translated into English by Rodney Livingstone (Lansdowne Press, Melbourne, 1966).

This book began, in my head, when I discovered, in a second-hand bookshop in the Charing Cross Road, *The Resolution Journal of Johann Reinhold Forster in Four Volumes*, edited by Michael E. Hoare for the Hakluyt Society (London, 1982). The London Library generously consented to acquire, at my request, Georg Forster's *Werke in vier Bänden* (Insel-Verlag, Leipzig, 1970).

I have also learnt much from Ulrike Bergmann's *Die Mesalliance* (Edition Büchergilde, Frankfurt am Main, 2008), Kurt Kersten's *Der Weltumsegler, Johann Georg Adam Forster, 1754–1794* (Francke Verlag, Bern, 1957) and Ludwig Uhlig's *Georg Forster, Lebensabenteuer eines gelehrten Weltbürgers* (Vandenhoeck & Ruprecht, Göttingen, 2004). Anyone wanting to know about Captain Cook is indebted to the great J. C. Beaglehole, whose *The Life of Captain James Cook* (Stanford University Press, Stanford, California, 1974) has been often read, together with Philip Edwards's selection of Beaglehole's edition of *The Journals of Captain Cook* (Penguin Classics, London, 1999).

Readers of these books will know that I have not invented very much in this novel. For dramatic effect – to increase the pace of George's brainstorm – I have brought forward the execution of Adam Lux to July 1793. In fact, he was beheaded in November. The characters of Major Manson and of Nally have been made up, and I have followed what is only the inference of Forster scholars, that George and Caroline Michaelis had an affair. After the Germans reoccupied Mainz, Caroline was briefly arrested and imprisoned in Kronberg. Her friendship with George was one of the charges brought against her. She was rescued by one of her admirers, August Wilhelm Schlegel, who took her to live near Leipzig until her son was born. She later became Schlegel's wife at Jena.

George's exquisite drawings are still in the British Museum. Incidentally, although all German books call him Georg, his father registered his birth as George and called him George. Though he published his German books as Georg, he published in English under the name George, and – anyway, I came to know him, and to love him, as George.

Each section begins with a quotation from *The Rime of the Ancient Mariner*. Mr Wales, the astronomer on the *Resolution* who got along so badly with Reinhold Forster, taught mathematics at Christ's Hospital, regaling his pupils with memories of the great voyage when 'ice, mast high came floating by as green as emerald'. One of those boys was Samuel Taylor Coleridge.

CAMDEN TOWN
May 2016